CRACKER

BEST BOYS

ALSO IN THE CRACKER SERIES

To Say I Love You

The Mad Woman in the Attic

One Day a Lemming Will Fly

To Be a Somebody

CRACKER

BEST BOYS

BASED ON A SCREENPLAY BY
Paul Abbott

ADAPTED BY
Gareth Roberts

St. Martin's Minotaur ✷ New York

ISBN 0-312-20498-1

First published in Great Britain by Virgin Books,
an imprint of Virgin Publishing Ltd

First St. Martin's Minotaur Edition: March 2000

10 9 8 7 6 5 4 3 2 1

CRACKER

BEST BOYS

ONE

Bill was the only male in the machine room. He'd seen the girls' calendar, displayed with prominence next to the snack machine. May was impossibly muscular, with sea-green eyes and golden-toned Californian skin, and stood with his back to the camera, head turned provocatively, the deep blue water of a distant lagoon lapping around his knees. And the girls were as bored as Bill was, so he should have expected this.

The Cheltex factory took up one half of a large industrial estate. Bill was here on work experience, the first he'd been trusted with. Responsibility, the office had told him, a reward for his improved behaviour. As it turned out, the responsibility consisted of hefting heavy fabric rolls off a pallet in the stores and into a trolley, then pushing them down to the big machine room for the cutters. He'd started yesterday, and for a while the routine of it had soothed him. He kept busy, concentrated on the new world around him, working out who was who, chatting with the fork-lift drivers, trying to appear normal and ordinary, and the thoughts that troubled him at other times receded. It felt good to be among fresh faces. But the day went on, the novelty faded, and by the afternoon he was thinking again, his mind turning over and over, always along the same spiral path.

Diane. Where was she? If she could see him here, with next to no qualifications, pushing a trolley for this pittance, would she then realise what she'd done? Would she then listen? He thought of Diane's house, the house in Urmston, his only home. Nobody who lived in such a house would end up working in a place like Cheltex. If she'd let him stay, he'd probably be doing sixth form now. Without Diane he was nothing, so he might as well be working here. The repetition started to crush him and he felt out of control, helpless in the face of his destiny. The only good thing was the job got him out of the common room at Wiverton House, and away from all the gobshites and rejects in there, and away from his roommate, who was a right tosser. It was good to be alone and unscrutinised.

The journey from stores to machines took him along a draughty and empty corridor, and he found himself thinking stupid things to fight the tedium, twisting the trolley over small bumps in the flooring and watching the wheels clatter on the concrete just for something to do. Having worked out that no-one was interested enough to check on him or his performance he often stopped and listened to the echoing radio. The factory's high ceilings made each bright pop song melancholic and taunting, the music overlaid by the incessant clucking of the machine girls. Their conversations never went further than their husbands and their kids. New babies, sons and daughters leaving home, marriages. Bill tried not to listen. Pinned above the machine room door was a big cartoon-rabbit-shaped card on which had been written *Jo Sharp gave birth to a baby girl 26th April mother and daughter doing fine.* He avoided that also. Whenever he caught sight of it he felt a familiar wave of anger rising in him, and pictures of Diane coming back into his head.

The last few times he'd been up to the machine room there'd been a noticeable change in the atmosphere, an unspoken tension. The girls were quieter, and their chat sounded artificially bright and mocking. Something was being planned, and now, as he returned and made his way between the work tables, he caught one of the younger ones and her mate laughing. What was funny? He blushed and his heart beat faster. It was stupid, but they scared him.

Quick as he could he finished the job, unloading the fabric on to the supervisor's table, and wheeled the empty trolley away. At the edge of his vision he saw the two girls, still giggling, stand up, and was vaguely aware of other chairs being scraped back and the descent of a strange, expectant silence. He pushed through the plastic sheeting and out into the corridor.

The sheeting rustled behind him. 'Billy, isn't it?' asked a female voice. Her companions tittered. Just for a moment he wanted them all to die or disappear.

'Bill,' he muttered, and kept his head down.

'How old are you, Bill?'

'Seventeen.'

'That's all right, then. That's a nice pair of keks you've got on, Bill.'

He increased his pace. They were closing on him, he could sense them, smell their cheap scent.

' 'Cause, you see, we're that dedicated to our job, like –' more sniggers '– and we're really keen to see how the competition's doing. We like to take a really close

3

look at garments produced by other manufacturers. We have to keep ahead of the game, don't we?'

He wanted to turn round and tell them where to go, but there were too many of them. The other girls were hooting at the wit and daring of their leader.

'And Billy, hope you don't mind, pet, but our Gloria here –' there was an explosion of laughter at the expense of the slowest-witted of their company '– our Gloria has noticed a revolutionary cross-stitch on your arse.'

Bill stepped up his pace, judging the distance from here to the stores. Another ten yards of corridor.

'And when our Gloria gets the bit between her teeth, you should see her. She has to chase her husband around the garden for it, you see.'

More laughter. Bill started to run, still pushing the trolley.

'Get him!' shouted the ringleader.

A riot broke out.

Bill threw the trolley to one side, intending to block their pursuit. He heard it overturned, and a jubilant cry, but by then he was already pounding into the stores. He tore round a pillar, his trainers thumping hard on the concrete, his breath coming in gasps. He passed one of the fork-lift drivers, who stood clutching his sides at the spectacle, and then darted into one of the long storage aisles at random. The clatter of high heels and the babble of feminine laughter resounded around the bays. Textile bales and pallets whipped by on either side. He came to a junction, changed direction again, sped away confident of escape. The noise of the girls receded.

Bill smiled inwardly. He was younger and faster than them. He was better than them.

He sped into the loading bay at the far end of the aisle, intending to run for the main exit and the outbuildings. They weren't going to have their fun. His dignity was safe. He'd hide a while and get back to the job. He didn't want attention on his second day.

The women were waiting for him, faces alight with ignorant glee. They charged forward as one, soft, flabby arms outstretched, and he was claimed. Struggling crazily, kicking and swearing, he was brought down, not gently, grappled into a trolley by tickling, sticky fingers. The big lights on the ceiling blinded him. The women were all over, reaching under his tee shirt, pinching and squeezing. He felt his belt slide from the buckle, his button undone, his fly yanked down. The metallic rasp of the zip brought out a cheer and much clapping. He shoved and flailed, remembered the glow of amusement, of envy, on the fork-lift man's face, wondered why this wasn't enjoyable.

His trainers were pulled off. He kicked again, tried to bring up his knees, but the jeans were pulled over his legs, and away. There was a surge of triumph, a bellow from the mob as the ringleader displayed them, shook them, made them flutter like a pennant above her head.

Bill let his head fall back. Their grip on him relaxed, and he hung his head in shame, pulling his tee shirt down over his pants and trying to stand. The stupid bitches. Their chatter hung in the air. The jeans were waved about again. The ringleader danced from foot to foot, her face flushed.

'Oi! What's going on there?'

The shout was frighteningly loud, sudden, military. The girls' noise stopped instantly, as if cut off by a switch. The ringleader's face fell, and abruptly there was a different kind of tension in the air.

Bill looked up, scared. Odds on that he was going to collect a bollocking for this one and be thrown out. On only his second day. That'd fulfil all the office's expectations. A bloke was walking confidently in from the loading bay. He was tall, well-built, upright, in his late twenties or maybe early thirties, with a firm jaw and short dark hair. He looked in good shape to be foreman at this crappy factory, and despite his predicament Bill felt himself responding to that shape.

The newcomer's eyes swept over the scene. He addressed the ringleader, fixing her with steel-blue eyes. 'Linda.' His voice was deep and gravelly, traces of a Northern Irish accent.

Without a word of explanation, as if she knew that would be useless, she threw the jeans back to Bill. Her eyes were cast down, and Bill took pleasure from the way she'd been so easily dominated by the supervisor.

'You,' said the newcomer, nodding to Bill, the steel-blue eyes connecting with his for a second. 'Get dressed. Well, Linda?'

'Just having a bit of fun, Mr Grady.'

'A bit of fun.' He gestured towards the machine room. 'Well, now you've had it. Get back to work, the lot of you.'

The women obeyed, and filed silently back through the aisles. Grady called after them, 'And I'll warn the canteen you'll be ten minutes late for your tea break, yeah?'

He walked towards Bill, who had found his belt and was buckling himself back up. Then he tucked his tee shirt back into his jeans and retrieved his trainers. 'Who are you, then?' Grady asked. His tone was unforgiving.

'Bill Nash. I started yesterday.' He looked up, but kept his face down. For some reason he couldn't bring himself to look into Grady's eyes. A hot tingle of embarrassment burned round the back of his neck.

'Work experience?' The question was laced with scepticism.

Bill nodded. He wanted to protest that this wasn't his fault, but this guy, he could tell, was a hard case. Any reply would sound feeble. He prepared himself for the worst, pictured himself trailing back to Wiverton House and the drubbing that would follow. Nobody would understand, nobody could, nobody ever did. What was wrong with him? Was he a bad person? Why did he always have to take the shit?

'Well, you'd best learn to think faster or run faster, eh?' said Grady. 'If it happens again, you're out, OK?'

Bill nodded again, almost not believing what he'd heard.

'Beat it.'

'Cheers.' Bill trailed away, still shaken by the assault and the memory of the alien, uninvited hands groping him. His mind was turning over, emotions whizzing through his body. He hated it all. This place was worse than school. He didn't belong. There was nobody for him. Nobody could understand. And now back to those women and their talk of husbands and babies, and family, always family. Well, he had a family, a real family, a family that had wanted and loved him, and would want him and love him again, no matter what he had to do to make them see. He had nobody else. Diane had to be made to understand.

7

He was conscious of being under scrutiny. He turned and saw Grady, who'd plainly been watching him walk away. Their eyes made contact, and Bill again wondered why he almost couldn't bear to meet that blue gaze. It wasn't only fear of the sack. There was a frightening truth in the glance they exchanged. Bill felt half terrified, half intrigued.

He'd been given a second chance. Nobody had given him such a thing before. Nobody had been interested enough. And there was interest in Grady's eyes.

TWO

Funerals. In the last couple of years Fitz had seen too many, and been involved, indirectly, in lining up a good few of the corpses.

He stood, this soggy Thursday afternoon, just inside the cemetery gates, having crept into the churchyard through some railings (fortunately there was a big gap). He was smoking and trying to ignore the fool Irish band wheedling over the way and the fool pressmen gathered in the road outside. There'd been a crowd of them buzzing at the door of his own home minutes after Jimmy Beck's ultimate act of self-pity, and the nuisance had continued, on and off, since. Questions on his way out, questions on his way in. He was asking enough of himself. The biggest: why was he here, now? He felt no grief for Beck (no more than anybody else, he suspected), and moreover there were clients to be seen, and money of his poor dead mother's to be thrown away on all sorts of futile pursuits. The answer came back immediately. This funeral was going to be emotional, in all the wrong ways, and that would make it interesting. Irresistible, and valuable research. He pictured himself briefly as a big black fly hovering around an especially messy turd.

The pressmen started to make a lot of noise, and

Fitz turned his head to the road. Wise's shaggy bulk appeared in the midst of the journalists, his arm waving over his head in a swatting motion. 'Ey, ey, ey!' he bellowed. Fitz wondered quite why the sight of this unremarkable middle-aged detective chief inspector should have aroused the assembled horde to such excitement, then registered that Wise was not alone. A tall, elegant, dark-haired woman was at his side. She was gorgeous, perfect skin, hair cut to a fashionable bell under a turban-like black velvet hat. Her body had the characteristic leanness of the Irish. These better features went a long way to disguising her identity as Beck's sister, Aileen. Fitz watched the pressmen crowding her.

'Why'd he do it, love? You're his sister, aren't you? What drove him to do it, do you know?'

Her face hardened. She looked between her inter-rogators, her expression scornful. Flashguns went off.

'Can you just give us a few words, love? Five minutes, that's all we're after. Come on, love –'

'Ey, ey, ey!' Wise again, shooing at the nearest journalist. 'Come on, lads. This is a private service. I'm within my rights to have you moved on. Take a look behind you.' He nodded back to a row of uniformed police down the road. The pressmen ignored him. 'I'll count to three!' At his side Aileen Beck bristled.

'Come on, love, can you just give us a few words –'

She snapped. Furiously she came forward, her move-ment so violent that the pack moved back a little, in unison. 'Who took it?' she demanded. Her voice was throaty, strongly accented. 'Who took the picture of him jumping?' The pressmen quietened but the flashguns kept popping. 'Who printed that?' Her eyes swept around the little group. Fitz was impressed by her directness. Her expensive clothes, her forthright tone, what did these make her? Doctor? No, she didn't have the right kind of zeal in her eyes. And she'd done her research, she knew the man she was looking for, had sought him out and given him an earful previously. She pointed at a face in the crowd and bellowed, 'Him. That bastard was there when my brother took his own life. I'm sure he's more clues as to what happened than anyone in the family.' She raised her voice. 'No, all the family got were dental records and personal effects. So save your arsehole questions for him.' She lowered her voice. 'And be very careful what you put in print. I'll sue the first one who deviates from absolute fact.'

Ah, a lawyer.

There was a moment's silence, which Wise used to regain control. 'Like I said, the service is private.' He ushered Aileen into the cemetery, and they crunched up the gravel drive leading to the church. Fitz watched them pass, perturbed a bit by the woman's strength of character. Not at all what he'd expected, and how he hated surprises.

He turned to follow them, emerging from cover, and at the sight of him the pressmen got themselves excited again. 'Fitz, Fitz!' they shrieked. 'Can we just have a word? Did you know DS Beck very well, Fitz? What about David Harvey? How was he connected to the murders of Jean McIlvanney and the other girls? Fitz! Fitz!' In the last few years Fitz had learnt to put this lot to the back of his mind. Celebrity was meaningless to him, couldn't enrich a personality as assured as his. In the end all it did was make you more comfortably miserable.

Calm returned. He walked slowly towards the open plot, into which Jane Penhaligon, immaculately turned out (and that was interesting, she must really have thought out that outfit, laboured over the details), was staring. Perhaps she was wishing she'd had the guts to do the deed herself. That would have given her tragedy a sort of resolution; it's what she'd intended, once. A week had passed since Beck's death, a week in which compassionate leave had twice been offered to her and twice refused. Instead she'd made a point of showing up and going through her routine. Rooms heavy with mutters went quiet when she passed through, head held high, gaze level, dealing superefficiently with every problem. On a visit to Anson Road Fitz had seen her on the phone, fielding press questions about the nosedive as if she'd been merely a bystander. He knew why. Now more than ever it was crucial to cover any sign of weakness. So she stood at the graveside, absolutely still.

Temple and Skelton joined her, trying to show some remorse and concern in their faces. Trying a bit too hard, thought Fitz, all things considered.

'How're you doing, Jane?' asked Skelton. 'You OK?'

'I'm fine,' she said evenly, but there was real strain in her voice that she couldn't disguise, and Fitz couldn't stand another moment of these poker faces. In many ways today was a day of rejoicing. He was rejoicing anyway; when everyone had gone home he might go so far as to spit in the grave. 'Oh, for God's sake, Moneypennyhaligon,' he drawled as he drew close. 'Get a grip, you sour-faced bimbo.'

Her head whipped round, her eyes wide with shock. Not here, they were saying, not now! Skelton and Temple flinched.

'Well, you're sick of the platitudes,' Fitz continued, casually. 'And, as we both know, everybody's blaming you, anyway.' He nodded towards Temple. ' "She was there when it happened, she didn't stop him making the big leap, did she?" Crap, and we both know it. They know it. So don't let them rub your nose in it.'

Temple shook his head and hissed through his teeth. 'You're a sick man.'

Fitz smiled. He liked it when people said that. 'Come on, now. Why not say it and be proud, eh? "I helped him die – Jimmy Beck, the Eddie the Eagle of British law enforcement." '

Temple's back was already turned. Skelton followed him. Fitz felt a momentary surge of frustration (at their piousness? at himself?) and slammed the flat of his hand against a handy tombstone.

'It isn't them,' Penhaligon told Fitz, 'half so much as that.' She pointed to a couple of floral tributes laid at the foot of the grave. The first was innocuous enough. *In our hearts forever, Mum and Aileen.* You could hardly begrudge the relatives, who hadn't seen the bastard in years. But the other wreath, larger and more expensive-looking, read *JIMMY* and the card affixed said *Remembered with honour, Greater Manchester Police.*

'I bet they didn't include you in the whip-round,' said Fitz.

'They don't include me in anything.' She started to walk towards the church.

Fitz finished his cigarette and, when he was sure

no-one was looking, threw the glowing butt into the grave. 'The flames already.'

The service, thankfully, was a short one, and no tears were shed. An atmosphere of strain and confusion prevailed. Fitz was amused by the officiating vicar, who tied himself in knots in an attempt to be meaningful and kind. A fatuous exercise in self-deception, these proceedings. Nobody was ready to confront the facts about Beck, who'd been miserable, callous and ultimately pathetic.

Fitz had witnessed Beck's plummet from the warehouse rooftop, he'd been standing only feet away, and a tremor passed through him whenever his mind's eye flashed up the image of Beck stepping off the ledge into nothingness, dragging the terrified Harvey alongside him. A scene Fitz's mind had refused to accept, so kept rewinding and playing back; one of the common defence mechanisms of the human consciousness. Sometimes a different version was provided, and he saw himself herding Beck and Harvey away from the edge, into the arms of Wise and the waiting SWAT team. That moment of decision resounded with possibilities. And if Beck had lived, even more of an embarrassment for Wise, and an added torment for Jane Penhaligon? Perhaps taking that big step had been the noblest, kindest act of his life. It had drawn the nation's attention, and attention was essentially what the man had always craved.

An enormous, crystal-clear picture of the two bodies, smashed across the bonnet of a police car, had blotted out all but a tiny block of text on a tabloid front page. LAW AND ORDER? ran the headline, picked out in white.

14

The feature inside ran to seven pages, eighty per cent speculative. Fitz merited a blurred, long-lens photograph, outside his house, in dark glasses with middle finger aloft, run with a list of his achievements. It was Wise who got the majority of the stick, both from the papers and from Allen, the Chief Super. Fitz had made his excuses to Judith and gone in for the row, not wishing to miss the opportunity to score a point.

'You lose an officer, the officer takes a suspect with him!' Allen had screamed, a pulse pounding against a purple temple. 'And you say you couldn't see this coming?'

'Jimmy Beck,' Wise protested, 'had been at this nick more than ten years.'

'We're wide open for a lawsuit,' Allen continued. His finger stabbed at the front-page picture on Wise's desk. 'Can you imagine what Maggie Harvey's solicitor is going to do with this?'

'All respect, sir –'

'I've got the Federation on my back, I've got the press on my back, I've got the Chief Constable on my back –'

Wise slammed a huge fist on the desk and rose. 'I didn't push him over! I didn't ask him to top himself, you can't land that on me!'

Allen smirked. 'It was you who didn't have the brain to diversify your inquiry, to take in other suspects.' He pointed at Wise. 'You let Harvey go. You were responsible for Beck taking Harvey, a member of the public, down with him.'

'Harvey wasn't a member of the public, he was a killer –'

15

'Your name's on the investigation –'

'He was a killer,' shouted Wise, 'and you let him go!'

'Because you had no evidence,' said Allen smartly.

Wise shook his head. 'You authorised his release before we had time to gather enough bloody evidence.' He picked up the paper and shook it. 'So don't you try to park all of this up my arse!'

Fitz felt like clapping. He watched as Allen fumed, the rest of the team kept their heads down, and Wise's expression changed to a glare that combined defiance, outrage, and the realisation that he might have crossed an important line.

Allen spoke again, softly. 'I don't think you've got the equation worked out here, Charlie.' He poked Wise in the chest, punctuating his words with a prod. 'You don't get a say. All right? All right?'

Wise straightened. 'Sir.'

Allen leaned closer. 'You ever speak to me like that again, I'll park your head so far up your arse that you'll be singing *Dixie* every time you fart.'

'Sir.'

With that, Allen grabbed his hat and emerged into the incident room, in which everyone but Fitz was keeping their head down. Contrarily, Fitz fixed Allen with a wide grin, just to let him know.

'And what have you got to be smiling about?'

Fitz shrugged. 'Relax. Let it out. That's what I told Beck. It's what I tell everybody. Some of them listen, and some of them don't.'

As it turned out, neither Allen nor Wise was in particular danger of losing his job. Culpability had been shifted onto the staff of the convalescent home that had cleared Beck fit to return to duty. In their turn they'd come up with a psychiatric report which classified their former patient as secretive and unpredictable. Fitz had a quiet laugh at that one; he'd marked Beck down as a potential suicide two and a half years ago. The looming inquiry into Anson Road's handling of the Harvey case lost much of its threat, and Wise's team got on with the task in hand, preparing the case against his wife for the CPS. A task they'd be returning to after the funeral.

The service finished. With Temple, dressed in a designer suit (the man had the most extraordinary wardrobe for a plain-clothes officer), and Skelton (who'd responded to the death, as he had to everything else, with unremitting openness) among the pallbearers, the coffin was taken out. Fitz watched it being lowered with a sense of relief, and he couldn't help but glance across at Jane Penhaligon to study her reaction. She was staring into space, a tiny smile on her lips.

Proceedings adjourned to a nearby Irish pub, brown and smoke-filled and noisy, with another traditional band in its corner. Fading daylight filtered weakly through frosted glass. Fitz found he didn't mind the music half so much in these surroundings. To him the world always looked far rosier from inside a pub, whatever might be going on. He'd intended to slip away quietly before now, but the appropriate moment hadn't come, and he wanted to keep an eye on Penhaligon. Well, someone had to look after her. She was at the bar when he entered, handing over a fiver. She received very little change, and when she turned round Fitz saw why. Was that a triple vodka? She walked past without catching his eye, stirring the ice with a parti-coloured cocktail umbrella. Something had changed inside her. There was a new and dangerous set to her features, as if Beck's funeral had settled the ground and she was ready to move on. She needed the drink for a reason. Oblivion? Not likely. Drink excuses one; she was preparing to cause a scene, to let something out. He recognised the tactic. It was part of his own arsenal.

'I'll have a water,' he told the barman, who responded with a blank glare. 'Just water, thanks.'

The barman looked him over doubtfully. 'Are you sure?'

'The stuff that I drink is more mature than the dead man ever was,' he replied. 'And I wouldn't offend a good whisky. Water.'

He felt a tap on his shoulder. Wise was at his side. 'Aileen Beck wants a word with you, big lad.'

Fitz swallowed. 'Christ.' He turned to the barman. 'Make that a double water.'

On his way over he passed Penhaligon, empty glass in hand, making her way back to the bar. She kept her eyes fixed straight ahead, not looking at anyone or anything. Building herself up to blow. Fitz thought fondly of his younger days, of slugging down triple measures in under a minute. Everybody needs nostalgia, as he was fond of telling Judith; even the self-destructive mark their path to inward immolation with fond moments.

Closer up, Aileen Beck's was an even more memorable face. She had her brother's jawline, in her firmer and full of character. Fitz pictured their past, imagined Jimmy's frantic efforts to keep up with her. Another woman, perhaps the first, to have bettered him, emasculated him. Expecting the worst, he raised a quizzical eyebrow.

'Hello, Fitz.' Her voice was warm, patient. 'Please sit down.' He sat, and kept silent, still unsure. 'You know, Jimmy barely wrote,' she said. 'He only called once in a blue moon, and never for long. But it was your name that came up most often. I just wanted to put a face to a friend.'

Fitz worked hard to suppress a giggle. 'That's all right,' was all he could say.

'To tell you the truth, I imagined you were an Austrian. You know, Fitz sounds a bit like Fritz, and you being a shrink. You obviously made quite an impact on him.'

Fitz thought back to the sanatorium (*'There's nothing wrong with me'*), to the panic attack (*'Women need rape, Penhaligon needs rape'*), to the rooftop (*'This is a dying man's statement'*). 'We talked at length about several things.'

Aileen nodded, uncertain how to take this. She went on. 'He took real interest in your work. Particularly when his friend was killed.'

'David Bilborough, yes,' said Fitz, sipping at his drink.

'Jimmy didn't seem the same after that. He called even less. I knew he'd been hurt by it, but it was all I could do to offer my support, and he didn't seem to want to know. It was just like him, though, cutting himself off.' She smiled weakly. 'You know, he was just twelve when he first said he was going to be a police-man. Not wanted to be, going to be. We thought it was a great joke. I mean to say, if you'd known him then, it was such a rich irony. He was always in trouble for something, mixing with the wrong gang. He never started anything, mind, but he was always in there somewhere. But I never doubted he'd do it. He had a good sense of right and wrong, you know.'

Fitz almost remarked that such rigidity could be a handicap, but two things stopped him. One, he didn't want to break Aileen's idealised vision of her lying, raping brother; two, there was a disturbance over at the bar. He heard snatches of raised voices, Wise's and Penhaligon's. He'd been right to come along.

'Will you behave,' Wise was saying. 'This is meant to be a bloody funeral. You're still on duty. How many have you had?'

'I don't see that's your concern,' said Penhaligon. She drained her second glass. Six measures in six minutes. 'When you're ready,' she told the barman.

Fitz became aware that Aileen was staring at him wist-fully, mistaking his distracted expression for melancholy. 'Look, Fitz, I don't want any details. Not today. But did Jimmy go wrong somewhere?'

'Yes,' he said.

'Badly wrong?'

'Yes.'

She took a card from her bag and passed it across. Fitz studied it. Aileen Beck, of St Martin's Chambers, Belfast. He'd been correct. 'There's another sister, isn't there?'

'I'm sorry? No, there were only the two of us.'

20

'Ah.' Fitz pocketed the card. 'Only he told me his sister was a nurse.'

'Did he?' It really hurt her, but it was no surprise. Her shoulders stiffened in resignation. And that proved it, that she knew her brother's character. She knew that Jimmy Beck could never let a woman get ahead of him. 'Good old Jimmy, eh? Well, hopefully you'll ring me when you've time to talk.' He nodded.

The ferment at the bar was growing louder, and gradually the surrounding conversation died away. Penhaligon was knocking back another neat vodka. Wise hissed loudly, 'Jane, nobody forced you to come back. You didn't have to come here today.'

'Oh, I did, sir.' She smiled and said loudly, 'I wanted to watch him burn. I was disappointed when I realised it was a burial.'

Wise signalled over his head. 'Skelton, take her home.'

'I'm going nowhere.' She fixed Wise with her most formidable glare. Fitz was impressed. It was the first time in a week she'd looked anyone in the face. 'I want promotion,' she said, loudly and simply.

Fitz decided to intervene. Nodding an apology to Aileen he sidled over and took Penhaligon lightly by the arm. 'Not exactly the best time to cause a scene, Jane.'

'Don't be such a bloody hypocrite.' Her cheeks burned red. 'I deserve promotion. Not because of –' she faltered '– what happened, but because I've earned it, because –' she turned back to Wise '– it should have been me, last year, after Bilborough.'

'Will you keep your bloody voice down?' hissed Wise.

'Will you stop telling me to shut up?' Her voice slurred. 'If I've got something to say, I shall bloody well say it. All right?' She moved away from the bar, swooned and nearly collapsed.

Fitz straightened her up, nodded goodbye to Aileen – 'Nice to have met you' – and walked off with his ex-lover under his arm.

Bill couldn't keep calm. The factory girls seemed to blame him for the trouble, and muttered darkly in his presence, but he didn't mind. Things felt different now. He kept on with his job, pushing the trolley back and forth, machines to stores and load, stores to machines and unload, only now his heart was thumping and he was short of breath. His encounter with Grady weighed heavily on his mind. In those brief moments the world had opened up. It wasn't his imagination, somehow he just knew. He didn't have to be a reject, he could get away from Wiverton. He could belong.

At six the buzzer rang and the girls rose from their machines and shucked off their aprons. Bill watched them collect their cards and clock out and his head spun with thoughts of Wiverton and its dark and crowded common room. His room, his tosser of a roommate. He couldn't talk to him or anyone else there. Nobody understood, they had the wrong idea about him. They watched everything he did and saw it in the wrong light, in a twisted way. Always bringing up the past without once trying to see what it meant. He wanted to show someone his real self, make a proper friend with someone who knew about life. He wanted something more than that, too, but right now he was unsure about that.

He joined the queue for clocking out. The girls at the front were filing out into the forecourt, to husbands and waiting cars. Through the main door Bill saw the beginning of the long road leading back towards Wiverton, thought of himself trudging down there in the fading light alone as he had the night before. Even the image of it felt like a closing in. In that moment he made up his mind. He was seventeen. It was time he took control, showed them he could make his own choices. He wouldn't return. He'd thought about it all afternoon, and had a plan worked out. He wasn't daft and now he had a mate. The look they'd shared had been significant. It couldn't be ignored, it was the start of something.

He waited for his turn, stamped his card, put it in its place on the wall with the others, then immediately turned about and entered the machine room. The bustle of the day had ceased, and just a handful of women worked on a smaller bench, on specialised tasks. Bill swallowed, gathering the nerve. He wasn't sure how to go about this. All he knew for sure was that Grady wasn't going to reject him.

He walked across to the work table and watched Grady guiding one of the women in her task. He had his supervisor's coat off and his sleeves rolled up. Bill watched him, admiring the latent strength of his body. He wanted to learn more, discover everything about the man, be his mate.

Grady looked up. Again Bill saw the flicker in his eyes, a nervousness, a sensitivity no-one else could see. There was a lot in those eyes. 'You forgotten something?'

'I was thinking.' This time Bill held his stare. 'I could do some overtime.'

'You're not on the list. Go home.'

Bill pointed to the cutters. 'They're going to be running out of rolls soon. And you're not going to bring them up, are you?'

Grady frowned. There was a moment's silence. Then he gestured towards the stores and said, without smiling, 'Go on, then.'

Bill grabbed a trolley and set off, his heart thumping. He'd done it. His days at Wiverton were over, and his new life was beginning.

Fitz decided he didn't like the prospect of an inebriated Penhaligon. Nobody enjoys staring into the reflection of their own worst flaw. While he tried to hail a cab, she was bent double against a wall, shaking her head to clear it. Bit late for that now.

'You know what I'd like?' she asked. She sounded as if she was about to vomit.

'No.' He held out his hand, and another cab sped by. They didn't look like good business, he had to admit.

'I'd like you to take me home . . .' she began, drawing out the words.

Fitz frowned. Another surprise. At any other time he'd welcome the offer (the prospect of a resumption of their erotic union had dominated a section of his subconscious for many months) but he knew better than to trust to drunken ramblings. He couldn't count the number of times he'd got pissed and fallen in lust with the most unlikely people. Drink and former friends should never be mixed.

'I'd like you to take me home,' she drawled on, 'put me into the shower, dry my hair, and take me to bed.'

The idea was tempting but sense prevailed. 'I can't.'

'You *can't*?' She stood up as best she was able and tottered over. 'Christ. Who is this talking? Mr Mothercare? Mr Early bloody Learning Centre?'

'The baby's got nothing to do with it,' he said, truthfully, he hoped.

She laughed. 'Oh yeah?' Staring him right in the eye she continued, 'That baby wasn't exactly planned. If Judith hadn't got pregnant you'd never have got back with her. If the kid means nothing, prove it, come on, prove it. Sleep with me.' She threw her arms up in the air.

'No.'

'Crap the baby means nothing.' She poked a finger into his stomach. 'You can fake lots of things, Fitz, but you can't fake that, not with me.'

He held her stare. 'I won't sleep with you because you've been through a lot, and now you've been drinking, which gives you an opportunity to overcompensate. You think you need it; you don't. Besides which, you're not ready yet.' Another cab approached and he hailed it successfully.

He saw the hurt in her eyes as the truth he'd spoken sunk in. She slapped him, hard, across the face with the back of her hand, yelled, 'Oh, just piss off, Fitz, just piss off,' and climbed into the back of the cab.

Fitz gave the driver the address and whispered, 'Look after her.' Then he watched the cab pull away and fade into the city traffic with a genuine (he hoped) sense of sadness and loss.

● ● ●

Judith, Hoover in hand, caught herself in the hall mirror. The image exuded unhappiness. In the lamplight her face looked pale and lined and her body haggard and shapeless. Right after leaving hospital she'd gone out and without thinking bought three pairs of wool leggings. If there was no need to leave the house, without a pram anyway, what was the point of glamour? On trips to the park she passed groups of much younger women with their own babies and swerved into the cover of hedgerows to avoid them. Always the same questions if she stopped, and the forced cheeriness of her replies made her sick to the heart. Pregnancy and childbirth made one public property. This was like being plunged over ten years back in time, and all her achievements, she realised, counted for nothing. Often she thought back twelve months, to the demands of career, to her office and her workers, to a life lived without Fitz, and stifled tears at the prospect of vanished potential. Once she'd made a difference, now she was back to being just a reproductive machine. Her feelings for the child changed by the minute. Constant love, yes, but also spells of indifference and frustration. Already the off-spring reminded her of its father; he was bigger than Mark or Katie had been, with great ballooned-up cheeks and rolling eyes. She caught the baby staring at nothing one morning and the features were a perfect impression of his dad after a binge. And were his wails laced with a trace of Scottish accent? The possibility of having helped to bring a second Fitz into being only added to her load of depression.

She heard footsteps coming along the drive. Fitz's, and she didn't like their confidence. To see him sober at the moment of her greatest weakness felt like an insult. She knew why. Because it wasn't going to last. She had seen many of these spry periods, which ended always in unreturned calls, mysterious absences and abrupt financial crises. If she got some of the hurt in now, she thought, and did not allow herself to be gulled, then the inevitable fall wouldn't hurt so much. She turned on the Hoover and swiped it aggressively across the hall carpet, making a pattern of deep grooves.

The door burst open. He stood on the threshold, his vastness almost obscured by a huge object wrapped in brown paper. She tried not to look up and started doing the stairs.

'Hello,' he called, wiggling his fingers under her nose. 'Hello, planet Earth calling.'

She stretched out a toe and clicked the Hoover off. Without looking up she unplugged it and started looping up the lead. 'What do you want?'

He smiled and ripped off the wrapping. Judith winced inwardly at the sight of the painting. A couple of weeks ago she'd have loved him for this. She sunk deeper. For what did her interests or individuality matter now? Who cared what she liked or despised? The gift was a cynical ploy. He was gearing up for a return to his old ways and this was the opening gambit. There was nothing worse than when he spent his winnings on her.

He finished the unwrapping. 'It's for you.'

She ignored him and put the Hoover away under the stairs.

He pursued her. 'There's meant to be a protocol here. "Thank you, darling" and a stiff drink. A bit of gratitude, you know.'

27

Keeping her voice low, because she wasn't going to rise to him until the last moment, she said, 'If your mother's money meant sod all and your winnings even less, how grateful did you expect me to be?' She turned to him. 'You promised. Or don't you remember the birth of our child?'

He wagged a finger, his expression hurt. 'Wrong. Wrong. I put the deposit down for this weeks ago, just after the last big phone bill.'

She considered. His hurt sounded genuine.

'I wasted this money when we were absolutely skint.' He added emphatically, 'As a present, for you.'

What did it matter if this was the truth? 'Shucks,' she said flatly, 'you shouldn't have.' She went into the kitchen and flicked on the iron. There was a big pile to get through. The baby lay quietly in a corner, staring across at the bright colours of the television. They'd watched a lot together recently. The jackpot on *Wheel of Fortune* was looming. The finalist was in her early fifties, looked saggy and deadbeat, with split ends of straw-coloured hair. Judith felt a rush of sisterly empathy for her as the wheel spun.

Fitz had followed her. 'We buried the bastard.'

'Really.' She started ironing. The wheel was now a whirling rainbow.

'Wise thinks,' Fitz carried on, 'he can get us through the inquiry unscathed. It's the court case that'll be the real nightmare.' He rubbed his hands. 'In the dock again, I can't wait.'

'Oh.' The wheel had come to rest. The jackpot question was taken from its envelope.

Fitz sniffed. 'Are the drains blocked?'

'No.' The big prize question was asked.

'Has Mark got his shoes off?'

'Mark's gone out.' The contestant pondered.

'Baby's crapped, then,' said Fitz.

Judith left the iron and with one hand removed a nappy, wipes and a tube of cream from a changing bag. She picked up the baby in her other hand, and deposited both loads onto him. 'You know how, I'm sure.'

She returned to the ironing board. There was much jubilation, shaking of hands and presentation of cheques. Her soul sister had picked up thousands. Judith smiled for her, and paid no mind to Fitz, who mumbled as he left the room, baby in hand.

Grady chipped at the woodblock, his brow furrowed in concentration. Regularly he checked his work against the print he was following. The curved section at the bird's wing-tip looked difficult, and he shook his head ruefully at the prospect of copying it. Sometimes you have to know your limits, he thought. He was a good draughtsman, a fine worker, but no artist.

He returned the chisel to its case and brought his fingers up to his tired eyes. The only light came from a small lamp angled over his work table and his head was swimming. On certain nights he could continue working until two or three without noticing, and when he stopped it was like coming up for air. He might lose himself in the sculpture, spend an hour scraping away precisely at a particular part. The detail and concentration were important, because he couldn't allow his mind to wander.

He turned off the lamp, pulled off his tee shirt and jeans, and threw himself, exhausted, into bed. The headlights of a passing car picked out the bareness of his bedsit. When the bed was pulled down there was almost no floor space left; his work table and easy chair took up the rest of the room. The furnishings belonged to his landlords, the Franklins, a middle-aged couple who lived in the room across the hall. There was one other tenant, on the upper floor, a nurse at the General. Grady tried to avoid making the comparison between this place and his previous accommodation, a two-bedroomed bungalow on the estate at Bretherton. In the main he tried to avoid thinking about himself at all.

He was, after all, disgusting.

Little by little he fell into half-sleep, his thoughts dwindling. Undisciplined, his mind roamed free, throwing up half-forgotten faces, irrelevant memories, illogical strands of ideas. The world faded, and all the while there was one face and one thought dominating him. The boy, Bill Nash. For a second a thought pushed itself up to his forebrain and a rush of responses, lust, sadness, anger, followed in its wake. He saw himself walking in from the loading bay that afternoon to the sound of Linda and the girls on one of their riots, expecting to find them pissing about with one of the fork-lift drivers. He saw the blue jeans in Linda's grasp, waving above the heads of the crowd. He saw Bill's legs, kicking, strong and young, dusted with pale down, the flash of blue underwear.

He sat up in bed, gasping, pushed his hands back up to his strained eyes and rubbed. Awake again. Now he remembered Bill's backward glance as he walked off, his plea for overtime. Grady had avoided him all evening, kept his eyes away from the lad as he pushed the empty trolley away to stores, told himself to ignore the fluttering in his chest whenever the plastic sheeting rustled and the boy returned. Now, sitting in bed in the dark, he felt vile, a contaminating influence. His body was responding to his sickness, out of his control, an erection straining against his briefs. A voice somewhere far back in his head was urging him to abandon decency. Abandon it because the boy had looked back. Because the boy was interested.

He was still contemplating himself when the hall telephone rang. The Franklins, his landlords, had already given Joyce a warning against late-night calls. There hadn't been such a disturbance in weeks. Glad of the distraction he got back into his jeans, went into the hall and lifted the receiver.

'Yes?' he whispered, looking anxiously over at the Franklins' door. A muffled groan and a thump came from their bedroom. He didn't want to wind them up.

'Mr Stuart Grady?' an officious voice asked.

'Yes.' He swallowed, illogically connecting the voice of authority to his thoughts of a minute before.

'Mr Grady, I'm Constable Pallden. There looks to have been a break-in at your place of work. Alarms have gone off. We have you down as the keyholder, can you come over quick as you can, sir?'

'Right away,' said Grady. 'There in five minutes.' He dressed hurriedly, grabbed his keys, and dashed out. Secretly he was pleased. Without this interruption the night could have been one of his worst.

He arrived in the forecourt to find a police car and two uniformed coppers moving around by the loading bay doors, shining their torches upwards and around the big windows of the factory. One of the interior electronic alarms was bleeping incessantly, the sound continuous, nerve-incising.

Grady got out of his car. One of the coppers came across. 'Mr Grady?'

He nodded. 'What's going on, then?'

'There's a broken window by the loading bay. We reckon they're still in there. Got any computers and that inside?'

Grady nodded. 'Couple in my office, another one in the orders and accounts room.'

'We thought so. They'd have to be daft to try and get any of the lifting gear out. It's a bad job, anyway. Kids, I reckon.' He gestured apologetically to himself and his comrade. 'Back-up's on its way, two minutes.'

'Right you are.' Grady pulled out his keys. 'Well, there's no other way out.' He led the copper round the corner to the main doors, punched in his security code, opened both locks and swung open the door. Behind him he heard another police car drawing up and footsteps moving swiftly over the tarmac.

'You don't have to come in with us, sir,' said the leading copper.

Grady bristled. 'I can handle myself all right. And you'll need someone to show you about.'

The copper considered, looked him over, nodded. Grady led the way into the darkened factory.

In the night it could have been a different place. The familiar smells of sawdust, cotton, dye and oil seemed sharper, and the storage aisles and abandoned fork-lifts gave the place the air of an abandoned ship. And someone was hiding here, waiting out, hidden away, ready to run. Perversely the thought gave comfort to Grady; the proximity to threat was refreshing. His nostrils flared as he led the coppers down the shadowy aisles of the storage section, ever watchful, towards the machine room and the offices. Torchlight played against the stacked rolls of fabric, revealing a big industrial vacuum cleaner, a newspaper, the chute leading to dispatch. In the night these ordinary things were made to seem strange. Grady felt a thrill run across his shoulderblades. A trespasser, an unwanted presence, might resist. Might even put up a fight. There could be more than one of them. None of the coppers following him looked capable of hitting back with the necessary force. Grady felt useful, for the first time in months, because he could hit back. He was trained. His heart beat faster. He recalled his youth in the ATC, night exercises, slipping in and out of cover, every sense alert.

He entered the machine room and flicked on the striplights. The copper shouted a warning. Nobody about. He turned to the leading copper and shook his head, then jerked a thumb over his shoulder to indicate the admin office at the far end of the room. The copper signalled his understanding, and motioned to two of his men to follow.

Grady strode silently towards the office door. He peered through the window. Nobody in view. They must have hidden away, didn't realise there was only one way out. They were trapped. And if they wanted to fight, let them try. He tensed and relaxed his muscles, recalling his training. He longed to take a run-up, kick the door in. He longed for a weapon.

This was life. He'd forgotten how much he missed it.

'I'll take in there,' said the copper, gesturing to the accounts section, on the far side of the rows of machine tables. Grady nodded and made for his own office.

He turned the handle of the door and swung it open slowly, without a squeak. The striplights outside reflected off the dormant screens of the computers. The coppers had got it wrong, then. Maybe this was just a case of kids mucking about.

He sensed a movement and tensed. Just perceptibly he caught a flicker of activity in one corner, somebody sitting or lying half under the desk. Without thinking, he raised one hand to the light switch and felt with the other around the desktop, searching for the knife he used to open letters. This could be anyone, possibly armed. He wasn't going to take any chances about that. His fingers trailed over sheets of paper, his out-tray, his pencils. He found the knife, curled his fingers around it, raised it to shoulder height, and flicked on the lights.

Bill Nash lay on the floor, looking up, dazzled by the light.

Grady swore, quietly. A rush of emotions passed through him at the sight. Those brown eyes, they were beautiful, there was no other word, beautiful. The boy was lying between two rolls of fabric taken from the stores, with his head leant up against a smaller bale as a pillow. Lying next to his makeshift bed were a couple of empty Coke cans and a discarded plastic sandwich wrapper.

His anger evaporating, Grady threw the knife back on

the desk. 'What the hell are you doing?' he hissed down at the boy. He knew he ought to report this. He would, if this was anybody but Bill, who looked up at him now with his pleading expression. He felt an enormous tenderness for the lad, wanted to scoop him up, press his beating heart against his own chest, cradle his perfect head against his own shoulder. Instead, aware that the coppers were coming closer, he whispered, 'Bill, you'd better start talking.'

'I'm on a ten o'clock curfew. I didn't get back 'til eleven. I got kicked out.'

'You didn't have to do the overtime, you daft sod.'

Bill propped himself up on his elbows and looked him straight in the eye. 'I wanted to,' he said.

Grady felt the world spin around him. This was all wrong. Things like this just didn't happen.

'Anything in there?' one of the coppers called. 'Mr Grady?'

Grady stood for what seemed a long moment on the threshold of the office. His sense of duty screamed at him to drag Bill out into the machine room. Then his mind ran through the consequences. The boy would be nicked. Curfew, he'd said. That meant he was already in some kind of trouble. If he got into more Grady would probably never see him again.

He looked into Bill's shining eyes and backed out of the office, closing the door as he went. 'They've touched nothing in there,' he told the coppers. 'Could be just kids buggering about, couldn't it?'

The leading copper nodded. 'Probably scarpered when the alarm went off.' His colleagues were returning from the factory's darker corners with nothing to report.

He turned to Grady. 'When's your working day start here, then?'

'First shift clocks in at seven thirty. Flexi-time, you know.' His pulses were racing. Over his shoulder he could sense Bill's presence, as if he could feel his warmth.

'Right,' said the copper. 'We'll keep one eye on the place until then, OK? I don't think they'll be back. You'd better reset the alarm.' He looked Grady's muscular frame over. 'You all right to lock up again?'

Grady felt a flash of irritation. 'I said I can look after myself.'

The copper nodded. 'I'm sure you can. Work out, do you?'

'I keep my hand in,' said Grady.

With a tip of the head the copper summoned his colleagues and they left the machine room. Grady waited anxiously as their footsteps receded. Only when he heard, distantly under the alarm, the sound of two car engines firing up did he turn back to the office.

He stuck his head through the door and into the darkness. 'Pack that stuff away and come on.'

He heard Bill shifting. His slender outline was just discernible in the light spilling from the machine room. 'Have those coppers gone?'

'Yes. Now come on.'

'Where are we going?' He started to roll up his makeshift sleeping bag.

Grady swallowed. 'You can kip over at my place.'

Bill sighed with relief. 'Cheers, mate.'

'Only this one night, you mind.' Grady raised his voice. 'You can get yourself some digs right away, do you hear?'

'Sure. Whatever. Cheers again.' Bill moved into the light. Grady pulled his eyes away from the lad's tee shirted frame and led him out to the loading bay. His hands were shaking.

The journey back was spent in silence. Grady kept his head straight, his eyes on the road. He battled to suppress the force of his physical reaction to his passenger. The boy even smelled fresh, lovely. Being near him was for Grady like staring into a pit of vileness. Descend once and you could never climb out. This was all so terribly wrong.

The car pulled up outside his digs. He pulled out a packet of cigarettes and offered one to Bill. He accepted. Their hands touched briefly as it was passed across and the contact was electric. Again he kept his eyes away from Bill's as he lit the cigarettes.

'You on probation, then?'

'No. Halfway house. You know, Wiverton?'

'Halfway from what?'

'Children's home. Sowerby Park.'

'Come on, then.' Grady got out of the car. A downstairs light was on in the Franklins' flat. In the morning he was bound to hear something about this. 'And keep your voice down. I don't want to disturb anyone, right?'

'Right.'

They walked towards the front door. Back in the open air Grady felt a slight lifting of his spirits. He was, he told himself, just doing someone a favour. No great significance in this. Anybody would have done the same. Any kind-hearted person. Trouble was, he was not and never had been kind-hearted. Looked at in any other light this situation looked exactly what it was.

Christ, how he loathed himself.

He let Bill into his flat and right away collected a beer from the fridge. Behave like a mate, he told himself. Don't let the weakness show. Act the part, do what a man would do. He threw another can to Bill, casually. Mustn't think, mustn't talk. Just forget it all, get to sleep.

Bill accepted the can, pulled the ring, sighed and sat at the edge of the bed. Grady's double bed.

A disgusting image entered Grady's mind. 'You'll have to kip on the floor,' he told Bill hurriedly. He opened a drawer and threw down a sleeping bag.

Bill smiled. 'Thanks.' He slid off the bed and started to unroll the sleeping bag.

Grady downed his beer in five gulps, undressed, and got between the sheets. He listened, waiting until Bill stopped moving about, heard the zip of the bag being done up, then reached out and clicked off the table lamp.

There was a horrendous silence. Grady turned in his bed, creaking the springs. A moment later Bill shifted, rustling the quilted fabric of the sleeping bag. In the distance a train went by. The only other sound was the ticking of Grady's alarm clock.

Grady stared up at the ceiling and prayed for forgiveness. In the street it was so easy to walk by, to look away. In this proximity his body was screaming for release. He was sick.

He heard movement. What, he wondered, if Bill got into the bed with him now? How would he react?

Which part of him would triumph in the end?

He licked his lips and propped himself up on his elbows. 'What are you doing now?' he whispered.

There was no answer. Grady flicked the light back on.

Bill, wearing nothing but his pants, was leaning on the work table. His slender upper torso was smooth, with only a few tufts of hair about his chest. Grady stared at the tiny pink discs of his nipples, imagined kissing them tenderly, flicking at the little hairs with his tongue. 'What are you doing?' he repeated.

Bill pointed out the carving. His face was alive with interest, with ambition, life, strength, the vitality of youth. 'Did you do this?' He picked up one of the gouges from their case.

Grady swung himself out of bed. 'Don't touch it,' he hissed.

Bill put the gouge down. 'What's it going to be?'

Grady pointed out the line drawing he'd been working from. 'It's called a lanner falcon.'

'I wish I could do something like this.'

'So do I.' Grady managed a small laugh. 'A mate got me into it, when I was in Cyprus.'

'You were in the army?'

Grady bristled. Scenes from the past flashed through his mind. Cyprus, Jackie, a broken beer glass, fists flying, the last day at Bretherton, sitting apart from the other lads in the refectory. 'You don't have to be in the army to go abroad.'

'Your sleeping bag's got a serial number on it,' Bill said precociously. He looked up at Grady with thinly disguised admiration. 'You ever have to kill anybody?'

Grady was amused. 'Dozens of times,' he said tersely.

The look on Bill's face was a picture. Then he raised a finger and snickered. 'Get away. If you really had, you wouldn't say.'

Grady didn't like the way they were talking. It wasn't right. Too friendly. They barely knew each other. They were alone but he felt as if the world was watching them, and saying the wrong thing or behaving in the wrong way would damn him forever. He said, as loudly as he felt he could (he didn't want to disturb the Franklins), 'You're not completely stupid, then? So why did you break into the factory? You must have known it was alarmed.'

Bill said softly, 'I knew you had the keys. I knew you'd have to come and get me.' As he spoke he moved closer. His gaze passed briefly over Grady's exposed chest, his sharply defined muscles and curls of thick hair, and smiled shyly. Then his eyes moved back up and connected with Grady's.

They held the look for several seconds. Grady felt the world turning again. Boys do not behave like this, I do not behave like this.

He moved back to his bed. 'Get some kip,' he said. 'You'll need your energy if you're looking for digs tomorrow.' He put the light out again.

Bill found it hard to keep his eyelids down. Grady was ex-army! And built like an outhouse. He thought back to the factory, the look on Grady's face when he'd put the office lights on. The man was afraid of nothing. He'd been abroad, seen a lot of things, knew the workings of the world. Wasn't a thick squaddie, though. That carving took real skill and patience. Bill knew he'd never be able to do something like that.

Yes, Grady was brave and strong. He could show the way, better than anyone at Wiverton. Best of all, he was interested. They were going to be good mates.

They were going to be so good together.

THREE

Fitz examined the client on the other side of his study desk. Only nine thirty and the bloke was opening up his soul. Getting confessional in the morning, a sign of real distress. It was true, most problems do go away over-night. They come back in the afternoon and you're depressed again in the evening, suicidal by nightfall. Only the most screwed-up can ignore the alleviating trill of birdsong. Spring sunlight filtered through the blind, giving the room a neutral, clinical ambience in spite of the disorder of his files and books.

'It's like, well, I'll be walking through a crowd of women,' said the client, crossing and uncrossing his legs, 'and I'm thinking, well, she might be here. You know, the one I'll fall in love with, the one who'll fall in love with me.' His knees shook. Fitz looked at his face. Young for twenty-nine, with silver, square-framed specs and traces of acne. There were far uglier people with splendidly rumbustious private lives (naming no names). Whither, then, the problem? 'None of them look at me,' the client went on. 'Not directly. It's as if I'm completely transparent, or a member of some alien species or something. And they know how nervous I am, when I do talk to them. They're being friendly and being kind. That makes it worse, you know, somehow. I mean, what woman would have me?' He looked over at Fitz. 'I just want to open my mouth and speak.'

Fitz waved a finger. 'Saying?'

'Well, just something like "I want to buy you a drink." '

'Why don't you?'

'They'll laugh. Like they always do.'

Fitz slapped a hand down on the desktop. 'For God's sakes don't censor your fantasies, Eric, or we'll never get you through that packet of three.' The client managed a watery smile. 'Look. You know the girl you want. You're desperate to make contact. Imagine the scene when nobody laughs. When she looks at you as if that moment's completely shared, and she's relieved you said it first.'

Eric looked doubtful. 'Well, I've tried . . .'

'Come on,' said Fitz. 'Come on, say it now.'

'I can't.'

'Say it, now.'

Eric took a deep breath. 'I think I love you and I want to buy you a drink.'

There was a loud squelching fart. Fitz gestured apologetically to the pram in the corner, reached over and rocked his new son gently back to sleep. 'I'm sorry. I'm sure that wasn't personal.'

Grady woke, and the world felt different. In the daylight Bill's sleeping face looked angelic. He craned his neck to watch, and lay for a few minutes simply looking at the sleeping boy and considering the future. There was nothing swish about the lad. He moved like a bloke and talked like a bloke. Best of all, he wasn't going to let anybody stop him. He'd seen what he wanted and gone for it brazenly. And what he wanted was Grady.

An impossible thought entered Grady's head. What if he just went over now, pulled down the zip of the sleeping bag, kissed Bill awake? Bill was brave, he could show the way. It's what the boy wanted, wasn't it? There was no other explanation for his behaviour. He hesitated a second, and the next moment the prospect seemed unspeakable. It was daft, but he felt as if his mother, and his old mates, and Jackie and young Michael, could somehow all see him now, as if they had a camera scanning his life and were just waiting for him to succumb. He heard names, insults, dirty stories, pictured the shame of discovery, the way such things were seen. The sick way you had to be if you did such a thing. It wasn't for him. He knew he'd never be able to make such a move, and with the realisation came a hollow, lonely feeling.

Bill, aware somehow he was being watched, opened a sleepy eye and groaned. 'Hiya.'

Grady grunted in reply. 'You want breakfast?'

'If it's going. Ta. Can I have a shower?'

Grady pointed to the kitchen. 'There's a bathroom through there. There's a bath with an attachment, that's all.'

'Fine.' He started to climb out of the sleeping bag, every detail of his perfect young body revealed in the light. Afraid he might weaken, Grady threw on a shirt and jeans and made for the kitchenette. As he cracked two eggs into the pan a smile broke out on his face. He didn't know why. What was going on? He felt hesitant and expectant. This was, he sensed, the very beginning of a long, long journey. It wasn't going to be easy but at last he was starting. Bill passed behind him. He heard the shower turned on and his smile broadened. A feeling was pushing itself up from deep inside, something good, something positive, at last. He had a guide. He wasn't alone any more.

'I'm not due in work 'til this aft,' he called over his shoulder. 'It's all right, I'll cover you.' He felt he should remind Bill to look for digs. The idea seemed suddenly ludicrous.

'Do you want to do something, then?' called Bill.

Grady's heart pounded. His eyes flicked between the bathroom door and the frying eggs. Through the frosted glass of the kitchenette's window he could see the houses opposite, lined with silver birches, ordinary people walking by, all as it had ever been. But just here, inside his tiny rotten bedsit, the world was changing. *Yes*, he wanted to shout back, *yes I want to do something. I want to grab you naked from the shower, throw you onto the bed and shag your brains out.*

Instead he called back, 'I suppose we could go swimming.'

There was a knock at the door. Three sharp raps. He cursed and turned the gas and the radio down. Had to be Mrs Franklin, to have a go about last night. All he had to do was apologise ardently and explain about the burglary. But she mustn't see Bill. She'd charged Joyce extra rent for having mates from the hospital over and he couldn't afford either the extra money or an argument. He hated confrontation. He closed the door that partitioned off the kitchenette and bathroom, kicked the sleeping bag into a corner, and made to answer her. On

45

the way he smoothed down his bedclothes.

He opened the door, keeping it on the chain. She was in her dressing gown and bare feet, but fully made up. She had an ignorant, brassy air. Still, she was his landlady and he had to put up, as you do. 'Yeah? Look, I'm sorry about the phone call, but I –'

'Rent,' she said.

'I stuck it under your door last Friday. Did you not –'

'And the rest.' She smiled, raised a roguish eyebrow.

Grady took the chain off and opened the door. 'Sorry, what do you mean?'

She remained on the threshold, leant against the jamb. 'Can I smell a fry-up? You never cook breakfast normally. She's obviously worth it. That's fifteen quid you owe me.' She raised her eyebrow again, not without good humour, like they were sharing a joke.

Grady swallowed. 'Look, I don't know what you're talking about, I've –'

'Look, you're a nice bloke, Stuart. I'm not saying you can't. I'm saying to you, like I said to Joyce, guests have to be paid for. Fifteen quid.'

Grady heard the kitchenette door open and turned. Bill was walking through, wearing just his jeans, towelling his hair, his upper half still wet, gleaming in the morning sun. 'You got a hairdrier?' he asked.

Mrs Franklin's face twisted, became a mask of hatred. She recoiled physically from the door, unfolded her arms, stared. Grady felt his temples starting to pump again. 'Now I'm saying you can't,' she spat. She pulled her eyes away from Bill. 'Get that thing . . .' She stared at Grady. 'Get that *whore* out of my house, right now.'

Grady's mouth ran dry. He saw Bretherton, a broken beerglass, Jackie and young Michael. 'He's a mate from work,' he said, trying to sound natural, reasonable, but he was stuttering. 'He'd – he'd nowhere to go, he had the sleeping bag, I didn't think he'd ... I mean, I'll give you the money at the weekend if you –'

'Sixty,' she said.

Grady couldn't answer. He caught her eyes, saw the loathing in them. It was a terrible thing.

Bill came forward, shoulders pushed back aggressively. 'You what?'

Mrs Franklin ignored him. 'Sixty,' she told Grady, 'or you sling your hook.' Again she looked between him and the half-naked Bill. 'No, actually, I don't hold with this at all. Shirtlifters in my house.' She pursed her lips, shook her head, hissed through her teeth. 'You want treatment, you do.'

'He's a mate, a mate from work,' Grady stammered. There was a roaring in his head, a shortness of breath, his knees felt weak.

'A mate from work, yeah? See these feet?' She pointed downward. 'I'm Sandie Shaw. Never guess, would you?' She sneered. 'The only women you've ever had in there have been and gone in half an hour. Well, that's not normal either, is it?'

Bill strutted forward, shouted, 'Why don't you shut the frig up?'

She shook her head. 'If you're not out of here – you and your little rent boy – in two minutes, I'm ringing the flaming police. How old is he? You need locking away.' She turned her back. 'And you still owe me sixty.' She exited sharply.

Grady followed her into the hallway. Music was coming down the stairs, faintly, from Joyce's flat. 'Mrs Franklin, don't do that. We've done nothing wrong.' He reached out, put a hand on her shoulder, raised his voice, felt his anger rising, redness gathering behind his eyes. 'Mrs Franklin, please –'

She pulled away, spun round and caught him under the jaw, not lightly, with a bunched fist. 'Don't you lay a hand on me, you filthy bleeding pervert!'

Bill was at Grady's shoulder. 'Who do you think you're talking to, you silly old slag? We've done nowt wrong.' He pushed past Grady, his hand raised. There was something in his hand, an object that glinted. 'Who do you think you fucking are?'

They were now at the open door of her flat. Grady saw what happened next but his mind refused to take it in. Everything around them was so ordinary. The stairs, the music, the rattle of a train passing. She raised her fist again, intending to strike Bill; the boy raised an arm to protect himself; his hand was gripping that object, something long and metallic; its sharpened end caught the junction of arteries at Mrs Franklin's wrist; he realised it was one of his carving gouges; blood spurted in a livid red fountain over her pale skin.

'Sweet Jesus!' She fixed Bill with a desperate smile as blood pumped from her wrist, trickled down her arm. 'You've done it now, you little shit. You've had it now. They'll have you now.'

Grady saw Bill's face change at these words. He saw a raw, pure, masculine strength and dedication, an anger mixed with horror that was both terrifying and beautiful.

Bill lifted the gouge again and next second stuck it

up, up into her chest. Her bloodied arm came up. She shrieked once, ghoulishly; Bill fell against the jamb of her open door. His arm jerked back, withdrawing the implement. She fell against him, smearing his still-wet body with her blood as, with horrifying slowness, she slipped to the floor. A thick band of gore was wiped across him, trailing across the back of his neck, over his nipples and down his front. He gasped, his mouth pulled back over his teeth, sweat pouring from him.

Grady watched without speaking, without thinking, his mind blank, as she crawled into her flat, trailing blood across the stippled surface of her transparent carpet protector, the absorbent towelling of her dressing gown soaking wet and red, making her way across the room, heading slowly and inexorably past the mini-bar with its '50s kitsch figurines, past the huge speakers of the ancient stereo, skirting the pink-tasselled rug, to the small glass prism table on which rested the chunkily vulgar marble-effect telephone.

He heard Bill at his shoulder. 'Oh God, oh Christ. They'll send me back. I'll be sent back.' He was whimpering, almost crying. 'They'll send me back.'

Grady snatched a glance at his blood-spattered partner. The boy was snivelling, his face contorted. 'Do something,' the boy whispered, glancing frantically between Mrs Franklin's pathetic, mewling, groaning form and the hall stairs, the music drifting down. 'Come on, Grady, for God's sakes, do something!'

Grady looked back at Mrs Franklin. She'd reached the phone, was lifting herself up, moaning, spitting and sobbing all the while. She grunted with effort and knocked the receiver off its cradle. He watched as she

49

raised her arm, stretched out a bright stained finger, inserted it in the 9 of the dial, twisted . . .

'Do something,' sobbed Bill. 'Please, Grady.'

Grady felt something break inside him. He realised he knew exactly what to do. There was a choice. A choice between standing by Bill and betraying him. In the end it would only mean betraying himself, destroying any chance for the future. He wanted to prove himself. The world was wrong, he was right. It was time to be brave, to show Bill his strength.

He snatched the dripping gouge from Bill and strode over to Mrs Franklin. Then he bent down, found his mark, remembered his instruction in unarmed combat, stuck the weapon into her left side. Once, twice, three times. She made a horrific gurgling noise and crashed to the ground like a slaughtered pig.

Grady stood back with the gouge in his hand.

The supermarket was like an assault course. Judith felt extra-sensitive, the rattle of trolleys and beeps of checkouts getting to her. She found herself going down an aisle she'd ignored for years, baby care, and ground to a definite halt at what awaited her. It hadn't been like this with Mark or Katie. Starter nappies, boy nappies, girl nappies, big boy nappies, big girl nappies, inbetween nappies, non-leak nappies, dry-weave absorbent nappies. Her senses reeled with the overload and her grip on the trolley's crossbar tightened, knuckles whitening as the baby within, as if reacting to her bewilderment, opened its eyes, took a look at the noise and the colour, wrinkled its blubbery, Fitzlike face and began to bawl. Every face in the aisle turned to her, and the faces were young and fresh and feminine, and the bodies they belonged to were super-slim, like Stick Insect's, like bloody Penhaligon. Judith stood transfixed, shushing automatically at the baby through gritted teeth, wanting to shriek with rage at the embarrassment. The baby dismissed her attempts at reassurance and carried on wailing.

Another shopper bumped into her, sending the trolley spinning off to one side. 'Sorry, love,' said a voice. 'Are you OK?'

'Yes, yes, I'm fine,' Judith said, flashing a smile. *No, she wanted to scream. No, I am not fine. The father of this child is a drunken overweight slob with an obsession for death and disaster. He's had an affair with a stunningly attractive and much younger woman. Because of him I've been threatened by a masked killer in my own home. And now, just when I thought I had broken away, this child has led me, unsuspecting, back into the trap.*

She pushed the trolley on past the nappies, not looking where she was going. Another shopper crashed into her, there was more concern, more staring. She felt herself flush. A murmur rose.

'Will you all just –' she began, then removed the baby, hoisted his sling over her shoulder, and kicked the empty trolley away viciously with one sandalled foot. Then, muttering her apologies, she pushed through the silenced company and fled through the checkouts, empty-handed and stifling tears.

Bill reached out and patted his mate on the shoulder. 'You were brilliant, Grady, you were brilliant.'

His friend's face was haunted, his steel-blue eyes unfocused. They were crouched in the hallway, facing each other, their heads close, their lips almost touching. Bill knew what had to be done, but now Grady had faltered halfway through the task. And they had to move fast. 'Come on. Few deep breaths. A few deep breaths. Got to keep calm, yeah?'

Grady nodded and obeyed him. His knuckles tightened on his side of the plastic sheeting.

'We . . . We . . .' His head shook and he turned away from what lay between them, the splattered mess, its twelve stones weighing down the carpet protector.

'We had to do it, Grady,' said Bill. 'Look at me. We had to do it. And we've got to do this, so come on.' He looked frequently over his shoulder, up the stairs, to the source of the music. The other tenant was a nurse, working a late shift. Might come down any second. They had to get on with things. He removed his hand from Grady's shoulder and took up his side of the bundle, getting a firm grip. 'Come on. One, two, three!'

They lifted the weight, and half-stood. The body of Mrs Franklin sagged, smearing the clear plastic. Tiny rivulets of red trickled off the edges, speckling droplets on the cracked lino of the hall floor. Bill kept his head straight, focused on the matter in hand. He told himself he could get jumpy later. All they had to do was keep calm and stick together.

They reached the cellar door. Grady angled himself, bringing his hand round to the knob, and twisted. Without saying a word he led the way, taking one step at a time. Halfway down he balanced his side of the load against the damp brickwork, reached out and flicked a switch. Bright white light came from a naked bulb, shining off the blood now matted down Bill's side. A shudder ran through him at the sight but he forced it down and followed Bill the last part of the way.

In silence they laid the body gently down. It came to rest in a tangled heap, the arms and legs twisted, the head lolling back. Bill flinched at the face, at the eyeballs and open mouth caked with dried blood. The body rolled over as Grady withdrew the plastic sheeting from beneath her and folded it under one arm.

'We've got to get the blood off the hall floor,' Bill whispered. He took deep breaths, deep draughts of musty air. 'Then they'll think someone got in and did her in.'

Grady nodded again and led the way upstairs. Bill followed him back into the bedsit. Without saying a word he watched as Grady filled his washing-up bowl with hot water, squirted in some Squeezy and ripped open a packet of J cloths. He looked Bill over, head to toe. 'Get your trainers off,' he told Bill.

Bill looked down. A couple of small red dots had dried across the laces. He slipped them off and threw them under Grady's work table, where the half-finished falcon still sat. He turned back to his mate, looked him in the eye, smiled broadly. 'You think of everything,' he said. 'You're brilliant.'

Grady looked down. 'Shut up and come on.'

They emerged into the hall. Armed with a J cloth each they scrubbed at the hallway floor. Bill worked away, untroubled, trying to force his emotions down. It was weird, but in his mind he kept seeing himself and Grady from above, as if he wasn't really a part of what

53

had occurred at all. The past day kept flashing through his head – the boredom of the factory, his fears of the common room at Wiverton, slipping through the broken window and into the office – and he couldn't see any pattern, any sense at all. He looked across at Grady, watched his elbow pummelling back and forth over the lino, studied his expression. His face was set, toughened. He'd done this for Bill's sake, to keep his mate out of trouble. It was the proof Bill had been looking for. They were together now and nothing would stop them.

He returned his concentration to the matter in hand, searching the hall keenly for more spots of blood. The worst area was where they'd stopped, halfway along, and he worked hard at that, rubbing like crazy to get the stains out. The blood had dried really quickly, gone purple and sticky. Bill was accustomed to the sight. He'd seen enough of his own blood.

It took them five frantic minutes. Grady stood up, pacing the hall, searching for signs. Satisfied, he picked up the bowl and gestured to Bill to throw in his cloth.

They returned to the bedsit. As soon as the door closed, Grady pointed to the bathroom door. 'Shower.' His eyes roamed over Bill's red torso. 'Shower.'

'Yeah.' As Bill passed him he put out a hand to his face, rubbed the backs of his fingers across Grady's stubble and smiled. 'Brilliant.'

'Shower,' growled Grady, recoiling slightly. 'Shower.'

Bill got out of his jeans and pants, climbed into the bath, turned on the taps, took the full pelt of the water, closed his eyes. He turned a full circle. When he opened his eyes he looked down and watched the last of the blood running down the plughole, the water turning from brackish brown to clear. He brought his hands up to his face. Him and his mate had done good work. It was time to show people he couldn't be pushed about, and now he had a friend to help him with that.

He emerged from the shower to find a fresh pair of jeans and a clean tee shirt waiting for him. Both were a bit too big for him, but he enjoyed the feeling he got when he put them on. They smelt of Grady. He felt a part of the man.

Grady was waiting for him. His eyes were wild and sweat was pouring down his face.

'If she'd phoned the cops,' Bill blurted, 'they'd have sent me back to Sowerby Park.'

'Sowerby Park?' Grady asked, his voice a monotone.

'You know. The home.' Bill felt tears brimming. His voice faltered. 'I can't go back there, I can't stick the place. They'd have kept me 'til I was eighteen.'

Grady flinched. 'A year?' He sank into the chair at his work table. 'You daft bastard. You killed someone for the sake of a year.'

'I stabbed her. It was you that killed her,' Bill pointed out. 'I've had twelve years of it. I'm not going back.'

Grady covered his face with his hands. He said viciously, 'It's better than spending another twelve years in prison.' His shoulders heaved and he leant back in the chair, laid his palms flat on the table and stared first at them, then the falcon.

'It's all right,' said Bill. 'We'll both be OK. You weren't due in work this morning, were you? So you're covered. I can just say I slept rough. No-one's going to find out. We've just got to get out of here. You can come back home tonight. Say you went swimming. No-one knows you're even in here, do they?'

Grady leapt up, nostrils flaring, eyes turning from incomprehension to anger. He reached out with one mighty fist, grabbed Bill by the collar of his tee shirt, shook him. 'You stupid little bastard. Got it all worked out, haven't you?' He pointed to a couple of bin bags lying by the door. 'What about all of that, eh? What about all of that?'

Bill looked. His bloodsoaked jeans lay in one of the bags, along with the J cloths and the plastic sheeting, covered in their fingerprints. A towel was wrapped around the weapon. 'We just dump 'em,' he said, licking his lips. 'Couple of streets away, we'll just dump 'em.'

Grady shook him. 'What? What?'

'Nobody'll look.' Bill stared him right in the eye again, smiled. 'Nobody'll look. They'll just think someone came in and did her in. They won't bother to look.' He reached up and removed Grady's hand. At his touch the older man pulled back, shuddered.

'Right.' Grady nodded. He picked up one of the bags, knotted it, threw it to Bill, picked the other one up himself. 'Right, come on.' He turned to face the hall.

They heard the front door slam.

Phil Franklin returned from Kwik Save bearing gifts. Nowadays Mary proscribed any deviation, no matter how slight, from her list and demanded sight of till receipts as proof. She counted out two tenners and counted back every penny of the change. In these small ways they were going to rebuild some trust. A couple of years ago Phil would have viewed the thought of such acquiescence with horror, as a sign of his ultimate defeat. Much had changed, though. He persuaded himself he could see the sense of it. Well, he had no pride left.

He'd timed his return to coincide with a repeat of *The Rockford Files*. There was just time to put the shopping away, display his receipt to Mary and make a brew before it started. He'd been fortunate today. She liked to begin each day with an act of violence and it was often hard for her to find an excuse. Most days she waited for him to incriminate himself, perhaps by dripping a tea bag across the freshly wiped surface of the pedal bin or by clipping his toenails without putting paper down first, and then set to. But this morning she was gearing up to confront Stuart, the downstairs tenant. Having a woman over. Phil envied him. There was a bloke who wouldn't let himself be pushed around. Kept himself in good shape, off the booze and away from the bookies, didn't let himself get dominated by a bird. Secretly he reckoned Mary fancied the bloke and was envious. Not that a young fit bloke like Stuart would look twice at a clapped-out bag like his wife.

The door of their flat was open. 'Only me,' he called, kicking it shut behind him. He walked through into the kitchen, aware as he passed of a strange sticky feel to the lounge carpet. The protector had been taken off. Perhaps she'd spilt something. 'Mary,' he called gingerly. There was no reply. Probably slipped out for a second. He dumped his carriers on the surface, sloshed the kettle about to check the water level, grunted his approval, and flicked it on. Then he started unpacking, sorting the groceries into four piles, just as she liked.

Cupboard things, fridge things, freezer tray things and bathroom things. He put the receipt to one side, arranged the change in order of denomination on top. His task complete, he wondered again where she'd got to. Couldn't be far, not leaving the door open, she was scrupulous about locking up. Still, best not to inquire. He'd only get more trouble.

The kettle boiled. He poured the hot water onto the bag and watched it float to the top of the mug. He didn't like weak, milky tea. Some people had the bag out so quick there was hardly any point putting it in. While he waited he might as well put the telly on. He returned to the living room, picked up the remote control from the handle of his armchair, opened the flaps of his cabinet, and pressed the standby button. His portable flickered into life. The news was just finishing, the weather was coming on. He was right on time. But what if Mary came blundering in in five minutes? He'd lose the thread of the plot. These American things weren't complicated, but even so.

He nipped back to the kitchen, lifted out his tea bag, whipped it into the pedal bin taking special care not to leave drips on the surface, opened a carton of milk from the fridge things pile and poured. Nice. He went back to the lounge, settled in his armchair, sipped, slid a coaster onto the occasional table – Mary was particular about markings on surfaces – and turned up the volume.

As the programme started he heard a faint sort of tapping from somewhere.

'Out, quietly,' Grady whispered, opening the bedsit door and beckoning to Bill. He poked his head through a fraction, stared across at the open entrance to the Franklins' flat. Any moment the daft old bastard would see the bloodspots on the carpet. They had to get away. He estimated it would take only ten seconds to get out of the house.

A noise came from the cellar. A dull, heavy thump. Then another.

'Mary? Is that you?' Franklin called into the hall.

Grady felt his own facial muscles spasm. 'Shit, shit,' he whimpered, backing into his own room, stumbling into Bill.

Bill regarded him with concern. 'What is it? Grady?'

'She's alive.' He wept, terrified. The thing that had been his landlady, the insides split open, the body drenched in blood, was living, had dragged itself up the steps, determined, reasoning. If she spoke they were doomed. 'She's alive. Can't you hear her? Christ, the cellar . . .'

Fear flashed across Bill's face, then he seemed to relax. 'Nah,' he said. 'She's finished.'

Franklin's voice came from the hall. 'Mary?'

Phil wondered vaguely if next door were having more alterations. He emerged into the hall, his mug of tea in hand, and searched out the source of the noise. Definitely inside the house, the thumps were odd, irregular, not the firm decisive sound of a nail being hammered. He glanced upstairs. Joyce's music drifted faintly down. The thumps weren't coming from Stuart's room, and besides he'd be at work by now.

He called again. 'Mary, is that you? What are you up to?'

In reply there was another, much louder, thump. Phil turned round just in time to see the faint vibration of the cellar door. He set his mug down and hurried over. 'Mary, are you in there?' he called. He turned the doorknob. 'Mary, have you –'

He pushed the door open.

It slammed into something.

He looked down at a pink-smeared, unrecognisable mess, from which two blue eyes stared. Strands of peroxided hair were matted to the forehead. He held the glance for a moment, then she was gone, losing her grip, tumbling down the steps, face down, her head banging against the risers.

'Jesus Christ! Jesus!' He moved forward, tantalised, filled with unthinking horror, put his foot down on the first step. It was slippery, slippery with blood. He screamed, lost his balance, and fell down the thirteen wet, unyielding steps. 'Jesus! Mary!'

Bill pulled Grady into the hall, gesturing frantically to the front door. They flattened themselves against the wall, bin bags in hand, sidling along inch by inch, terrified.

A stomach-churning scream, hollow and drawn out, the most revolting sound Grady had ever heard, came from the cellar's open door. He sneaked a quick glance, and saw the brown imprints made by Franklin's shoes on the lino. He'd trodden in his wife's blood. Then there was a second scream.

'Shit, shit.' Tears were now streaming down Grady's face.

'Come on,' Bill whispered, tugging his arm.

60

They made for the door. Joyce turned her music up – she must have thought the Franklins were just rowing again. The ceiling thudded. Franklin started to sob ferally, each strangulated sound ending with a high-pitched howl.

'Help me . . .' The words were drawn out. 'Somebody . . . help me . . .'

They were right at the front door, seconds from freedom.

A blur of red and blue appeared through the frosted glass. Grady pulled Bill back, whimpering as the figure came closer.

The letterbox rattled. A free paper was poked through, fell to the mat. The music throbbed, Franklin wailed again. The blurred figure moved off.

Franklin delivered a hideous anguished bellow. 'Help me, somebody . . .'

The blur returned, stretched out a hand, tapped the glass. 'Hello?' a woman's voice said. 'Hello, is there anyone in there? Are you all right in there?'

Grady swore and scurried backwards, pulling Bill with him, back into the bedsit.

The front doorbell rang. The deliverywoman hammered on the glass. 'Are you all right in there? Are you all right?'

Grady felt the bin bag fall from his hand.

Jane was at her desk, putting witness statements in some sort of order to send to the CPS. The Maggie Harvey trial was going to be difficult for everyone. Ironically, the press had chosen to paint Jimmy Beck a hero. An ordinary, old-fashioned copper driven quite literally to the edge. In a way, that helped her. And Fitz had been right, she was glad of Beck's death. Imprisonment would never have been good enough for her peace of mind. As she'd discovered, she couldn't kill him. Suicide was the only useful gesture he could have made.

Temple sauntered over to her. His posture showed concern, but with none of the clumsiness of the previous day. 'All right there, Jane?'

'Perfectly.' She bound the bundle of papers together. 'I can hold my drink, you know.'

'It's been a bad week for us all.' He smiled and sat at the edge of her desk. 'Was that a platitude?' She smiled back, conscious as she did so of a familiar sensation passing through her body. Its return, after many months, both delighted and upset her. It worried her also that Temple's new, informal mode of address seemed motivated by something other than desire. His eyes conveyed a mix of pity and interest, and she wondered why. He was like a scientist staring at a specimen slide.

Over his shoulder she was faintly aware of Skelton talking loudly into his phone and scrabbling furiously for a pencil. A moment later he made straight for Wise's office. After a pause she shrugged and said, 'Fitz says whatever he likes whenever it suits him. At a funeral he's going to be disrespectful, at a party he's going to be morbid.' She handed him the bundle. 'A fully paid-up, card-carrying member of the awkward squad. These are for the CPS.'

Temple nodded. 'Uh-huh. Everything's in here?' A shadow of doubt crept across his face.

'Everything to show what a total cock-up was made, yes,' she replied, but she was smiling.

Wise burst out of his office, Skelton at his side. He clapped his hands for attention. 'Right, right. We're on the road again, lads. Nine Banville Street.' To Temple he said, 'Alan, call Forensic and detail an incident van. Skelly, check this Phillip Franklin's form. Jane.' He exchanged a glance with Skelton before going on. 'Jane, get hold of the big lad.'

Through the leaves of Banville Street's line of silver birches Fitz saw, as the taxi turned the corner, the reassuring spectacle of flashing blue lights, lines of tape, and gawking bystanders. Getting to be a home from home. The house the activity surrounded was late Victorian, detached and unworthy of note, large but unkempt, with a poorly tended front garden across which most of the police vehicles were parked. Penhaligon and Temple were hovering about an incident van, and a uniformed copper was interviewing a woman dressed in an anorak with a paper delivery satchel slung across her shoulder. A Forensic team were zipping themselves into overalls and an ambulance crew were tending to a bloodstained man in a threadbare cardigan.

He paid the cab, made a mental note of the fare for tax purposes (he always did this and always forgot) and strode briskly to the waiting Wise. 'And what can I do for you today?'

'Mary Franklin, deceased,' Wise said grimly. 'Woman who delivers the free papers heard screams. About an hour ago, that was. When the local station got here they found hubby in the hall covered in blood, wife in the cellar. He

63

says he fell down when he discovered her. I reckon he fell down when he was dumping her.' He clicked his fingers at Skelton and a couple of sheets of paper, still warm from a photocopier, were handed over. 'He's got form for beating her up.' He started to lead Fitz to the front door. 'They started divorce proceedings six months ago, then he moved back in. All I need to know is if he's capable of murder.' The last sentence was pronounced as if the matter was purely perfunctory.

Fitz grunted. A wife beater, distressingly ordinary. Easy to crack, as their crimes made evident. 'Show us the way. I can always get a hard-on for thirty pieces of silver.'

Jane forced down her reaction to the sight of the bloodstains around the cellar door and got on with the job. She climbed the stairs to the source of the techno music. The electronic bassbeats made the landing carpet vibrate. There were doors on either side of the landing; one was slightly ajar, and through it she saw an empty single bed and a dresser. She knocked on the other door, hard, several times.

Finally it was opened. A Jamaican woman, in her dressing gown, appeared. 'Yes. What do you want?' Her eyes roamed suspiciously over Jane, and she glanced towards the stairs, aware for the first time of the activity in the house.

Jane flashed her badge. 'I'm afraid there's been an incident. I'm DS Penhaligon. Can I come in, please?'

The woman narrowed her eyes in suspicion. 'I'm sorry, you'll have to see the landlady.' She moved back.

Jane stuck her foot in the door. 'She's dead,' she said, waiting for the reaction. She'd seen enough murderers, she reckoned she could smell guilt. It was nothing tangible, perhaps a slight tension in the features. She thought of Beck.

The woman knew nothing, that was plain. Faltering a little she crossed to the top of the steps and looked down on the mass of policemen. 'Oh God. Is she all right?'

'I told you, she's dead.' Jane pointed to the door, through which the music continued its thump. 'Now, please can I come in?'

On entering the dingy hall Fitz was pulled up short by the spectacle of Malcolm, Anson Road's favourite pathologist, dressed in a tuxedo, with a flower in his lapel and a hanky in his top pocket. 'Bloody hell. Is that compulsory dress now, in case the papers turn up?'

Malcolm sniffed and straightened his dickie bow. 'Pathologists' luncheon.' He wasn't smiling and when he looked down Fitz could see why. The body was being hauled out of the cellar by the white-overalled Forensic men, who worked with studious expressions to lower her into a bag. His own air of cheer evaporated for a moment and he swallowed convulsively. 'That was a long marriage, I'll bet,' he said, averting his gaze from the twisted mess.

'How do you mean?' asked Malcolm.

'I mean he must have really bloody hated her. Lead on.'

Checking his gold-plated watch, Malcolm led Fitz and Wise through a door on the opposite side of the hall and into the Franklins' flat. The door opened right into the living room, and Fitz blinked once, gathering his faculties, and then swept his gaze about the place, taking in the details. Interesting. And very bizarre.

'Having taken a major wound, I'd guess to the front,' Malcolm said, 'she bled between here' – he indicated the door – 'and here, over some sort of carpet protector, I reckon.' He indicated the telephone. Between these two points were a drizzle of blood spots, turning purple where they had stained a shockingly bright pink rug. 'There's a bad head injury, but there's a lot of blood in the basement. So she was still alive when she got dumped. He must have carried her through the hall and thrown her down, and that's when the head opened. I'd say she took a fall, almost certainly.'

Fitz was only half listening. He stood in the centre of the room, contemplating. This wasn't so boring after all. The scene around him looked like a microcosm of the marital state. His and hers, possessions and space divided almost equally. Two armchairs, positioned away from each other, one of them facing a big, matt-black TV set and video, the other facing a cupboard. The doors of the cupboard were half opened on a crummy black-and-white portable. Fitz recognised the grainy James Garner coming to the end of another case. On top of the cupboard were positioned a variety of flea-bitten stuffed animals, and above them was a cross-piece formed by two curved Turkish swords with dusty carved handles. He reached out and tested the blade for sharpness. As he'd expected, it was blunt. Then he turned back, examined the other side of the room, her side. Nipping carefully around the blood and the

Forensic man crouched there he found a mantelpiece decorated with family snapshots. The victim's mother, herself as a younger woman with her husband and a small child, the child, a girl, grown and with a husband of her own. There were some ornaments dotted about, mementoes of holidays and castles and crap of that kind, but tellingly nothing sentimental, no owls or kittens and the like.

Aware that his observations were, in their turn, being observed by Wise and Malcolm, he said, 'Cellar.'

'Y'what?' asked Wise.

'Americans say basement, we call them cellars,' said Fitz, sticking his head through a beaded curtain into the kitchen. 'It's a bit like saying "deli" when you mean "pie shop".' The kitchen surfaces gleamed, and there was a neatly arranged load of groceries on the worktop. He caught sight of a receipt and a smattering of change and smiled to himself. The poor bastard, he couldn't help thinking. That's where crawling back gets you. He withdrew his head and said to Wise, 'You say he's got form for assaulting her?'

'Two cautions and an injunction.'

Fitz looked around the lounge one last time. He caught sight of a large padded birthday card on the window-sill. *To the one I love.* Beneath was a pink heart and a smiling mouse in a waistcoat. He peeked inside. *Mary – Happy Birthday all my love – Phil.* The writing was grudging, cramped, the words bunched together. 'Do we know when this birthday was?'

'We will,' said Wise. 'What do you reckon?'

Fitz put the card down. 'You know, birthdays, Christmas . . .' He waved a hand effusively. 'All that togetherness, all that merriment, all those arguments. Bitterness, another wasted year.'

'What an uplifting view,' Malcolm said.

Fitz glared at him. 'It must be all day of a job, the pathologists' luncheon. Weighing the steaks at the table, describing them, carving them up, trying to ascertain the exact cause and time of death.'

Malcolm gave him a superior smile. 'You'd be surprised at what subjects get covered.'

Fitz smiled back. 'No I wouldn't.'

Temple knocked at the door of the ground-floor tenant, not expecting a reply. There was none. Without thinking he flipped open his note pad and wrote GREATER MANCHESTER POLICE and Anson Road's telephone number, ripped off the sheet and posted it under the door.

It was halfway through when the door opened.

Temple looked up. Standing in the doorway was a tall, well-built, good-looking bloke in checked shirt and jeans. He looked together, confident, not the usual bedsitter type. A set of personal stereo headphones, the cheap sort with foam speakers, was looped over his head. He pulled them off. On the floor at his side was a tin of paint and a small brush. His eyes flicked between Temple and the note.

'I've been knocking,' said Temple.

The man pulled his headphones off, and music filtered out. Van Morrison's gravelly tones. 'What?' He looked over Temple's shoulder, registering the police uniforms, the hubbub in the hallway. 'What's going on?' He spoke with a soft Irish accent.

'There's been an incident. Can I come in?' He

68

advanced into the room. Shady, even for a bedsit, with a pull-down bed, a mirror, table and chair and not much else. A door on the other side of the room gave on to a small kitchen. The man was painting the skirting board. New arrival, most probably, and that Walkman had been no help to Mrs Franklin. This bloke was strong. If he'd heard anything perhaps she'd have stood a chance. 'You are?'

'Stuart Grady. What's going on?' His head turned curiously back to the hall. Temple had seen that look before. Ghoulish curiosity bored him as much as breaking bad news.

'There's been a murder, Mr Grady. Your landlady,' he said, lowering his voice respectfully.

'Mrs Franklin?' Grady gulped and set his paintbrush down. 'Good God. Where?'

Temple said nothing but his eyes flicked automatically towards the hall. 'How long have you been here?' he asked.

Grady shook his head, still shocked. 'Er, I don't know, must be nine months.'

'Today,' said Temple patiently.

'All morning. I nipped to the shop earlier. I saw her in the hall. She was fine.' He blew out his cheeks and scratched his stubble.

'You've heard nothing all morning?' Temple asked.

'Not a thing. I've been listening to tapes, you know, for a couple of hours.'

Temple nodded and made a note.

Something clattered in the kitchen. For a moment a doubt surfaced in Temple's mind and he tensed. Grady stiffened, his head whipped round to the inner door.

Then a teenage boy in a Man City top and jeans appeared, rubbing sleep from his eyes. 'Dad, what've you done with my trainers?'

'Where'd you leave 'em?'

The lad smirked and picked up a pair of trainers from beneath the work table. 'Thanks.' He nodded to Temple. 'Who's this, Dad?'

Grady looked down. 'Look, I'll tell you later, all right?'

'Is he a copper?'

'I said I'll tell you later.' The lad shrugged and walked back into the kitchen with a final glance at Temple, mumbling under his breath. Grady shrugged and hooked his thumbs in his jean pockets. 'Still can't believe it.'

Temple considered. 'Might he have heard anything?'

'Well, he didn't hear you, did he?' said Grady. The implication was obvious. He doesn't hear much. Temple found himself thinking nostalgically of his old neighbourhood in Glasgow, where everyone knew everyone's business.

There was a knock at the door and Penhaligon's voice. 'Alan, we could do with some help.'

'Right, Jane.' He readied his notebook. 'Listen, if we need a statement, when's the best time to get you to answer the door, eh?'

Grady checked his watch. 'Well, I'm due in at work in half an hour. I'm a foreman at Cheltex.' His voice faltered. 'Sorry, this is all a bit much to take in. What happened?'

'I'm afraid I can't discuss that, sir. Cheltex, that's the big textiles place down at the Bagley Road estate, yes?'

Grady nodded. 'Yeah. Er, is it all right for me to go in?'

'Sure.' Temple nodded to Grady, put his notebook away, and left the bedsit.

Jane was waiting in the hallway. Someone was shouting outside. He looked through the open front door and saw a short, swarthy middle-aged bloke in sandals and cardigan, swearing and backing away from Wise. 'That's Franklin?'

She nodded and led the way out. 'Resisting arrest. Any luck with downstairs?'

Temple shook his head at the general unfairness of life. 'It's sickening. The woman gets slaughtered in her own home, everyone's in, and nobody hears a thing. Bloke was wearing a bloody Walkman.'

They strode over the gravel to the gesticulating Franklin. Closer up, Temple saw the man was covered in his wife's blood and there were grazes and cuts on his nose and forehead. He was drooling, wisps of sweat-slicked grey hair glistening over his pate. 'I haven't done anything,' he protested, looking with wide eyes at Wise. 'My wife's dead, you bastards. I didn't do it, I found her.'

Wise laid a hand on his shoulder and pointed to the waiting wagon. 'Come on, Mr Franklin, we just need to ask you a few questions. Get in the van, all right?'

Franklin raised a hand, pushed Wise in the chest. Tearstains ringed his red eyes. 'I found her, you bastard, I found her!'

Temple stepped forward at a nod from Wise, twisted Franklin's arm up behind his back. 'This way, Mr Franklin, or you'll be charged with resisting arrest.' He steered Franklin towards the van, conscious of the stupidity of his threat. The feller was going down for ten years – three months wouldn't make any difference.

As he staggered by with Franklin straining against his grip, Temple caught Fitz's eye. His fellow countryman was sucking on one of his especially acrid cigarettes and staring at Franklin with curiosity and a kind of pity.

Grady felt Bill's arms slide gently about him. The boy's touch was repellent, sending equal measures of pleasure and disgust around his body. He recoiled at first, yet the simple human need for comfort overwhelmed him and he let himself be hugged. Bill then rested his head on Grady's shoulder and whispered, 'Smart. Look, I've put the bags in this.' He held up an old canvas holdall. 'There's no ID on it. We'll dump it miles off.'

Grady sensed movement at the window. He turned, shook Bill away. Through the net curtains he saw Mr Franklin, besmirched by blood, being bundled into a van by the young Scottish copper. Two fatter blokes were standing by, one bearded. His colleague, an enormous guy in a black suit, looked on, lighting a cigarette from the butt of the one he'd just finished. Franklin was swearing, kicking, shouting.

'If we can walk out now, we better had,' Bill said casually. 'We'll be all right, and we've got to get rid of this.' He dangled the holdall by its strap. 'If we hang about they might come back.'

The door of the van slammed. Grady watched as the bearded man slammed a fist on the side and it started away, out of the drive. The remaining police started trailing back to their own vehicles.

Then a sick feeling burst suddenly up from deep inside him. He clutched his throat as his stomach muscles inverted. He reeled for the sink, twisted on the taps, catching a brief sight of himself in the glass of the wall clock before he put his head down and retched, once, twice, a third time, clear fluid falling in strands from his mouth to be washed away down the plughole.

Bill touched him again. 'We had to do it. It's all right. Come on.' And the sickest thing of all was that the touch sent a shiver of desire through Grady's shaking body. He spat into the basin, turned off the water, and faced Bill squarely. The boy's hand trailed round to his front, to his lower chest, fingertips trailing against the pectorals, then down, lingering just above the button of his jeans. 'We had to do it.'

Grady coughed and dried his eyes with a shirtcuff. 'Let's go,' he said, pushing Bill's hand away.

FOUR

Fitz was in the interview room, picking at a Cornish pasty. Police catering was very basic and starchy, so he supplemented each bite with a swig of coffee and a mini-roll. Needed to get the blood sugar up for this one.

Penhaligon entered. 'Wise is bringing Franklin up from cells now.' Her eyes flicked to the detritus of Fitz's meal. 'Sure you've got enough there?'

'Oh yes.' He licked his sticky fingers, dabbed his mouth with a hankie, and threw the silver wrappers one by one into the litter bin. 'Good shot. So what's our man's story?'

'He says,' Penhaligon began, making no effort to conceal her scepticism, 'that he went to the supermarket at approximately nine fifty, and got back at about eleven. The receipt bears that out, he was at the check-out at ten forty. He heard a noise from the cellar, went to look and fell down the stairs after her.'

Fitz considered. 'The pile of shopping in their kitchen . . .'

'It doesn't mean anything.'

'It means he went shopping.' Fitz drummed his fingers on the desktop. 'He went shopping, came back, and murdered her. Why the shopping?'

Penhaligon shrugged. 'They had a row when he got back?'

'Presumably, presumably.'

Penhaligon came closer. 'Are you saying he didn't do it?'

Fitz chuckled. 'Of course I'm not. I'd just like to know why.' He held her stare a while longer. 'Drink, I expect. Knocked back a bottle or two in the park on his way home. People behave differently, you know, say and do things they don't actually mean.'

'Piss off,' she said quietly.

Fitz reached inside his jacket, took a card from his wallet and held it out it to her. 'Beck's sister. She's confused about his death. Well, she's a barrister. Logical brain, no room for abstract thought. She gave me this but I've no intention of calling her.' Penhaligon reached out and took the card, her face sombre. Fitz cursed himself for refusing her offer because he still felt for her, in many ways. He'd proved that by turning her down. Sleeping together, it would only have mucked her head up more, at this stage. At this stage. Hah! There lay an irony. It was all part of his plan to get back in there. Show you care, prove you're not the slob she thinks, then when the time for resumption comes things'll be much smoother. He was a mercenary bastard.

She tucked the card away in her jacket without saying a word.

There was a knock at the door and Wise entered. Following him was Franklin, in the company of a uniformed escort. Fitz regarded him. The man's wounds had been dressed and he still looked like the walking dead. There was a lack of spirit in his sloping posture and sunken eyes, some spark of life had snuffed out in there. Fitz had rehearsed his opening, and stood, clapping loudly.

'Man of the match, here he is, buy the guy a drink.' He sat, gesturing to Franklin to take the seat opposite. Franklin stared at him unseeingly. Fitz guessed he'd been given some sort of mild sedative. Even so, his lack of reaction was interesting. 'We're all jealous of you, Phil,' he said, shaking his head in mock admiration. 'Every normal man's fantasy. Give the bitch what she's asking for. Finally, *finally* show her who's the boss, eh? Stick her in the ground, smite your heart, say "I did that", and rot in prison with all the other brave men.'

Franklin stared across the table, bewildered. He blinked and said quietly, without emphasis, 'I didn't do it.'

Fitz smiled. Denial. Interesting response. Confront him with the facts. 'Two, no, three times before you've just beaten her up.'

Franklin shook his head. 'I didn't beat her up. We had fights.'

Penhaligon spoke, reading from a sheaf of notes. 'March '94. You broke her nose and ripped her earrings out.' She looked directly at Franklin, poised and calm. For a moment Fitz caught a glimpse of his Panhandle of two years before, the good times they'd shared before they got to know each other properly.

Franklin shook his head again. 'She was pissed out of her head. She came at me first. She wasn't frightened of me.'

'She took an injunction out,' said Penhaligon.

After a moment Franklin nodded. 'Yes. But she took

me back. You don't know her.'

Fitz sat forward. 'Why do you think she took you back, Phil?'

'She loved me.' For the first time he faltered, closed his eyes to hold back tears.

'In your dreams,' Fitz said cruelly, warming to the attack. It was like looking into a distorting mirror. He pressed on because he knew, just knew, what had happened. The amount of times he'd thought of raising his hand to Judith. 'You begged her to see that you'd changed. Yes, you'd gone wrong before and promised to be a good boy before, but this time –' he struck the desktop with his hand '– this time you really had changed, for good.' In his own mind he saw Judith's strained, sweating face, her agony as the baby was forced out, his promise to stop gambling, his broken promise. He knew he'd hit home because Franklin recoiled, staring at him as people did when he summed them up just after meeting them. It was not an unpleasant sensation. At such times Fitz felt almost like a useful part of human society. He went on. 'You didn't know it then, but by God, yes, you had changed. Changed for her. The household bills are all in her name. She didn't trust you with money any more.' He wagged a finger. 'No more gambling, and this time you couldn't – she had the cash, and that really got to you, didn't it?'

'I don't gamble,' said Franklin.

Fitz shrugged. 'Big drinker, then. You'd spent the mortgage enough times.'

'We haven't got a mortgage. It's paid for.'

'Ah, then a very big drinker. What was it, lots of

mates down the pub, "Franklin's flush, he's subbing the kitty"?'

Franklin recoiled and the tears returned. 'I've got enough.' He glanced over at Wise, who was starting to look a little nervous.

'Never again,' Fitz continued. 'No more sprees, no more wild nights. Mary got you to sign it all over to her, everything, in one moment of weakness. Suddenly, without screaming, without violence, she was squeezing your balls like a pair of lychees and you'd given her your consent.' He smiled at Franklin's reaction to his words. This was it, this was the truth. 'And that's why you killed her, isn't it, Phil? Because all you got from the deal was a crappy little portable and sex when she said you could. That was your new marriage. She'd finally overpowered you, using her mouth and her brains, and the worst thing of all was you'd given your consent.'

Franklin was sobbing now. 'Look, I don't need you to tell me what I am. I don't need you to say what Mary was. I went back –' His voice broke and he started swaying in his chair. 'I went back because she wanted me to. She wanted me, she loved me.'

Fitz held up a finger. 'Ah! But that was an error, wasn't it? Going back to what? Slavery, misery?'

'I stayed, because I loved her.'

Fitz smirked. 'Bollocks you did. You stayed because you'd nowhere else to go and no way of getting there. You're too old now, you're no looker, she's all you've got. And when the time came, and she said one little thing out of turn, reminded you of what you'd done, you cracked. Her death was your only way out, so you went ahead and did the deed and you killed her.'

Franklin's shaking hands started to unbutton his shirt. Before Fitz could react he had the shirt front open, and nestling on his abdomen was a two-inch-long pink weal of hairless flesh. 'I let them do this to me to stop me drinking.' He held his shirt open a second longer, then fell forward, his forehead bumping the table top, his upper half twisting, racked with grief and pain. 'I let them do it because I loved her. I loved her.'

Certainties crumbled around Fitz. 'An implant?'

Franklin nodded.

Fitz cast his eyes down, avoiding the gaze of Wise and Penhaligon, and lit a cigarette. Franklin's anguish echoed around the room. 'Bugger it,' Fitz said at last, and got to his feet. 'I'm sorry,' he told the figure splayed across the desk. 'I preferred you when I thought you'd actually done it.'

It seemed just like yesterday. Bill collected fabric rolls from the stores and delivered them to the machine room and the girls, Grady did paperwork in his office. Only today Bill was happy. He had a mate, he was no reject, he'd never go back to Wiverton. His mate had proved himself by killing the old slag. Nobody had ever given Bill anything before. Her death was a gift and he felt great for it. He carried on working, not bored at all this afternoon, because in his head he was planning. They should get away from the city, go somewhere. Abroad? Grady knew the world, he'd been to Cyprus with the army, he could work things. Nothing could stop them. They could go to France, America, anywhere. For money they could rob people, then they wouldn't have to work. They could get loads of money and stay in hotels.

He was thinking this as he brought a loaded trolley up to the large cutting table at the edge of the machine room. He leant over to pull out the rolls and a hand reached out and felt him between the legs. He pulled away, shocked, and there was an explosion of laughter from the girls. Everyone looked at Linda who sat back in her chair, rocking with delight. 'Just wanted to see what you'd got in your lunchbox,' she told him, to the great amusement of her mates.

Bill shrugged and smiled back. He was reaching for another roll when he noticed the girls looking over his shoulder, and quickly getting their heads back down. He turned and saw Grady stalking across the shop floor from his office, his face contorted with rage. 'Linda!' he shouted, jabbing a finger at her. Bill stood back, wary. Grady wore the same expression as he had this morning, as he'd brought the chisel down on Mrs Franklin. 'Linda, leave what you're doing, get your bag, get your coat and piss off. You're fired.'

The machinists looked up as one, aghast. Linda stared at Grady, eyes wide with shock, her lip trembling.

'You can't sack her for that,' said one of the cutters.

'What've I done?' Linda protested, looking between Grady and Bill.

Grady bore down on her. 'What you always do, Linda, which is to take it one step too far.'

'It was just a bit of fun,' said the cutter, putting her arm around Linda's shoulder. 'I'm a witness.'

Grady raised his voice. 'Every time there's trouble,

I've to come out here, and it's always you and I'm getting sick of warning you.' He jabbed his finger aggressively between her eyes. His eyes were bloodshot and his face was reddening, the veins on his neck standing out. 'So get your bag, get your coat and move!'

Linda stood up, crying, put her coat on, and shuffled away. Her mate gave Grady a filthy stare and followed her to the cloakroom. There was a prolonged silence. 'Well, get on with your work,' Grady said at last, and stalked back to his office.

His eyes connected with Bill's as he passed, and Bill felt a surge of emotion. An overreaction, yeah, but Grady was showing again that he cared, that he was interested. That mattered. They were linked, forever. They were together.

One by one, the machines started up again. A murmur rose around the machinists and several of them eyed him with disdain. 'What are you looking at?' he demanded, sticking out his chin. 'Eh? What are you looking at?'

'Someone likes you, don't they?' said one of the women. 'Someone likes the look of you.' She wrinkled her nose at him, her owlish eyes magnified by thick spectacles. Her red face wore a look of contempt. The other women muttered, stared at Bill. 'Got yourself an admirer there, ducky.'

Bill strode over to her, raising a fist. He felt the blood rushing to his head. 'Why don't you shut it? You know nothing about him! You know nothing about him and me!'

The women chuckled. Bill reeled from their stupid laughing faces and kicked his trolley savagely aside. He ran for the corridor, bursting through the plastic sheet-ing, skidding to a halt halfway down the long, cold, empty passageway. He leant against the wall, catching his breath. So bloody stupid. They could never begin to understand.

He heard a movement and looked up to see Grady, walking slowly towards him. His protector. 'She was asking for that. She's always . . .' He broke off, and his expression changed, his face dropping to a look of absolute horror and self-loathing. 'She's always pissing about – some of 'em don't realise what they're paid for . . .'

Bill put a hand on his arm to steady him, stroked him up and down. 'We can't stay here. We've got to get away.'

Grady snarled. 'Get away to where, exactly?'

Bill shrugged, trying to look cheerful. 'We can go anywhere we like.' There was an awkward pause. 'They'll nick her old man for it, don't worry.'

'Don't worry?' Grady's face crumpled again. 'Christ, an innocent man . . .' He pulled himself up, grabbed Bill by the collar, threw him up against the wall. In a terrifying whisper he said, 'Why did you do it? Why did you do it?'

It was the first time Grady had approached him, initiated physical contact. Bill felt the man's strong hands on him, smelt the warm stubbled cheek inches away, longed to reach out and caress him. 'We did it,' he said softly. 'Grady, we did it. Together, yeah? Together.'

Grady released him. 'You're right. We can't stay here.'

• • •

Wise used the gents as a second, secret office. He stood at the urinal, looking in the mirror at the huge black shape of Fitz, who was circling around the cubicles and smoking. Fitz was warming up, getting excited, drawing little patterns in the air with his cigarette. The sight gave Wise an uncomfortable sensation. 'I want to book Franklin,' he said.

'You needn't book him because he didn't do it.' Wise snorted and shook his head. 'Look, that guy's opened his guts up for her. He's had a boozer's brick installed. The things are vile, a last resort. If he so much as smells the stuff it makes him throw up.'

'What are you saying? What's that got to do with anything?'

'I'm saying that a man like Franklin would have needed at least a litre of firewater to have had the balls to do it.'

Wise shook and buttoned himself up. He started to wash his hands, soap from the dispenser making pink bubbles around his stubby fingers. He sighed. 'So he isn't capable of murder, is that what you're saying?'

Fitz nodded. 'He's certainly not capable of this one. The man's a mouse.' He shrugged and reached out a hand, grabbed a paper towel and handed it to Wise. His eyes were narrowed, forming wrinkles on his brow, and there was something brash and unconsidered in the way he pulled himself up. He was about to drop a bomb. 'Anyway,' he said casually, because all his grim pronouncements were casual, 'we're not looking for one murderer.'

Wise crumpled the paper towel. 'Y'what?'

'We're looking for two,' said Fitz, raising an eyebrow.

Wise smoothed his hair and led the way out. 'Oh no. Here he goes again, Russell bleedin' Grant. Nothing's ever straightforward with you, is it? I bet you even piss sideways.'

'We're looking for two murderers,' Fitz repeated, calmly.

'We've already got the murderer,' Wise said firmly, motioning him to keep silent as they re-entered the offices. 'And his name's Franklin.'

Grady stalked on to the forecourt, the rage burning behind his eyes. He knew what he could do now, he sensed the power in his limbs, a power to change the world. To change the world for himself and for Bill. His hands clenched and unclenched as he thought of Linda. He had no sympathy. For her, for all of them, it was all so bloody easy, wasn't it? Just walk out and grab what you want, where you want it. She'd never had to stop and think, never had to ignore the demands of her own mind and body. She'd never have to fight for an inch of respect.

He felt exhilarated, propelled by a force greater than himself. The new Stuart Grady could do things his old self hadn't even considered. Walking out, telling Linda where to go . . . The thought died. He'd killed, taken a life, got away with it. There was the difference. Bill. He'd killed for Bill, he'd do anything for the boy. All his deepest-buried fantasies were surging out into the real world, unstoppable. He thought of the years he'd wasted, the nights spent chipping away pointlessly at blocks of wood, and cursed his faint heart. Bill would show the way.

He took out his keys, waited for the clunk of the Montego's central locking, climbed in, sought the cassette he wanted from the dashboard, slid it into the stereo, and drove away. Away from Cheltex, away from routine, away from the crushing burden of his responsibilities. Tomorrow didn't matter. The music started.

Bill was waiting just outside the gates. Grady opened the door for him and he slid in, filling the car with his scent, the chewing gum and chocolate odour of healthy boyhood. He smiled. 'Let's go, then.'

Grady found it impossible to return the smile. The block was still too strong in his mind, a spiral of elation and despair that made his heart beat faster, his fingers tighten on the wheel. He grunted and slammed the car into gear, and drove away down the factory's long approach road.

'Drive properly or you'll get pulled,' said Bill.

They drove on, heading towards the city.

The body of Mrs Franklin, naked and cleansed of blood, lay white and blue on the slab. Water sluiced in a runnel around the groove at the slab's sides. Temple looked away, loosened his tie. For him, the routine horrors remained a trial, making him queasy. He glanced over the table at Jane, trying to judge her reaction. There was no measurable, noticeable response. He wished she would stop trying so hard to keep her wits, wished she could scream, let it all out. If he felt queasy at the sight of the body, what then did she feel? She caught his glance and frowned, refusing to share his shudder. She kept her attention on Malcolm as he rolled the body over on its front and prodded aside a roll of fat with a gleaming silver set of retractors. The bloke was tall, saturnine, resembled a ghoul, a grave-robber. The lab was filled with a respectful silence, green-masked operatives scrubbing and sterilising a set of implements at a basin, sending out invisible, sweet-smelling chemical clouds that mingled with the formalin.

The atmosphere was shattered when the door burst open and two dark and prodigious shapes entered, reeking of nicotine. Malcolm rolled his eyes heavenward at the sight of Fitz, who was getting pink in the face, and was gesticulating wildly. 'You've got to let the man go.'

'You've no evidence in support of what you say,' said Wise.

'Wrong. Wrong. You've got no evidence against Franklin, so let him go.'

Wise blinked behind his spectacle lenses. 'You're coming over soft-hearted all of a sudden. It's your wee lad, is it? Your missus has a kid and suddenly you're Maria von Trapp.'

Fitz sighed and stomped a foot. 'That is not true.' Temple caught a quick glance that flashed between him and Jane. 'You're holding the wrong guy, obviously, so it's obvious, you let him go.'

Wise tapped his own chest. 'I'll decide that, all right? It happens to be my job.' He shook his head. 'I should have let you stay at home.'

Fitz snorted. 'What, nick Franklin? Get a nice little conviction on purely circumstantial evidence, and the killers get away? Do you want that? Is that justice?' He pointed to the body. 'Is that justice for her?'

Temple spoke. 'Did you say killers?'

Wise waved a hand. 'Don't encourage him.' He turned to Malcolm. 'What do you make of it?'

Malcolm looked between him and Fitz and said, 'The weapon wasn't a knife.'

Wise nodded to Temple. 'The sabre, on his wall.'

'Was dusty and blunt,' said Fitz. 'Christ, it hardly takes Sherlock bloody Holmes . . .'

Malcolm held up the right arm, pointing out the severed arteries at the wrist. 'This happened first. Not directed, could well have been accidental. If I saw this on its own, I might almost say she'd tripped over and on to something, done it herself. But the other wounds are very different.' He rolled the body on to its side. Temple winced at the sight of the face, the open eyes and purple-lipped mouth. 'The weapon went into the lung here,' said Malcolm, pointing out the tiny puncture mark, 'but only just.' He turned the body on to its front. It made a revolting, wet sucking noise as its folds and sags flopped forward on the slab. A white finger pointed out a circular series of gouges on the lower back. Malcolm reached forward with his retractors, clipped the tissue between them, folded back the body wall a fraction. 'But these went through the rib cage and hit the back of the sternum, hard. Made their mark.' He mimed the action with his free hand, striking upwards. 'Judging from the angle, I'd say the husband brought the weapon down from above.'

Fitz stepped forward. His eyes settled on the lower back. 'Back of the sternum, how many times?'

'Three, possibly four. In quick succession.'

'Right, that's a lot of power.' He looked around himself, addressing Temple and Jane, pointedly avoiding

Wise. 'Back of the ribcage and the sternum. That's a powerful man, more powerful than puny Phil Franklin.' He raised his eyebrows to Malcolm. 'Eh?'

Malcolm blinked his heavily lidded eyes. 'Possibly.'

'But the first, the wrist, that was accidental, you say?'

'Possibly.'

'And the frontal attack was botched?'

'Shallow by comparison to what followed, yes.'

'Right, I knew it,' said Fitz, turning to Wise. 'That's two different people. If you've got the power to inflict that kind of damage, you are not going to get it wrong the first time.' Wise stared straight ahead. Fitz sought agreement from Temple, but Temple knew better than to give it and lowered his gaze. 'Look, to quote another disillusioned Jock, the first cut is the deepest. Because that's your fight or flight, your one chance. The rear attack, those three or four blows to the back, were driven, precise attempts to finish off a botched job. A stronger assailant, and that means a man. A man, a woman. Two killers.' He looked at Malcolm. 'Am I right?'

'Possibly.'

Fitz gestured to Wise. 'Don't let him influence you. Malcolm, come on. Two killers?'

'Possibly.'

Fitz threw his arms up in the air. 'I'm telling you. Two killers. A man and a woman.'

Grady watched the assistant swipe his Switch card along the plastic groove built into the till. A whirr, a click; the receipt chattered its way out and he was handed a pen. His signature felt alien and unreal, a product of the old world, and halfway through his surname he faltered and almost lost control. The electronic beat of the music from the shop's Tannoy seemed to thud inside his brain, and a wave of redness, of the anger, washed over him, threatening to claim him. Across the counter the assistant, young and slim, just a bit older than Bill, seemed to be laughing at him, looking into his head and judging him. He closed his eyes, gathered his wits, and signed the receipt.

Bill was waiting outside, looking through shirts on a sale rail. Around them the mid-afternoon, end-of-the-week activities of Manchester's shoppers continued unchanged. Grady was transported back twenty years, saw himself sagging off school, alone, wandering through the centre of Belfast and dodging truant officers. Now he had a mate to share the skive. He handed the carrier to Bill.

'What?' The boy looked inside and gave a broad, beaming smile. 'You're kidding?'

Grady shook his head, still uncomfortable in his new role. People might look, and see this, and draw conclusions. A bloke of his age handing gifts to a teenager. Already this afternoon they'd drawn stares. A couple of shaven-headed blokes in denims had tittered and whispered as they passed. People thought the worst, and nothing had happened. They'd done nothing wrong.

Bill pulled the box from the bag. Inside were a pair of Caterpillar boots. 'Wow! How did you know what size?'

'Same as me,' Grady said stiffly. He looked away from Bill's beautiful face. Right here, in the city centre, he wanted to reach out and grab, push the boy against a wall, kiss him deeply, put a hand under the tee shirt, explore.

'Thanks.' Bill's eyes glistened. He stared at the picture on the shoebox. 'Thanks, I really mean it, thanks.'

Grady pointed out the shirts on the rail. 'Are you wanting any of them?'

Bill shook his head. 'I'll keep this one.' He plucked at the hem of the City top he was wearing. Grady's top.

Fitz was addressing the incident room, a photo of Mary Franklin clamped in his hand. Temple looked non-committal, Skelton faintly amused. Of the others only Penhaligon seemed really to be listening, and he wasn't going to flatter himself that her interest was anything to do with his personal magnetism. She believed him more readily because she had a better mind and she needed to store ammunition for her future career. Results alone would make a difference with the promotion board, and as part of a team that had lost three officers through incompetence – crucially, for not listening to Fitz – she had to stick her neck out now, go with him if she wanted to advance. She was cleverer than Wise, she'd been cleverer than Bilborough. Her sex was the only reason she'd been overlooked, and she'd been punished enough for that already.

Temple raised a finger to address Fitz. 'Franklin and his wife rowed. He picked up a weapon, she fell forward accidentally, he struck again, something inside him snapped and he finished her off. Then he loads the body on to the carpet protector, lugs her down to the cellar. She's still alive, he opens the door and falls down himself, and the shock breaks him and he starts hollering. It fits every fact we know.'

'Crap,' said Fitz. 'Franklin was out, he went shopping. And he hasn't got the strength, the nerve or the intelligence to do any of that. He'd have run off at the first squirt of blood.'

'You think it's burglars then?' asked Skelton.

'No. Burglars would have stuck her and left her where she fell, just cleared off.' He waved the photograph at them. 'No, this was a man and a woman who risked being caught to dump Mary Franklin in the cellar. There were tenants in the house, both upstairs and downstairs, right?' Penhaligon nodded. 'Either of them could've opened their door at any moment. This couple were desperate, they panicked, they risked being caught. So they weren't new callers, so she knew her killers. They had no time to take the body elsewhere, the other people in the house could walk out, Mr Franklin might come back. They killed Mary and they dumped her. They were terrified.'

Penhaligon held up a black leather address book, of the kind with a pencil attached. 'They don't have many friends. There are no couples in here. It was Mary's book and the names are all female.'

'Check them all out,' said Fitz. 'She knew the woman, it's definite. The man is strong, if not big then well-composed, able to throw a punch. She's shorter and less substantial. And they're hardly Bonnie and Clyde, remember, just ordinary, healthy people that went too far. Now if you think you're on to them, target him, he'll be more vulnerable.' He warmed to his theme, looking around at them, captivating them.

91

Temple and Skelton were looking at him with more confidence now, the doubt erased from their faces. And Penhaligon was convinced, she was flicking through the address book already. 'She has the temper, she stabbed first. He finished the job to protect her, but – and this is the important thing – she stabbed first, that jab to the wrist and the frontal injury, that was her. She'll be harder to crack, so go for the bloke.'

Penhaligon looked up. 'There are about twenty names in here, most of them local.'

Fitz nodded. 'One of them'll be her.'

The door of the incident room opened with a definite push, and Wise strode in carrying a blue file and looking very pleased with himself in a grim sort of way. Fitz recognised that arrangement of the features and his spirits sank. 'Scrap that,' said Wise. 'We're looking for a single bloke.'

Fitz put a hand to his head. 'Look, it isn't bloody Franklin.'

'Perhaps it isn't,' said Wise. 'But a single bloke.'

'No, a man and a woman.' Fitz held up two fingers. Wise felt threatened, he was reacting badly, trying to reassert his authority. It was so pointless. 'Two.'

'One.'

'Two. Cha cha cha.' Fitz stood in his way, said in a low voice, 'Look, do you want justice? Isn't that some-where in your job description? Or do you just grab the nearest likely candidate, bang them away, collect your dues and slope off down the pub?'

Wise raised a finger. 'I can throw you off the premises.'

Fitz squared his shoulders. He raised the photo of

Mary Franklin and waved it in Wise's face. 'Listen, just listen to me. For her sake. I know, there are two of them.'

Wise reached inside the folder and whipped out another photograph. Fitz caught a blurred glimpse of a stocky bulldog-faced man, a mug shot, a prison number. 'Joshua Cooper. Mary Franklin's bit on the side, on and off since last December. He did three years for GBH, and last month he tapped her for a two-grand loan to pay his fines off. Last known address, fifteen Stamford Road, Moss Side.' He raised his voice, pointed to Temple. 'Alan, go and get him.'

Temple rose. 'Sir.' He and Skelton hurried away.

Fitz snatched the photo from Wise and thought quickly. The man in the pictures looked tall and strong, but where was the woman? It didn't make sense, either way. The frontal attack was weak, hesitant, misjudged. And someone capable of GBH wouldn't make a daft mistake like that. 'Wrong!' he thundered. 'You're wrong.'

Wise blew out his cheeks. 'We've checked with Mary Franklin's next-door neighbour. She saw her with Cooper, and Mary told her about the loan. It's evidence, eh? And on the evidence I'm more right than you are.'

Fitz gave his most patronising grin. 'On the evidence the economy should be working.' He pushed past Wise and out of the incident room.

Grady sat with Bill, at a table in the food hall of the Arndale. The new clothes he'd bought, a denim jacket and a pair of black chinos, felt good on him, and despite all that had happened today, the late afternoon sunlight coming through the atrium's glass rooftop gave him a sense of a new beginning, a sense of health. Surrounded by bright ordinariness, he felt the murder slipping further and further away in his mind, as if he'd only seen it on television, not been involved. Bill was right, they were going to get away with it. They could forget it, start a new life together.

He started to roll a cigarette. Opposite, Bill sat with his feet up on a chair, crossing and uncrossing his legs, looking down regularly at his new boots. He picked up a plastic menu from the table and scanned it through a new pair of Raybans. Grady didn't mind spending money on him. He'd saved enough from Cheltex, and that was on top of his forces dismissal payment, enough that he didn't miss the maintenance payments that disappeared from his account, direct debited, each month. Now he had somebody to spend it on, and why not? It was time to live. He finished rolling the cigarette and put it to his mouth.

Bill reached over and stole it with astonishing sleight of hand. It disappeared up his sleeve. 'Bet you didn't know I could do that.' He slipped it out, waved it across the table and smiled. 'I learned loads of tricks when I was a kid. I was in the Magic Circle. Gave me something to do.'

Grady felt uneasy, unused to this friendliness. He shifted in his chair and started to roll another cigarette, noticing an absence from his inner pocket as he did. 'Lost my matches.'

Bill laughed and produced them from his pocket, lit the cigarette he'd stolen. Without knowing why, Grady laughed back at him, hesitantly at first. Then he threw his head back and roared. Without anything around him altering noticeably, he felt life taking on a wider quality, as if the previous thirty-one years had been nothing but a lonely, aching dream.

Anson Road was filled with activity, a knot of officers grouped around a radio set to monitor Cooper's arrest, a board going up with Cooper's mug shot and various reports pinned to it, a blackboard being chalked with the legend JOSHUA COOPER d.o.b. 4.7.44. Fitz waited until Wise emerged from his office, putting on his heavy coat, Penhaligon trailing at his rear, before he swooped. 'Doesn't it occur to you you might be acting a little hastily?'

Wise glowered at him, refusing to stop. 'Haven't you gone home yet? It's six o'clock, you can knock off. Can I hear a baby crying?' He turned his head to Penhaligon. 'Tell cells to release Franklin, my authority. Take him home.' He stopped on the threshold of the incident room and added, 'And behave yourself, all right?'

Fitz smirked. 'What can he mean by that, I wonder?' he said to Penhaligon.

Wise ignored him. 'I mean, you keep your opinions to yourself, and you don't mention Cooper to Franklin.' He broke off, looked around the room. 'We don't want Franklin filing a complaint.'

'Ah, I see now,' said Fitz. '*You* don't want Franklin filing a complaint, because it'll land at your door. With that on top of dear Jimmy's departure, the Devil take his soul, this place might start smelling like the *Marie Celeste*, eh?'

'I said you could go home,' said Wise.

Fitz addressed Penhaligon. 'He's under pressure, so he's shoving the bad job your way.' She reacted to that but kept her eyes down. 'See his thread veins coming out? His job's on the line, he's staring into the abyss.'

Penhaligon blinked. 'Give it a rest, Fitz.'

'You heard her,' said Wise. He jerked a thumb over his shoulder. 'Now piss off home.'

Fitz looked between them. He wasn't going to let them do this. He'd had a wrecking tactic lined up all day, now was the time to deploy it. 'You see, Jane,' he said. 'He's forgotten about you. You're back to being the doormat again. Now you're sober he's forgotten about your promotion.'

She flared up, as he'd known she would, manipulated in spite of herself. She glared, first at Fitz, then at Wise, who remained framed in the doorway. 'Well? Sir?'

He shook his heavy-bearded jowls. 'When you stick it down in writing, like a grown-up, maybe.' Then he was gone, the force of his push leaving the doors swinging back and forth after him.

Temple waited for the right moment. He had a car covering the ginnel at the back of the terraces of Stamford Road, and he and Skelton were backed up by a team of three. They were parked at the far end of the street, outside a pub, in an unmarked car. Skelton had a pair of binocs out and was scanning the upper storeys. 'There's someone in there, more than just one. A bloke, and a woman.' As soon as the words left his lips he withdrew the binocs and exchanged a significant glance with Temple.

'Are you sure it's Cooper?' asked Temple.

'Can't see through the nets. Big bloke, though, it's got to be him.'

'OK.' Temple picked up his radio and clicked the call button. 'X-ray Tango three-four calling. Bring the wagon in, we're going in in two, over.' As he spoke he unclicked his seat belt and got out of the car. 'A bloke and a bird, eh? Perhaps everyone can go home happy today, eh?'

He walked briskly to the blue door of number fifteen, reaching inside his jacket for his ID. Skelton rapped on the knocker. There was no response. He knocked again. Out of the corner of his eye Temple saw the wagon turning into the street. The door opened. Cooper was a big bloke, a massively powerful hairy torso bulging out of a denim shirt, an earring, a couple of visible scars. Mary Franklin couldn't have stood a chance against that, the poor cow. The image of the white bloodless body flashed before him and he felt a rush of righteous anger. 'Joshua Coo–' Temple began to say, flicking his wallet open, but the bastard had clocked them and slammed the door shut.

'Shit!' Temple stood back, took a run-up as Skelton radioed the lads waiting at the back, and charged, cursing the damage to his suit as he shouldered the door open, wondering if he could claim it on expenses, wondering how he'd justify a three hundred quid tailors' bill to Wise. He burst into the hall, caught a confused impression of decay, neglect and an unfeasible number of household items – toasters, televisions, microwaves – littering the hall, and a woman in a dressing gown descending the stairs and shrieking, and Cooper bursting out through the kitchen into the yard, straight into the waiting team of uniformed coppers.

'Into the van!' he shouted. 'Come on!' As Cooper was manhandled past him and out the front, his brutal features twisted with rage, Temple repeated the litany of the arrest, automatically, forcing out the string of verbiage between gasps.

The woman on the stairs looked on in horror. 'You can't nick him,' she cried. 'He's looking after it for his mate. It's his mate's stuff, you can't nick him for that!'

Cooper snarled. 'Will you shut your mouth, Pauline!' Then he was out of the front door, across the tarmac, being loaded into the wagon. Wise's car had drawn up at the scene, and the boss was climbing out, surveying the arrest with approval. Temple walked out, following Cooper, rubbing his shoulder. It felt limp and dead, strangely unconnected, so he tried lifting it. 'Oh Christ!' The agony surged through him, like a hot brand-iron had been laid on his upper back. 'Christ!'

The wagon door slammed behind Cooper. Skelton thumped on the side and it drove away. Wise watched its departure with apparent satisfaction, then turned to Temple. 'All right there, son?'

'Sir,' Temple gasped. 'I think I've dislocated my shoulder.'

Before Wise could react, Cooper's woman darted out of the house, screeching and swearing. 'What the bloody hell do you think you're doing? It's his mate's stuff, it belongs to his mate, you don't need all of that bloody lot to arrest a man like that, what are you playing at?'

'All right, all right, calm down, missus,' Wise said, his features suddenly clouded with worry. To Temple he said, 'Get Skelton to drive you to the ozzie.' Temple nodded and lurched away.

The last thing he saw as they drove away, barely registering the outside world through a haze of pain, was Wise shouting and pointing at the woman, threatening her with arrest for obstruction. But Temple had served at Anson Road for long enough now to recognise the expression hidden behind Wise's anger. There was doubt, and when he caught sight of the stolen goods in the hall that doubt was going to grow.

The meal over – they'd had nachos and a plate of chips and two bowls of ice cream each – Bill was following Grady up the stairs of the multi-storey, back to the car. With his Raybans on he could hardly see in this light, but he wasn't going to take them off for a while. He'd always wanted a pair. 'I never got things like this in Sowerby Park,' he told Grady, making sure to smile really wide to show how much he appreciated it. 'We got really crappy things at Christmas, you know, things people had donated.'

Grady frowned. 'What, you never had Christmas presents?'

'Only rubbish ones. I got a Scalextric once, a proper set, and some A-Team figures, but that wasn't at Sowerby Park.' He felt a flicker of the past's pain, compared it to how he felt today, and was glad of the change.

Grady stopped on the stairs at a landing. He was frowning with interest, with concern, and Bill felt himself responding with pleasure. If only the bloke would make a move. He wanted to give him everything he had.

He might even have reached out himself, but he could hear people coming up the steps, kids' voices. 'From your parents?' asked Grady, gently, clearly aware he was treading on dangerous ground.

'It doesn't matter,' said Bill, surprising himself. 'It doesn't matter.' He felt a great weight lifting off him. 'Where are we going to go, then?'

Grady shrugged. 'We could go to the pictures.'

'All right.' They started walking up again, Bill a step behind Grady, looking longingly at the power in the older man's strides, the interplay of his denim-packaged leg muscles, the hair cut close, almost shaven, at the nape of his neck. It was like the past had never been, and Bill felt a sense of closure and a new life.

And then, without warning, the old life came rushing back.

Whenever he was out in town, which was rare because he had no money, Bill's eyes flicked automatically around the shoppers, seeking a certain set of familiar faces. The city contained millions, and the odds against him finding them were ridiculously high. Even today as Grady had led him around the Arndale he'd felt himself looking about, searching to connect. Now, as the moment came, as he stood on another landing, it wasn't a face but a voice that caused his breath to catch in his throat.

'Steven! This way!' a woman called to the kids, on the level below. 'Steven!' There was a childish giggle, a small boy making the noise of a plane, the sound of the doors on the lower level swinging open and closed. Bill felt his legs give way and he reached out for the stair-rail to steady himself. All these years he'd been searching, combing the streets, walking miles to find them again, and on the very day he stopped looking here they were. Without thinking he felt himself turning back, clattering down the steps. They might get away. He heard Grady calling after him.

He burst through the doors. And there they were. Diane and Brian, looking five years older, and healthier, well turned-out. The baby was grown now, a tiny boy in rumpled school uniform, being teased by Steven. Bill's eyes narrowed as he looked at the older boy, his smart haircut, his trainers, his leather schoolbag slung over one shoulder. His mouth dried as he walked towards them, as Brian unlocked the Volvo and the kids climbed in, as Diane put her shopping bags, from Toys Я Us and Jigsaw, into the boot. He had to say the right thing, keep it casual. He'd planned this for so long, rehearsed it in his head so many times. He rubbed his hands nervously against the sides of his legs, the niggling aftershock of the day's events blocked out.

'Diane,' he said simply. 'How're you doing?'

She spun round, and close up she still looked the same, only a bit older, and her clothes were posher. She was wearing a knitted suit, but her face was still kind and pink and motherly. Her mouth dropped open and her pupils contracted. 'Bill,' she said. He could tell she was shocked, but what was going to happen next? Could they be friends? Was everything going to be all right? They might invite him home, make tea. They could talk and be friends. 'We're . . .' The sentence died on her lips and she shot a glance at Brian, who was staring at Bill with a negative expression, like he was disappointed. 'We're all fine,' she went on, trying to sound bright, casual. 'How are you? You're looking well.' Her eyes swept over him, at his new jacket and boots.

'Great,' he said, forcing down his excitement. He mustn't lose them. 'What are you doing round here, then? Where are you living now?'

There was a horrible silence, and Bill felt things turning away from him. The kids in the car were staring out, fear on their faces. 'New boots, Bill?' asked Brian.

Bill ignored him, kept his eyes fixed on Diane. He gave a broad smile. 'Where've you moved to?'

'Look at the size of you now,' she said, stretching an arm out to the car door, letting her fingers rest on the handle. 'You're a young man.'

Bill wanted to weep with frustration. He couldn't let them escape, he'd never see them again. 'Where've you moved to?'

Brian stepped forward, around the front of the car. 'Bill, will you please not do this. It isn't fair.'

'Shut up, you.' Bill raised a shaking finger, felt himself losing control. 'Look,' he said to Diane, but she was opening the car door, 'look, I just want to know. I just want to see you.'

'Bill, you know that's not a good idea.' Behind her, Brian opened the driver's door, climbed in. 'You're looking really well.' Her face assumed a look of pity. 'I'm glad about that, I hope things are better now.' She got in, slammed the door, kept her eyes away from his.

Bill started forward, desperate, but Brian had started the engine and the car was moving out of its plot. The kids were looking out, uncomprehending. It pulled away, doing fifty at least, shot down the ramp. Bill made a mental note of the number plate and turned, sprinting back to the door, where Grady was waiting, looking confused and alarmed.

'Who is it?' he called. Bill pushed past him, tore up the steps to the next level, his heart pounding. 'Bill?' Grady rushed up behind him, took out his keys. They emerged on to the next level, where the Montego was waiting.

Bill snatched the keys. 'I'm driving,' he said, switching off the central locking and making for the right side of the car.

Grady grabbed his collar, took the keys back. 'Not in that state you're not.'

Bill leapt in the air with frustration, gestured furiously to the car. 'Come on, come on, they'll get away!' He slammed his hand down on the roof.

Grady pulled open the driver's door.

Fitz sat obstinately in Wise's office, listening to the police team on the other side of the glass partition going about their business. He was not going home. How many times did they have to go through the motions of doubting him? His insights had been proved correct on nearly every previous occasion. If they'd listened to him Bilborough might still be alive. They appreciated him only when it was too late, and even then grudgingly. Why? Because he was a pain, he was too much, he irritated them. That wasn't a good enough excuse. They should view him as a resource, a valuable one. When news came through on the incident room's radio that Cooper had been arrested and was being driven in Fitz gave a huge sigh. No, he was not going home, he

103

would see this one through. He felt a brief pang of guilt towards Judith. Their last contact hadn't exactly been meaningful, and he really was trying, that painting had been an honest-to-goodness gift, hadn't it? Or was she one step ahead of him? Best to call and settle things. He picked up Wise's phone, got an outside line and punched in his own number.

He got the sound of his own voice, which he adored most of the time. Not now. 'This is Fitzgerald. We're out. Leave a message and make it short.' He waited for the beep. 'It's me. Judith, I know you're there. Will you please pick up the phone and talk to me. I won't be home 'til later and I want to explain why.' He waited a few moments. 'Judith, pick up the phone.' His temper rising, he terminated the call and reached for another of the mini-rolls he'd got from the snack machine.

Judith heard the phone ring but made no attempt to answer. She was in Fitz's study, unable to read, unable to think, with the baby's bawling echoing from the front room and Mark's music coming from above. There were things to do, too many things to do. There was a steriliser overheating in the kitchen, a heap of washing soaking in the machine waiting to be pegged out, letters to write, a baby to be fed. Too many things, and she was doing none of them. She sat before Fitz's battered IBM, her eyes flicking over a fresh deal of cards in the solitaire pack, her hand guiding the mouse around its pad, the high-pitched tones as her points total grew bleeping through her screen-dazzled mind. This was, she reckoned, about her fortieth game of the afternoon. Often she lost track halfway through, if the noise got too much, and she dealt out a fresh deck. Her head was spinning with hearts and spades, and she began to make mistakes, overlooking connections, trying to put diamonds and hearts together. Every time she promised herself this would be the last game.

She didn't hear Fitz's message. The needs of the Greater Manchester Police were evidently greater than the needs of her or their child. Something sordid and unpleasant was happening, and the Stick Insect and her husband were investigating. How could she and the child compare?

The change in Bill was profound, and disturbing. There was a lot of traffic heading out of town, and Grady watched with growing unease as he wound the window down, stuck his head out, and nodded. 'About four cars in front, indicating to turn left.'

'Look, who is it?' he asked again, obeying the instruction, waiting for the turning and going left, heading for the suburbs.

Bill didn't reply, just sat upright in the passenger seat, straining to check the Volvo's intentions as they neared a roundabout. 'They're going right. Castlefield way.' He licked his lips, his hands drummed impatiently against his legs. 'Do you reckon he's seen us?'

'Bill, who is it?' Grady repeated, picking up the trail, easing the car off at the correct junction.

Bill shot him a quick glance. 'My family.'

'What are you doing sat in here?' Wise paused at the threshold of his office, pulled up by the sight of Fitz, sprawled in his chair. 'I told you to go home.'

Fitz rustled the magazine in his hand, laughter lines playing around his mouth. 'Just flicking through the staff rag. Reassuring reading, the letters column's a hoot.'

'Yeah, well you can go home now, all right?' He advanced threateningly. 'And get your fat arse out of my chair.'

Fitz didn't move, and his smile remained. He was looking past Wise, through the window. 'I can see your boss from here.'

Wise reacted by throwing himself behind a filing cabinet. He couldn't risk another confrontation with Allen. He hid as well as he was able, heard the office door open. 'Where is he?' Allen demanded, his tone sharp. 'And what are you doing in that chair?'

'I'm keeping it warm for his fat arse,' said Fitz. 'His lottery numbers came up. Shot out of the door with a year's supply of pile cream and a map of Jersey.' He gave a little laugh. 'It's a tragedy for the Channel Islands, don't you think, the lottery? They thought they'd cracked it, stipulating "rich". Now the Bank of Toytown's full of Scouse builders slagging off the plasterwork.'

There was a long silence. Wise saw Allen moving closer to Fitz. 'I can wait.'

'Oh dear. Has he done something wrong again?' Fitz pulled a mocking face, raised a finger. 'Don't tell me, Franklin's put in a complaint.'

Allen grunted. 'You're only here because you're good for publicity.' He made for the door.

Fitz called after him, a little angrily, 'The results don't count for anything, then?'

'Ours do. Tell him I want him.' The door swung to after him.

Wise poked his head around the edge of the filing cabinet. 'Thank you, friend,' he said in a voice heavy with irony.

Fitz beamed back at him. 'Pleasure.'

The housing estate was large and newly built, courts, avenues and ways, all in red brick with plastic window frames. Obeying Bill's instructions, and still unsure why, Grady slowed his car as it turned a corner into a long street. The prey, the Volvo, was parked neatly in a drive halfway along. Bill nodded excitedly at the street sign. 'Honeysuckle Road.' His eyes turned keenly over each house on the row facing them. 'Twenty-four, twenty-six, twenty-eight . . .' He was counting them off until he reached the Volvo. 'Thirty.' He clenched a fist, held it up triumphantly. 'Thirty Honeysuckle Road. I've found 'em.'

Grady brought the car to a stop and watched the family getting out of the car, the two boys getting under their dad's feet, the mother smiling affectionately at them and unloading the shopping bags from the boot. There was nothing in the least remarkable about them. Why Bill's interest? The woman looked too young to be his mother, and neither she nor her husband resembled him; the father and both boys were sandy-haired and thick-set, a contrast to Bill's wiriness. He killed the engine and turned to confront Bill, to ask for an explanation. But his companion was already out of the door and skipping across the road, cautiously.

Grady wound down his window. 'Bill, come back

here,' he called, keeping his voice low. 'C'mon, Bill. What are you going to do? Who are they?'

Bill was already backing up, following the path leading around the back of the houses. Grady considered waiting, considered driving off. Two things prevented him. One, the lad was in a heightened, tense emotional state, looked as if he might crack at any moment. What if he opened his mouth about Mrs Franklin? And Grady didn't care to think about the second reason. He swore, unclipped his seatbelt, and followed.

When the knocking began Judith felt her heart sink even lower. The daylight was fading and she had to squint to see the cards, which after several hours were starting to jumble themselves meaninglessly, her options whirling through her head, kings on queens on jacks, deal a new deck, change the design, maximise the screen. A familiar dull pressure was building up on her forehead, starting at the centre and spreading out, starting to pound, starting to pull her down. And now someone was knocking on the front door.

The baby started to wail again, this time even louder, its cries piercing her to the core, as if it sat in judgement, as if it was mocking her for the mess she was making of her life, this life of confinement.

She cracked, threw the mouse at the screen, sprang to her feet, marched out of Fitz's study, past the answerphone with its blinking red light, past the foot of the stairs and the thud of Mark's CD player, past the kitchen where the steriliser was still spewing out steam and a bundle of wet washing waited, and into the living room, to the pram. She'd left it facing the window, as you were advised to.

She wheeled the pram around, bent over, clasped its sides, looked into the eyes of her child, and screamed back, with force, letting out guttural cries, letting it know. The pram shook.

'Mum?'

She turned, raising a hand to her mouth, saw Mark, face full of concern. There was somebody standing beside him, moving into the room; Danny, Fitz's brother, who was staring at her in horror. His presence was unexpected. She hadn't seen him since the birth, and before the death of his mother he had been a rare caller. The arrival of someone who could reasonably be classified a stranger made her blush with fright and embarrassment. 'Uncle Danny's been knocking,' said Mark, looking past her anxiously, at the still wailing baby.

Judith was unable to speak. She took a breath and burst into helpless tears, feeling ashamed as Mark came forward, hugged her. 'Hey, come on, what's the matter?' he whispered to her shoulder, as she had so often said to him. He rocked her gently and for a moment she felt proud. She'd brought this one up half decently. 'What's the matter?'

Danny spoke. 'Have you had a drink, Judith?'

She shook her head. 'You should have called me if you needed help with anything,' said Mark. She pushed him away gently, still tearful, and he immediately went to look in the pram, started cooing at his younger brother as if he were a pet.

Danny looked her up and down, and shook his head

sadly. 'Come on, let's find you a drink and have a sit down. Wee Jimmy'll be fine.'

Fitz was right. The pious way his brother reacted to almost any emotional conflict was irritating in the extreme. But as he led her towards the kitchen, an arm placed protectively around her shoulder, she was glad of the simple bodily comfort.

Fitz took the back way out of the station, descending the flights of steps with a heavy tread, dreading home and the inevitable, unavoidable row waiting there for him. He entered the car park and saw Jane making for her plot. 'You couldn't squeeze an extra one in there, could you?'

'You're miles out of my way, Fitz,' she said, avoiding eye contact. Ah, she was trying to keep things casual. Silly move.

'Franklin's made a complaint, then,' he said, attempting to stir some reaction from her. She didn't respond, so he went on, 'Mind you, I would and all, if I got pulled off the street and a big fat drunken wreck of a Scotsman shouted at me until I started crying.' He followed her to the car. 'Did you take him back to his house?'

She shook her head. 'He's gone to stay with his daughter, in Cheadle.' She had the door open. He couldn't let her go. He put a hand on the door.

'You believe me, Jane?' he begged. 'You see it, don't you?'

She hesitated before replying. 'I follow what you're saying, but Cooper is the most likely suspect.' She made to escape again. Still he held on.

'No!' he said. 'Look, you're bleeding badly, you're heading for the phone. You've turned your back on your assailant. Why the hell do you do that?'

She climbed in, fastened her seatbelt. 'I've tried ditching my lover – Cooper. I've threatened to tell my husband and he's gone ape. He didn't mean to do it. I think he's too shocked or too scared to do it again.'

Fitz snorted, and kept his hand on the door. 'Hundred per cent cast-iron bollocks. Josh Cooper didn't kill her. Yes, he's served time for GBH, but if Wise had bothered to look a little closer at his file they'd have seen he was had up for assaulting a nightwatchman, together with three other blokes, part of a bungled robbery. Not the same thing at all.'

'But if she told him it was over, perhaps demanded her money back –'

'No. She wouldn't end an affair that never properly got started.' He waved his free hand effusively, now confident he was getting through. This time everything made sense, he knew he was right. 'Mary Franklin wasn't in love with this guy Cooper. She was having sex with another man, fairly openly I'd reckon – I mean, she told the neighbours, for Christ's sake. Just to help patch up her marriage. It was her way of sticking the jump leads on old Phil. He's a drunk, he's self-absorbed. She wanted to stir his envy, light the fireworks and get some bloody passion back.'

'Really.' There was a pause, then she said, 'Is that your version, or Judith's?'

Fitz leant over her. 'Two people murdered Mary Franklin. And you know it, you know I don't say these things for the sake of saying them.'

She shook his hand off. 'Oh, get in the car, Fitz. I'll take you as far as I can.'

Honeysuckle Road was at the very edge of the estate, and backed on to an area of scrubby woodland. Grady saw the blue of the City top through the bushes and walked forward tentatively, his senses alert. He came upon Bill, who was standing just feet away from the low wooden fence at the back of number thirty's garden. He'd calmed down, thankfully, and his hands hung at his sides, limp. His posture now looked more defeated than defiant. Grady followed his fixed, unblinking stare. The garden was spacious, with two swings, a small slide and a gnome-edged pond. The kids were mucking about, the older boy standing up on a swing and rocking back and forth, shouting and mocking his younger brother playfully. The father was visible, in the kitchen, unpacking groceries. Bill watched the scene forlornly, shaking his head every few seconds.

Grady felt uneasy. If someone came along, what would the pair of them doing this look like? A bloke and a boy in the bushes. He turned about, but the woodland seemed deserted in the twilight. A bonfire smell was drifting over the rooftops and there were shouts and cries from a distant playing field.

The father came out of the kitchen. 'Right, you two,' he called. 'Dinner'll be on the table in fifteen minutes.' His voice was forthright, middle-class. Again Grady looked doubtfully between him and Bill.

'Your dad's not on your Christmas card list, then?'

'That's not my dad,' said Bill, narrowing his eyes. 'That's Brian.'

Grady nodded. 'Your stepdad, yeah?'

'No.' Bill exhaled deeply, his shoulders heaving back and forth. Grady quelled his impulse to reach out and comfort. 'They're nearly my mum and dad.'

Grady was getting more worried. This was weird. 'Nearly?'

Bill answered slowly. 'I came to live with them when I was seven. Not here, they lived down Urmston way.' He shuddered again. 'One hundred and three Fairfield Drive, Urmston, M31. 061 824 1940.' There was a terrible, wounded sadness in his deep brown eyes. Grady felt his heart melting, a sticky feeling of compassion mixing with his suppressed lust. He hadn't felt this way since the age of fourteen.

Bill continued. 'My family, my new family. I'd been to loads of foster parents before, when I was younger. Josie and Alan, Maggie and Peter, Ian and Barbara, Norma and Wallace. They were a scream, they used to enter every competition going and the house was full of bicycles.' He returned his attention to the garden, and carried on, speaking matter-of-factly, not seeking pity. 'Then Diane and Brian. They were different, they wanted to adopt. That was unusual because I'd turned seven by then, that's usually too old. I knew how lucky I was. I was on my best behaviour and all that. I didn't want to spoil things.'

'You blew it?'

Bill shook his head and tensed up again, his nostrils flaring. 'I never put a foot wrong. I did the dishes without being asked, they used to say how good I was. And I tried really hard at school so they'd be proud of me. We used to go on trips at the weekend, the Lakes,

113

and castles and things. Even if I got bored I'd never say. They took me on holiday, we went to the South of France. Diane used to be a music teacher. I was learning the piano. I can still do *Fur Elise*.'

There was a lack of emphasis in his account that troubled Grady. 'So what happened?'

'Well, Diane got pregnant. They'd been trying for five years, and nothing. They'd just signed the first lot of adoption papers. P120, the green form. Then she got pregnant with him.' He nodded to the older boy, now climbing up the slide, and for the first time his face clouded with anger.

Grady felt himself responding to the tale, empathising. 'They booted you out?'

Bill couldn't answer. There were tears building in his eyes. 'Social services came to pick me up. I didn't know what was going on. They told me I was just going away for a few days. I was in the car, bawling my head off. I mean, I was only eight years old. I was screaming and calling for Diane and Brian. They stuck me in this room in Sowerby Park, with another kid. I couldn't sleep and I tried running away. A few days later they told me what had happened. I thought they were lying, I couldn't believe it.' The tears were falling now, over reddened cheeks. Bill kicked at a bush. 'Brian had taught me to use the phone, in case I ever got lost anywhere. I used to ring them up, promising I wouldn't get in the way. I said I liked babies.'

Grady took a deep breath and reached out, but somehow, in the second it took to reach Bill, the caress he'd intended became a mere tap on the shoulder. Still he couldn't express what he felt. 'Come on, Bill. Let's shoot.'

114

Bill smiled at his touch, but said, 'Not yet.'

'It's getting cold.'

'Go and sit in the car. I won't be a minute.'

Reluctantly Grady backed off, still looking about him anxiously.

Jane braked her car at a bus stop and turned to Fitz. 'Off you go, then.'

He smirked at her, infuriatingly. 'You're going in the wrong direction.'

'No I'm not.'

He shifted in the passenger seat, the seat belt straining against his massive frame. 'You've taken the wrong turning for your flat.'

'I'm not going to my flat.' At his raised eyebrow she leant across him, with difficulty, and unlocked his door. 'It's none of your business, really, Fitz, so please get out.'

He refused to budge, wagged a finger at her, assumed his diagnostic face. 'Canny. You refused me the lift, until you worked out you could do this to me, and I wouldn't object, but I'd be hurt, envious. You want me to ask where you're going?'

'Aren't you?'

He sat back. 'All right. Where are you going?'

'I'm going to Alan's flat,' she said evenly. Inwardly she relished the moment of shock on Fitz's features.

'Alan, as in Alan Temple?'

'He dislocated his shoulder, when he went to arrest Cooper. I want to see if he's all right, that's all.' She gestured to a looming bus. 'Haven't you got a home to go to?'

Fitz unstrapped himself. 'Clever. Testing the ground. You're thinking of taking up with him, you want to see how I'd react?'

She was accustomed to his accuracy. After three years it didn't hurt half so much, particularly when he only got it half right. 'You'll miss your bus, Fitz.'

He got out of the car without saying another word.

After several measures of Scotch Judith was pissed enough to ramble. Danny sat on the other side of the kitchen table, and she didn't mind who her audience was. It felt good just to get things out. 'Have you ever read *The Midwich Cuckoos*? John Wyndham?' As she spoke she poured him another slug from the bottle. His car keys were on the table. Well, they could put him on the sofa bed. 'Alien babies take possession of the women in a village. At any cost they must be nurtured. The mothers try escaping but if they cross the boundary line, piff, they self-destruct. They're compelled back to the offspring, ripping their blouses open, pointing their sags and creases at the only thing they have any value for.' She laughed bitterly. 'Only a man could write that and pretend it's science bloody fiction.'

He laughed with her, but there was a forced quality to it that he couldn't conceal. He took another sip of his drink, looked around the kitchen. 'Is Eddie working? Do you know when he'll be back in?'

Judith felt her temper rising. 'If you can't be bothered to listen you might as well go.' She knew as soon as she said it how ridiculous she sounded.

He reached over and laid his hand on hers. 'Judith, I was just asking.' At his touch she felt unexpected

116

pleasure. Then, she was fairly far gone.

'That obviously runs in the family,' she said, shaking him off. 'I've nothing to say, nothing to make you feel better, I'm just asking.'

'I didn't mean it like that,' he said.

She thumped her drink down on the table and stifled a sudden rush of hot tears. 'I know, I know, but I can't help how I feel. I've lost my career for this child, and your bloody brother promised, he *promised*. No more gambling, for the sake of the child.'

Danny frowned. So, he was listening, taking an interest. She was still sober enough to realise that her conversation wasn't up to its usual sparkling standard. Maybe it was just the opportunity to score a point off Fitz that had roused him. 'He's gambling again?'

'Look behind you.' She nodded to the painting, propped facing the wall, still half concealed in its wrapper. 'And his mother's money too.'

Danny bit his lip. 'What did he do with it?'

'He threw half of it away in a casino. The other half went on the dogs.'

'The bastard,' Danny breathed, half to himself.

Judith stood, scraping her chair on the kitchen floor, yawning. 'Take it up with him if you like, I couldn't care less.' She grabbed the whisky bottle and set off for the lounge.

Bill reached out, hooked his fingers through holes in the plastic fencing. The new house was large, with a garage and utility room and mullioned windows. The middle window on the first floor was open, and through it he saw bright striped wallpaper and posters – footballers and a couple of pop stars – and a United scarf pinned across a wardrobe. That was his room by rights. As he watched Diane walked in, pulled off the duvet cover. The way she had of holding her head at a certain angle when she did ordinary household chores was like a bit of the past come to life. He thought he remembered everything about his time with them, but it was the little things, the tiny domestic details of a cancelled world that really shook him.

Diane looked out of the window and she saw him. The next instant she'd dropped the duvet and was out of sight. Bill knew what she'd do next. She'd call the office, like all the times before. Why wouldn't she listen?

In the grip of rage he ran through the woodland, tramping through patches of scrub, pushing branches aside, and he was on the tarmac of the estate. He ran round, not thinking, conscious only that he had to get back in there, make an impression, make a stand, make them see. He deserved their time.

He sprinted along the pavement, found the Volvo, ran up to the door, twisted the handle. It was locked. There was an open wooden gate leading to the garden. He darted through it, along a paved path at the side of the house, got into the garden. The kids and Brian were gone, she must have called them in, but the back door was open. He snuck through, heard her voice. She was on the phone. Brian was herding the kids upstairs.

'Ian McVerry, please.' Bill's fury grew. McVerry was his caseworker. Why did she have to call him, what was the problem? 'Well, can you give me the number?' He was the problem, he'd always been in the way. 'Then please will you call him and tell him to ring me urgently?' There was fear in Diane's voice and Bill found himself enjoying that. This was his moment, his time to make an impression on them, show them what they'd done, make them suffer for it. They were the only people in the world who mattered. 'Please, it's very urgent. It's Diane Nash.'

He prepared himself, put on his biggest smile, and walked into the hall. 'Hiya, Diane,' he said.

Fitz trudged towards his front door, crunching gravel, unsure which of his current crises were worth worrying about. His thoughts were crowded. He saw Mary Franklin's purpling body, Wise's shaking head, Penhaligon dismissing him from the car. The latter came to the fore most of all. She was testing her limits, laying down the ground, gearing herself up for a return to the real world. An inner voice niggled persistently, difficult to ignore. She didn't need him any more, that's what she was trying to prove. And she was right.

It was only as he put the key in the lock, and saw his brother's car parked outside, that Fitz remembered that his wife and new child might also be added to his list of problem areas. Then surely one day away didn't count, not if there was work involved. And he had tried to phone her, it wasn't his fault if she left the answerphone on.

As he walked into the hall another inner voice whispered that perhaps there was a connection between Danny's car and the unanswered call? He dismissed that instantly. Danny was too holy to let himself cross that particular line.

The television was on. 'I'm home,' he called. There was no reply. He entered the living room. The only light came from the TV. In the flickering patterns it cast he saw Judith, slumped sideways along the couch, her head buried in a cushion, a hand thrust out at an uncomfortable angle, an empty bottle of Jim Beam on the carpet. He crossed to the pram; it was empty.

A little nervously he went to the kitchen. Inside were Danny and Mark, listening to a match on the radio, sharing a pizza. He nodded to them, tried to suppress his guilt, refusing to let it show, refusing to let them better him. He'd been working, for Christ's sake, earning money. 'Where's Jimmy?'

'Asleep upstairs,' said Mark. He scooped up his pizza portions and left the room, avoiding Fitz.

Danny was staring right at Fitz with an all too familiar glint of righteousness in his eye.

'What?' said Fitz.

'You know what.'

'Oh, the money.' He crossed to the sink, poured himself a glass of water, trying to decide how to play this one. 'Yes, my money, left to me, for me to spend as I wish. Not Judith's money, not your money.'

'You promised her.'

Fitz stared back at him. 'What's it to do with you? I didn't realise you were qualified as a marriage counsellor as well as a twat. I mean where do you find the time?'

'Eddie, I don't think you know what you're doing to her.'

'Look, one day. One lousy day. Tomorrow things'll look different.' He barged past Danny. 'And is that your

120

car blocking the driveway? I presume you've seen how the baby's doing, I mean' – he smirked – 'that was your reason for coming round, wasn't it? Or did you just feel in the mood for a sermon.'

Grady counted off the songs on his cassette copy of *Common One*, smoking roll-up after roll-up and trying to put the day's events in some sort of order. Since yesterday afternoon the things he'd done had taken on an ethereal quality, as if he'd only observed them, not taken part. As the hours passed, and no retribution came, he'd allowed himself to wonder if they really were going to get away with it. He remembered his platoon leader telling him of time spent in Korea. You kill one man, and your hand shakes, your blood pumps. You kill another, the reaction changes. After your third, your fourth, killing starts to seem more and more like a job, a complex profession, and if you're the right kind of man then each life you take makes you stronger and cleverer. There's no better feeling, he'd said, not sex or booze, nothing compares to the exhilaration of winning a war. For the first time Grady understood that. He felt powerful.

The cassette reached the end of side one and clicked over. Irritated, Grady leant forward, pipped the horn. They had to get away. He was planning something. They could drive back into town, spend some more cash, book a room at the Midland and make a night of it. All Bill had to do, he realised now, was reach out for him, guide him.

Another car pulled into Honeysuckle Road, a blue Sierra. It passed him, came to a stop right outside number thirty, and a bloke got out. He was tall and bespectacled, with grey receding hair, and wore a flimsy brown leather jacket. As he locked his car door Grady registered the irritation on his face. He was muttering to himself, mildly bothered, and he walked quickly up the drive.

Terrified, Grady leapt out. Walking as nonchalantly as he could he passed the car, saw the blue sticker on the rear window. Greater Manchester Social Services. 'Shit,' he said, feeling his breath catching at his throat once more, the adrenalin rising. Then he lost restraint, legged it back up the road and around the corner into the bushes, pushing aside the shrubbery, clawing his way to where he'd left Bill.

Bill was gone.

Grady looked up at the sound of raised voices. It was getting dark now, it was past eight, and the window of the lounge was bright with electric light. Bill was in an armchair, his arms gripping the padded rests, shouting. Also present were Brian, the foster father, pacing the carpet with his head in his hands, and the social worker, who knelt down, trying to reason with Bill, his face a picture of condescension.

Grady froze, his new life crumbling around him.

Bill couldn't look at McVerry. On many occasions like this one he had, and his spirit was broken, and it was away back to Sowerby Park. No, he was staying. He was an adult, he had rights, all he wanted was to have his say and talk things through. McVerry was standing before him, hands on hips, and Bill knew without looking how he was exchanging resigned glances with

Brian and shaking his head in that condescending way of his. 'Come on, Bill. Come and sit in the car. You're trying my patience.'

'I don't care.' Bill tightened his grip on the sofa, dug the moulded soles of his new boots into the carpet. He stared past McVerry at the shelving unit, at the photos of Steven and the younger brother, smiling and chubby-cheeked in school sweaters against a neutral blue background. 'I want a cup of coffee. I want to talk. I want a cup of coffee.'

Brian muttered, 'Oh God.'

'Bill, look, you're scaring people, you're scaring me,' said McVerry. He reached forward, touched Bill lightly on the arm.

Bill shook him off, viciously, surprising himself with the force of the response. McVerry backed off slightly, raising his hands. 'If Brian and Diane don't want you here, you've no right barging in. What happens if they get the police? Because they could, you know.'

Bill screwed his eyes tight shut, and when he opened them up he found himself smiling, beaming at Brian. 'I've done nothing wrong,' he pleaded. 'I just want to come home, that's all. Fetch Diane, let me talk to Diane.' He knew Diane was the weak link, that she at least felt guilt. She knew it too, though; she'd taken off upstairs at the first sight of him. 'Fetch Diane.' He raised his voice, calling upstairs, not aggressively, modulating his tone to a gentle, familiar, childlike call, raising the pitch of the second syllable. 'Di-ane. Di-ane.'

'Oh, for Christ's sake,' said Brian.

His imprecation seemed to galvanise McVerry. He reached forward, grabbed Bill by the arm, very definitely this time, levered him off the sofa, twisted his arm behind his back.

'Let go of me!' Bill shouted. 'Piss off, get off me!'

'Come on, Bill.' McVerry applied greater force, pushing him out of the living room and into the hall. 'Come on, Bill.'

Bill tried to strike back, kick back, but McVerry must have gone on some bloody social services defence course. His hold was immovable, the strength behind it alarming. For the first time, as he was pushed through the front door that Brian held open, Bill realised how big McVerry was. With that realisation came a frightening new thought. McVerry was an opponent, an equal opponent. Bill was grown now, almost eighteen, he didn't have to obey this unrelated, uncaring stranger. He was strong enough to fight back. And he had a mate.

It was dark outside now, and he twisted his head, sought the Montego. The driver's seat was empty. He struggled again. 'Calm down, Bill, just calm down, OK?' McVerry hissed in his ear. This close Bill could smell the leather of McVerry's old, creaking jacket, the odour of imprisonment with the rejects at Sowerby Park.

Grady appeared from the darkness and at his approach Bill felt a thrill run through his body, an uplifting sensation of desire commingling with terror and the anticipation of violence. Grady's stride was confident and militarily precise, his shoulders pushed back, his neck jutting forward. 'Where d'you think you're going with him?' he growled to McVerry. Bill felt a rush of exhilaration. His mate was looking out for him, taking his side. 'Let him go.'

124

'Who are you?' asked McVerry, still steering Bill towards his car.

'He's my mate,' Bill spat. 'I'm allowed mates, aren't I?'

McVerry relaxed his grip slightly. Bill twisted free, moving to stand with Grady. He was shaking all over with emotion.

'Social worker?' asked Grady, his eyes narrowing.

'I'm taking him back to Sowerby Park,' McVerry said patiently, reasonably. The way he spoke when he was doing something wrong.

Grady nodded at Bill. 'Look at the state of him.' He addressed Bill. 'If you don't want to go with him, get in mine.'

Bill glowed with pride. Against Grady McVerry was powerless. Together they could defeat him.

McVerry looked between them, studying Grady. 'Bill, this is serious. I'm warning you, for your own sake. Why's a bloke that age want to be your friend, eh? You're a good-looking lad, put your thinking cap on.'

Grady seemed to balloon at his words, strode up aggressively, inches from McVerry.

'He's here,' said Bill, 'because I want him to be.' He moved to join Grady, slapped his mate across the back, sneered at his opponent, his enemy, his equal enemy.

McVerry shook his head. 'I'm not arguing with you any more, Bill.' He started walking away, trying to make out he'd lost his cool when really he was frightened. It felt good to see him like that, on the losing side for once. It felt good, but it wasn't enough. 'Just get in the car.' As he spoke he looked over nervously at number thirty. All the front lights were out, no help was coming from that way.

Bill followed him to the car. He couldn't stop now, he had to hurt. 'What's wrong with that, McVerry? I picked him, he's my mate. What's wrong with that?'

McVerry turned at the car door, raised his hands. 'OK, mate.' He looked behind Bill, at Grady, disgust written across his face. 'I'm washing my hands of you.' He opened the door, climbed into the car. 'You can do what you bloody like from now on.' He fired the engine, and the motor's splutter acted as a lever on his anger. He shouted, 'What you do with your arse is your own bloody business.'

Bill couldn't let him get away, not after that. He ran forward, started kicking the door panel, frenziedly, clicking at the handle, straining to break the lock. 'You're scum, McVerry! He's my mate, I picked him, all right? Not you, not the bleeding office. I picked him because I say where I go next, McVerry, not you!'

McVerry was shouting back. 'I'm ringing the police.' He addressed Grady. 'And I've got your number, pal.' He crunched the gearbox and was away, tearing along the quiet, suburban tree-lined road.

'Bastard!' Bill screamed after him. 'Bastard!' Without thinking he ran for Grady's car, jumped in, found the keys still in the ignition, turned them. Grady was only half in himself when Bill put his foot down, screaming wildly, chasing after McVerry's disappearing tail lights, hammering on the horn.

Diane Nash waited until the shouting, the screaming and the roar and screech of engine noise had passed, and turned the landing lights on. The kids were crying, faces clouded with fear. Steven's arm was extended protectively around his brother's shaking shoulders.

Brian came up the stairs and she met his eyes. 'I'm not asking you this time,' she said. 'We're moving.'

Grady was breathing hard, the familiar awful redness building up behind his eyes. They'd turned on to the main road, and McVerry was in sight, trying to get back into town. Street lights flashed by on either side, the wind roared as Bill put his foot down, overtaking another vehicle, getting right on the tail of the Sierra. The danger was like fuel to Grady, making him restless, empowering him, stripping away the lies, the half-truths, the compromises he'd made for the sake of other people. This was his world, his and Bill's world, and he'd do anything to help the lad.

It was as Bill wrenched at the wheel to overtake McVerry, tears of rage running down his scrunched red face, his body quivering, that Grady realised he really was in love. He called to mind the casual violence of his first love object, Gerry Mackay, who'd boasted of killing a copper. It was a wonderful, brutal, shining thing, the destructive power of the adolescent male. His own weakness paled beside Bill's strength.

They zoomed across a flyover, still not quite level with their enemy. They approached a row of cones marking out road works. Bill increased his speed, driving like a demon, scattering them one by one, knocking them flying like skittles, the road a hail of orange blurs.

They reached McVerry's side. Bill leaned across Grady, saw the social worker's terrified face. 'You're gonna die, McVerry!' he screamed. Grady relished the physical contact with Bill's trembling body. 'You're gonna die!'

McVerry felt cold waves of terror passing through him. The boy's face was agonised, turning purple, the eyes thin slits of malignance, just feet away. The Montego came closer, bumped against the Sierra, shook him, scraped the paintwork. He glanced over his shoulder, saw his briefcase lying on the back seat, his mobile within. He weighed the risks. If he stopped he was dead. That bloke with Bill was big, dangerous-looking. He raced ahead, putting his foot right down, willing for a police siren to suddenly appear. But the main road was almost empty.

He shot off down a side road, waiting for the last possible moment and wrenching the wheel around. The streets spun dizzily about him. There was a crunch from somewhere in the engine, the brakes squealed, but he'd gained time. Bill followed him, a few yards back.

There was a pub ahead, on a street corner. Lights flashing, music blaring, shouts and the murmur of conversation. McVerry slammed on his brakes, crashed to a halt in a plot on the small forecourt, leapt out and ran for the saloon door, registering the Montego screeching up at his rear. There was a banner and balloons hanging over the door.

The place was packed, sweltering, he had to push his way through. Male bodies, densely boxed, the smell of beer and sweat. There were cheers in time to the beat. McVerry looked about wildly, checking behind him, searching for sanctuary.

'They're trying to kill me!' he shouted.

He could barely hear himself. There were more cheers, shouts, raised glasses. The men were all looking up, at a raised stage, at a stripper and the birthday boy, a hairy rugby type. She was undressing him, timing her moves, unbuttoning him to the rhythm, smiling with mock seductiveness. The crowd roared as she pulled off his shirt and threw it away.

'He tried to bloody kill me!' McVerry grabbed the nearest reveller. 'Call the police! Please, call the police!' The lad shrugged him off, intent on the spectacle.

McVerry looked over his shoulder. Through the smoke-filled air, just for a second, he saw Bill's vengeful tear-stained face.

He turned and ran, pushing wildly through the crowd, making for where the side door had to be, by the gents. He lowered his head, charged through the tightly knotted groups of leering men, wrenched the door open, fell through, down a flight of steps, his own breath resounding in his ears. All trace of individuality, of common concern, was stripped from him. He became a creature compounded of nothing but animal terror. As he emerged into the chill night air the birthday crowd went wild, whistling and clapping.

Outside was a yard of scrappy waste ground. He ran forward, searching for a way out. Ahead was a high-walled dead end. He turned, intending to run around the other side of the pub.

Bill was standing before him, holding a brown beer bottle.

McVerry recalled his training, raised his hands in a

placating gesture. He thought frantically, searching for a strategy. All foster kids wanted reassurance, wanted to keep out of trouble. And he knew how much Bill hated confinement, hated the law. 'If you stop this now, Bill, I'll say your mate led you on. It's not your fault, he led you on. Nothing will happen. Nothing will happen to you.'

Bill tipped the bottle from side to side, tantalising McVerry, advancing slowly. The beer sloshed out, forming small puddles on the churned-up asphalt. 'Nothing ever happens to me,' he said, dangerously calm.

An amplified voice came from the pub. 'Let's hear it, lads, for the lovely Sheena!'

Bill lost concentration, turned slightly.

McVerry sprang, kicked the bottle from the boy's hand, heard it smash. He leapt, wrestling Bill to the ground, knitted his fingers in Bill's hair, slammed his head against the hard surface. He felt the strength flow out of him, his anger erupting after thirty-odd years of measured liberal care and patience and compromise. 'You stupid, stupid little sod,' he cried, slamming Bill's head up and down, up and down in time to his words. 'Nine bloody years and you just can't let it go, can you?' He felt warm blood trickling through the boy's hair, trickling between his fingers. 'Why can't you just let it go and give us all some peace, for God's sake?' He pulled himself back and up, breathing deeply, his inner turmoil blotting out his senses.

Something moved behind him.

He turned. The older, bigger bloke was moving towards him. He was twisting something between his bunched fists, a strap or something. A belt. McVerry whipped

130

round. Bill was standing up, reaching for the broken bottle.

There was nowhere to run. He sank down, whimpered, pleaded, looking between them. The older man was implacable, a psychotic glint in his eyes. Bill, his head and football top wet with blood, raised the jagged glass.

They moved in as one, and McVerry felt his face being smashed to pieces as the breath was slowly squeezed from his throat.

FIVE

Penhaligon was back at Anson Road at seven, prepared for a long day. Work was her best comfort, she'd known that since school. And the sight of Wise's shaking head as he opened the door of the cells to her knock was reassuring. Cooper was a dud, then. In all likelihood Fitz was correct. Another plus point for her, another black mark against Wise. She'd bring it up at her promotion board.

'He doesn't know a bloody thing,' said Wise, nodding over his shoulder along the yellow bricked corridor. He was in his shirtsleeves and there were red rings around his eyes. 'He's got another ten birds on the go. Thought he was being nicked for handling. He is, now. Seventeen bloody toasters in his kitchen. His current totty dropped him right in it. Takes us no further forward.'

Jane nodded. 'What about Fitz's idea, sir?' She kept her tone neutral. 'I've got Mary Franklin's address book, I could go through it.'

Wise leant against the wall, studying her. 'You thought he was right about this couple business?'

'He's been right before, sir. That's all.' Her face hardened. 'There's no personal reason, if that's what you mean.'

'I didn't say that, Jane,' said Wise. There was an awkward moment. Cooper's gruff, booming voice echoed along the corridor towards them, the words muffled by the low ceiling. She knew what Wise was thinking, and moreover he was correct. She was out for evidence against him. At last he demurred. 'Go and get on with it, all right?'

Bill's really was an angel face in sleep. Grady opened his eyes to it, saw the gentle rise and fall of the boy's chest, heard the assured rhythm of his breathing. In the night he'd dropped off and his own head was resting on Bill's shoulder. He felt comfortable there, in the few seconds before his thinking brain kicked back to life and he realised what this might look like. There was nobody about for miles, he'd made certain of that, but there were people in his head all the time, even now. Jackie, young Michael, his parents, Gerry Mackay, all looking down on him, seeing him cuddling up to a seventeen-year-old boy. So he blinked, and shook his head to clear it, and sat up in the passenger seat.

The car was parked in woodland, and it was concealed on either side by tall trees. There was silence, stillness, disturbed only by the birds and a distant rumble of city traffic. He sat in contemplation, feeling strangely tranquil, and still very tired. His body ached in many places. There was a searing muscular pain across his shoulderblades. He called to mind McVerry's final moments, the belt about the neck choking off the man's pleas, the bottle in Bill's hand going back and forth, back and forth into the face. Bill's expression, bestial, grunting with savage joy, a parody of orgasm. He killed the thought, reached over to shake his partner awake.

Bill opened one eye and smiled. 'Hello, Grady,' he said weakly, and raised an arm to touch him. Grady pulled away. The sleeve of the Man City top was dark with McVerry's crusted blood.

Jane was at her desk, writing out the names and numbers from the address book and checking them against computer records. Her own face was reflected dimly in the screen. Vaguely she was aware of other members of the CID team making their way into the office, chatting about nothing, keeping their conversation unnaturally bright, as they always did around her. Skelton set a plastic cup on the edge of her desk and smiled. She nodded back, kept her eyes on her work. It remained impossible to relax with them. Soon, if things went her way, with her in control, it might change.

She sensed Temple's presence before he spoke. He was standing over the table, shoulders hunched like a teacher inspecting the work of a pupil. His left arm was in a sling. 'How are you?' she asked.

'It's OK, it's been reset. I'll have this off in a couple of weeks. Doctor said I can't move it about too much. I'll have to stick to desk work.' He paused. 'Er, how are you?' Again, that tone of gentle inquiry, and again the sensation that he was holding something back, that his interest was more than that of a prospective sexual partner.

'I'm fine,' she replied, in a monotone. Not ready, not yet.

Wise burst into the office, looking more harried and tired than ever. 'Incident,' he called. 'Must be open bloody season.' He nodded to her. 'Leave that.'

'Sir,' she protested.

'You're coming with me,' he said firmly. 'Another murder. Back of the Hope and Anchor, Morris Street.' There was a collective sigh, a murmur, scraping of chairs, activity. He turned to Skelton. 'Go and get him, meet us there.' Skelton nodded and hurried off.

Wise's eyes swept over Jane as she stood, turned her screen off.

Morning. Fitz had spent an uncomfortable night on the sofa, which could barely contain him. There was no sense in forcing things with Judith. After carrying her up to bed last night, not without some resistance on her part, he'd nipped back downstairs, thrown a blanket over himself and collapsed. His dreams were full of dead purple faces and beautiful women turning him down, and his sleep was punctuated by several anxious moments. Right now there were plenty of things for him to be worried about, and it was difficult to prioritise. Who to curse first? Judith, Wise, Danny, Alan Temple for moving in and wrecking his schemes for Jane Penhaligon?

He fell off the sofa, decided he couldn't be bothered to haul himself up on it again, went to the kitchen, threw a couple of glasses of water over his face. Right, he thought, make a domestic gesture. There were dirty plates all over the surfaces. He rolled up his sleeves and set to, squirting liquid into the bowl. A series of thumps and a despairing, low-voiced groan came from directly

135

above. Ah, movement, she's stirring. Right, be considerate. He filled the kettle, flicked it on, arranged things nicely. As an extra touch, to demonstrate his thoughtfulness, he started up the baby's steriliser. The stairs creaked. He slid his hands into rubber gloves, immersed them in the suds, scrubbed at a plate.

Judith came in, slammed the door. She picked up a dirty glass, leant over him, and filled it from the cold tap. He heard her down it, mentally willing her to speak. If only she'd say something, open up first as usual, he could react and play innocence. She gulped the water down, tossed the glass into the bowl, and slammed out again. His plan had failed.

Secondary strategy. Play the mature, concerned husband, offer help. He followed her, drips cascading from his pink-gloved hands. She was ascending the stairs again, deserting him, purposefully. 'Don't you think we should talk?' He made his voice a model of contrition.

She replied without turning round. 'Again? That'd be twice this year. I'll need more warning.'

The phone rang and Fitz snatched it up. 'Hello.'

'Dr Fitzgerald?' The voice was tentative, familiar. He struggled to place it.

'Ah, Eric. You want to make another appointment?' He flipped up the phone's aerial, carried the call into the study. 'Let me just take you through to the sanctum.'

'No, Doctor,' said Eric. 'I was just phoning to say I did it.'

'Did what?' Fitz searched his memory. He couldn't recall yesterday's meeting. Much had occurred since then, he'd pushed the more routine events to the back of his mind.

'I saw a girl and I went up to her and told her how I felt.'

Fitz's heart sank. Had he really advised that? 'Right, great.'

'She told me to bugger off.'

'Ah, right.' The doorbell rang. 'Look, Eric, someone's just come to the door . . .'

'You just want to get rid of me. You're not interested.'

'Look, Eric, I really have to –' The line went dead. 'Stupid bastard.' Fitz ran to the door, to find Katie, baby brother in hand, had beaten him to it.

Skelton stood in the porch. 'Hiya, is your dad in?'

Fitz pushed past her, finger raised in triumph at Skelton's disappointed face. 'Cooper's a dud, am I right?'

Skelton sighed. 'A bloke's been glassed outside a pub. The boss just wants you to have a look.'

Fitz didn't move. 'Ah, but Cooper is a dud, I saw that look in your eye. Wise has cocked up again, he'll drag you down too, and you don't want that, do you?'

'I'll drive you there,' said Skelton, moving back to his waiting car.

'Wait just a moment.' Fitz turned to Katie, nodded to the baby. 'Hold the fort for an hour will you, love?'

She sighed. 'Dad, I'm going round to Clare's.'

'Well, get Mark to look after Jimmy. It's time the shyster put in some work.'

Katie dropped her eyes, awkwardly. Fitz had an odd feeling he was missing out on something. 'Mark's out.'

'Out?' Fitz grabbed his jacket and shrugged himself

137

into it. He realised he hadn't taken a shower, and hoped he didn't smell too badly. 'It's Saturday, he's never out before the beer mats.'

Katie hefted the baby up. 'I've got to go to Clare's, Dad. We're rehearsing an assembly, it's important.' She shot him a look of pure venom. Fitz glanced up the stairs, shuddered at the thought of increasing Judith's rancour. Skelton beeped his horn.

An idea occurred to Fitz.

Grady watched Bill from the car. He was back in the driver's seat. The boy was dousing his shirt in a stream that ran through the woods, scrubbing his hands with leaves. McVerry's blood flowed away, down to the river.

Grady's mind was a blank. It wasn't the same as yesterday, after Mrs Franklin. This time he felt justified, that justice had been served. He felt renewed, strong.

Bill straightened up, started to flick the top like a whip, to dry it. Grady told himself that what he felt as he looked on was merely admiration, envy for a real survivor, a lad half his age that could look after himself in any situation. He knew that was only half the picture. Bill's perfect shoulders and hairless chest were visible again, and his prick was throbbing at the sight, threatening to overwhelm him, urging him to abandon all morality and decency, his masculinity.

He turned his head away, clenched his fists tight on the steering wheel. 'Bill!' he called. 'Bill, we've got to get on.'

Bill smiled, waved, slipped his top back on and

climbed the incline back up to the car. 'Where are we going then?'

Grady waited until Bill was sitting in the passenger seat. 'I need my cheque book and a few other things. Change of clothes.'

'Back to yours?'

Grady nodded and fired the engine. He followed the dirt track leading back to the main road. 'Then we'll hide away for a few days.'

'Hide?' Bill frowned. 'We ought to get away, out of the country. We could go abroad.'

Grady snarled. 'They'll be looking for us, soon. If we try anything like that they'll pick us up, easy. If we keep low for a few days we'll stand a better chance.'

Fitz reflected how odd it was to be valued; academics were generally despised, often rightly, and a practising shrink regarded at best as a necessary eccentricity of the medical profession. As Skelton's car turned off into a long backstreet, and the bustle of scene-of-crime activity outside the pub became clearer, a sense of pride swelled somewhere in Fitz. In this area of his life he felt vindicated. Everything else was a bloody mess, but this was his stomping ground.

Penhaligon walked around the corner of the pub, a clipboard and pen in her hand, displaying all her alarming efficiency. She greeted Fitz as he climbed out of the car, and said straight away, 'The cleaners found him this morning.' She walked back the way she'd come, leading Fitz around the pub to the back yard, which was not much more than a few square yards of walled-in waste ground. It had started to rain, very gently, and a plastic sheet was being hauled up over a shape in one corner, Wise directing the operation with Malcolm, all in white, scraping about for clues. 'There was a stag party but the manager reckons there was no trouble.' Fitz looked back briefly at the pub's windows, at the balloons and streamers.

'There was no trouble at my stag party,' Wise grumbled as they joined him. 'It was the next thirty bloody years that were the problem.' Fitz sensed the genuine bitterness of the statement. Wise looked beaten, and he was staring at the sodden shape on the ground with an expression of resignation to the confusion of life. For the first time Fitz realised that the puddles he'd been skirting round were composed of blood not water, and surprised himself with an involuntary shudder. The blood led messily from the centre of the yard to the corner, where it formed a red aura around the head.

Satisfied the protective sheet was steady, Malcolm reached for the dead man's shoulder, and very carefully, almost tenderly, turned him over.

Above the denim shirt and threadbare tie there was no face. It had been removed, destroyed, in its place a shattered mess of bone and gristle and blood. The mouth had been slashed across, the lower lip cut in two, the tongue, black with blood, lolling out. One eye was open, the white of the eyeball slashed across. Malcolm leant forward, felt for the lid with a white plastic finger, and closed it.

'Christ Almighty,' said Wise. Fitz took a quick look at Penhaligon. She faced the sight with apparent calm. 'What the hell did that?'

Malcolm produced a metal instrument with a tweezer-like end and removed a sliver of something. He held it up to the light of the drizzly May morning and squinted. 'Amber glass. Beer bottle?'

'Sir,' said Penhaligon. She pointed a few feet away, to the base of a scrappy, weed-ridden hedge that grew at the base of the wall. It was infested with crisp packets, condoms, and cans; she pointed to the broken neck of an amber bottle.

Wise clapped her on the back. 'Well done, Jane.' He whistled to the Forensic team, who were approaching, bags at the ready. 'Over here.'

Fitz returned his attention to the body. Malcolm opened the man's jacket, felt about inside, withdrew a wallet. He flipped it open, took out a card. Fitz caught a quick glimpse of an ID card marked Greater Manchester Social Services. 'Ian McVerry,' read Malcolm, speaking loudly to get Penhaligon's attention. She heard him, noted the name. 'I think he's a social worker.'

Fitz couldn't resist. 'A social worker, and we're looking for a motive?' As soon as he'd said it he knew he'd made a mistake. Penhaligon turned her back on him. Malcolm averted his eyes and handed the wallet to a waiting adjutant. Then he returned to the task in hand, lifting the head slightly.

Fitz smelt something. 'Good morning, Temple.'

Temple's voice came from behind him. 'How d'you know I was here?'

Fitz turned and smiled. 'Caught your aftershave blowing down wind.' He gave an exaggerated sniff. 'Sure you've splashed enough on today? Or is this a new tactic to overpower the fleeing criminal?' He kept his tone light-hearted, and even so his envy shone through. He felt a brief pang at the sight of the sling. 'How's the arm?'

'It's OK,' he said. He looked briefly between Fitz and Penhaligon.

Wise was detailing Skelton to contact social services for details of McVerry. He came back over, spoke to Malcolm. 'Any news?'

Malcolm looked up. 'There are cuts all over the head, face and neck. The neck was under pressure.' He pointed out a bruised band around the dead man's Adam's apple. 'A three-inch belt, I'd say. That's probably – er, possibly the imprint of the buckle.' Fitz leant forward, thinking. 'And it's strange, but . . .' He lifted one of McVerry's hands. The fingers were splayed, and there were tufts of hair beneath the nails. 'That looks to me as if it could, er, possibly, be human hair.'

'What's all that in Scouse?' asked Wise.

Fitz answered, his excitement building. 'It means he was attacked from in front and from behind.'

Malcolm raised a finger in correction. 'He was *secured* from behind *before* he was attacked from the front.'

Fitz slapped his hands together. 'Just like Mrs Franklin.'

'Eh, eh, eh,' said Wise, motioning for him to pipe down. He hissed, 'They were killed five miles apart. Mary Franklin had nothing to do with social services. You can't bring these two together.'

Fitz gave a long-suffering sigh. 'Frontal attack, rear attack. Two people.' Wise shook his head. Fitz smirked.

'You've charged Cooper then?'

Wise shuffled uncomfortably, stuck his hands deep in his pockets. 'Shut it.'

Penhaligon was interested, though. 'I thought you said Mary Franklin was attacked from the front first?'

'Doesn't matter. One's stronger than the other.' He indicated the body. 'This social worker, he's got hair in both hands.' His mind was racing, the thesis formulating as he spoke it. God, this was good, the adrenalin flowed, he was working, doing, making himself useful. 'He's having a fight. He thinks he's dealing with one person, the weaker person.' He followed the puddles of blood back to the centre of the yard. 'Right, he's overpowered that person and he's banging his head on the ground over here.' He demonstrated the motion, knotting his fingers together, bringing his arms up and down. 'The guy from behind, the stronger one, comes up. He takes the social worker by the neck with the belt and garottes him, holds him still for the guy with the bottle.' He rubbed his hands together, enjoying the silence he'd created. The entire incident team had stopped what they were doing to observe him. 'Emotionally,' he concluded, 'it's identical to Mary Franklin's murder.' The resounding silence that followed was deeply pleasurable. Even Wise looked half convinced.

Penhaligon said, 'Except you just said him.'

Fitz blinked. 'Eh?'

'He was banging *his* head on the floor, you just said. I thought we were looking for a man and a woman?'

Fitz wanted to grab her and kiss her. The elements fell into place in his mind. 'I did say that. I was wrong.'

143

He looked at the body. 'A man wouldn't do it, wouldn't bash a woman's head on the ground like that.'

Penhaligon raised an eyebrow. 'No?'

'No,' said Fitz conclusively. 'He'd belt her, slap her, grab her. This was a young bloke, a boy, a teenager.' He avoided her gaze. 'One older, one younger. One taller, one shorter. Could be father and son.' He looked around again, pleading with his face. Wise was contemplative. Temple looked ill, and was turned away, his good hand clutching at his injured arm. 'Well?' He turned to the pathologist. 'Malcolm?'

Malcolm waited, and nodded. 'It fits the facts as we know them.' He added hurriedly, 'About this incident.'

Before any of the others could reply a wail came from Skelton's car. All heads turned as one in surprise. Fitz shrugged. 'Excuse me.' The baby continued bawling as he scurried in his ungainly way back around the pub. Wee Jimmy was in the back, in a baby seat, howling, red-faced. Fitz levered the infant out and took a feeding bottle from his pocket. He tested the contents and stuck the teat in his son's mouth. 'There you are, you have a good suck.'

Wise and Penhaligon appeared. Wise was openly incredulous. 'What's that doing here?'

Fitz gazed down at Jimmy's tightly screwed-up eyes. He thought of Mark, how they'd regarded each other in the kitchen last night, and shook his head decisively. 'No, not father and son. I think this is a new relationship. Mrs Franklin discovered something that caused a row big enough to warrant her murder. Now, then, what is there to discover about a relationship? Only sex.'

Wise frowned. 'Sex?'

'Yes. She discovered them having sex, a man and a boy. That's what the row was about. That's why she got murdered.'

'Look, what is that doing here?' Wise asked again.

Fitz grinned. 'That –' he nodded to the baby '– is what we shrinks call dissociation. You ever seen a guy pushing a pram with one hand? It's to prove they've only half weakened.' He cooed at Jimmy, pulled the teat from his mouth. 'It's the first symptom of premature ejaculation and athlete's foot.'

Grady parked the car a couple of streets away from Banville Street, between two other vehicles in order to conceal the number plate. He turned to Bill. 'Right, keep your head down.'

'Are you going to be long?'

'Not if I can help it.' Grady pointed a warning finger. 'You stay here, right?' He reached into the back and his hands closed around the tyre lever he kept there, in case of trouble.

He got out and walked slowly, nonchalantly, to his digs on the corner, holding the lever flat against the side of his jeans. Through the nets he could see a television on upstairs. That'd be Joyce. There was no sign of activity from the Franklins' flat. The garden bore the marks of the police vehicles. He couldn't be sure the police weren't keeping an eye on the place, even if Mr Franklin had been arrested. All it took was a bright spark to link his departure from work with the murder and they'd be after him.

Carefully, after looking around casually, Grady stole along the pavement that ran along the side of the house.

It was mid-morning, nobody about, no sound apart from distant voices on Joyce's television and the patter of drizzle. He reached the back of the house, the extension, took a run up and sprang. Using a length of guttering as a prop he pulled himself up, swung the full weight of his body onto the extension roof. There was a window up here, open just a fraction, which lead onto the landing. He removed his boots, lifted the tyre lever and set to work to prise the window further open, quickly and quietly.

Temple drove through the rainwashed streets, his bad arm throbbing and his mind racing. Father and son. If Fitz was right (and, he kept reminding himself, nothing had been proved), then his career in the force was more or less over. He'd interviewed two suspects, let them go, and they'd killed again. His demotion, and subsequent transfer to Anson Road, had been the result of a horribly botched drugs bust up in Glasgow, when as a direct result of his misjudgement the gang had fled the country having destroyed any evidence against them. There'd been an inquiry, and he'd been given a final warning. Any more errors and he was out. Now, as he pulled into a side road adjacent to Banville Street, his breath was coming in short gasps and there was a burning sensation around the back of his neck. He wasn't certain of his own motive for sloping off. If Grady and his son were in he'd have another word with them, put the pressure on. If they weren't he'd look about, search for clues, anything to get himself back in favour. He pictured himself calling for Wise on the radio, saying he'd acted on a hunch, found the murder weapon. He'd still look a fool but there'd be some reward.

He parked the car, got out and walked towards the house on the corner.

Grady moved soundlessly along the landing, passing Joyce's room. He recalled the laughs they'd shared, little pleasantries exchanged on the way in and out. There was no returning to that world.

He descended the stairs swiftly, each creak appearing to resound with the force of a firework. There was no response, no activity from above or below. Briefly, he wondered what he'd say, what he'd do, if Joyce did emerge from her room. Already he could feel the return of the tension, the redness behind his eyes. The lever hung heavily in his hand, a weapon, an instrument of power.

The journey through the hall was agonising. Essentially everything was much the same as it had been since he'd moved here; the stairs were dusty, the window at the far end by the cellar door needed cleaning, there were remnants of Blu-Tack on the wall. But as he crossed to his door, found his key and entered, the violence of the previous day returned to the forefront of his brain and he saw once again the pathetic spectacle of Mrs Franklin, lowing like a wounded animal as she crawled away.

His room was undisturbed and empty. Gently, satisfied there was nobody in here lying in wait, he closed the door. His old kit bag lay where he'd left it in the corner. He threw open a cupboard and started to pack, stuffing as many clean clothes as possible in the bag, taking care to select things for Bill's use as well.

Suddenly there were noises from the hallway, the crack of the front door being pushed open, and footsteps. Bill? No, the steps were tentative, made by heeled shoes.

Grady leant the bag against the wardrobe, dropped to the floor, his hands and knees on the dirty brown carpet, and shuffled behind the sofa, edging his way to the opposing corner. The footsteps were coming closer. He reached out with one hand, lifted a square of carpet. Beneath was a loose section of floorboard. He dared not lift his head, kept his eyes fixed on the flea-bitten back of the sofa as his hand scrabbled with the floorboard, prised it up, reached inside.

There was a knock at the door. 'Mr Grady?' said a voice, a voice he recognised from its Scottish accent. The copper who'd interviewed him yesterday morning. A sensation of horror ran through him with the realisation that the door to the flat was open. 'Mr Grady?' There was another knock.

Grady's fingers delved into the cavity he'd uncovered, and closed around the cold metallic butt of a standard issue domestic service revolver, Webley 455 Mark 6. He lifted it, clicked off the safety catch, clutched it to his chest, buried himself in the carpet as the door clicked open.

'Mr Grady?' The copper was only feet away. He weighed the gun in his hand. Out of the corner of one eye he caught a glimpse of expensive-looking, sharply creased trousers as his opponent searched the room, looking everything over. The tin of paint and the brush were still down by the skirting board. He watched, almost whimpering with fear and terror, as the copper knelt down and examined them, turning the brush over in his hand. Grady couldn't see his face, but knew at this distance he had only to look over, to the other side of the sofa, and he'd be seen. He tried to remain calm, assess his options. The copper seemed to be alone. Easy to take him out, a wounding shot to the knee or the elbow. He didn't intend to kill, he never had. Without warning the image of McVerry's shattered face came back to him and he stifled a nervous exclamation.

Was the copper ever going to move?

Eventually he stood. Grady closed his eyes with relief as he heard the intruder moving to the kitchenette. Gently he raised himself, twisting over until he was back on all fours, and lifted his head a fraction over the arm of the sofa. He glimpsed the copper in the kitchenette, splashing his face with cold water, and muttering to himself, inaudibly, in the way people do when they think they're alone. One of his arms was in a surgical sling.

Grady swallowed, raised the gun, as the copper moved back into the main room, shaking his head dry and cursing under his breath. The tip of the revolver he kept angled upward, mentally willing the man just to leave, just to go. Again he lingered in the doorway, looking about for what seemed to Grady an agonisingly long period.

Then, abruptly, with a final shake of the head, he was gone, closing the door with a decisive click.

Grady fell back on the carpet, clutched the gun to his chest, stared up at the ceiling. Dust tickled his nostrils and slowly he sat up, breathing hoarsely, allowing the tension to flood out of him. Then, not far away, he heard radio noise. 'X-ray Tango three-four, come in please. Report your position. Come in, please.' He crawled over to the window, lifted his head over the sill, and saw the copper moving back to his car, pulling out the radio on its coiled wire, barking something back into it. Then he got inside, awkwardly angling his damaged arm, slammed the door and drove off.

Slowly Grady stood up. He wrapped the revolver in an old tee shirt, jammed it on top of the clothes piled into the kit bag, collected the tyre lever, and departed the way he'd come.

Temple drove back to Anson Road in a cold fury. There was nothing in Grady's flat, nothing new. There was a sofa bed and a sleeping bag in a corner by the table; plainly his son was staying with him temporarily. When he got back to the station he'd check records, see if Grady had form. He kept telling himself that only Fitz's word, based on supposition, laid any suspicion in that direction. And Fitz had been wrong before, hadn't he? According to Jimmy Beck, anyway.

Bill sat in the car, listening to the radio, trying to find a station that agreed with his mood. Grady appeared around the corner, shoulders hunched forward aggressively, eyes darting from side to side, a massive canvas bag slung over his shoulder. He opened the back door and threw it in. 'Change of clothes for you in there.'

Bill leant over, ferreted about. As Grady got in and they drove off, he pulled at an old black tee shirt. It looked OK, and he liked to wear Grady's clothes, it made him feel a part of his mate. He was pulling at it when it fell open, and a gun fell out on to the seat. His heart leapt at the sight and he reached for it, weighed it in his hand, checked the barrel, saw the loaded chambers. 'Sound. Where d'you get this?'

Grady answered curtly, sounding irritated. 'Put it back.'

Bill obeyed. He didn't want to wind his mate up. He smiled and started pulling off his top, preparing to change into the tee shirt. 'Is it yours?'

Grady waited a few seconds before replying. 'When I came out of the army, I got told the only work you're fit for is private contracts. Security, nightwatchman, that type of thing.' He grinned sardonically. 'I've seen what happens to exes working for security firms. Some bastard comes at you and all you've got is a uniform and a torch. I'm not used to that.' He reached forward, changed gear with a decisive movement.

Bill looked him over, looked between him and the gun, comparing them favourably. He reached for the black tee shirt. 'You ever fired it?'

'Not at anybody, no. On exercises and that, target practice.'

'Are you a good shot?'

Grady frowned, and his eyes flicked nervously over at Bill's exposed torso. 'Put something on, for goodness' sakes.'

It was one of Fitz's many bad habits to sum people up at a glance, and Janet Emery presented no problems on that score. She was McVerry's supervisor, although a good twenty years younger than he, and as she led him and

Penhaligon towards his office her expression was cynical and untrusting. He pondered on this as he looked about, at the meticulously arranged wall charts and personal performance markers. She was bright and young, a product of the Blair era, socially concerned, yes, but with an eye for the techniques of the market, for tangible, provable results. She was showing all the stock reactions to grief (he was put in mind of Skelton at Beck's funeral), but he sensed her true reaction. The death of a colleague was irksome because it messed up her schedule.

'Ian was called out of the case conference at about eight o'clock,' she told them. She opened the door of his office. 'I saw him take the call in here.' Fitz entered, raised an eyebrow, and shot Penhaligon a significant glance. Because the room was empty, stripped virtually bare, McVerry's earthly possessions – trade journals, a holiday brochure, a framed photograph of his wife – packed neatly into a large box on the windowsill.

'So he left when?' asked Penhaligon.

'He didn't come back into the meeting, so I suppose about five past eight.' Fitz felt her scrutiny of him, her disapproval as he started to riffle through the box.

A large black Filofax was jammed in a corner. 'Is this his office diary?'

She snatched it from him. 'That's confidential. There might be clients' names and addresses listed in there.'

'We're investigating a murder, the murder of your colleague,' Penhaligon said patiently.

'It isn't my place to offer our clients as potential suspects,' Emery said frostily.

Fitz felt his hackles rising. 'You ever worked in a hairdresser's?'

She frowned, taken aback. 'No. Why?'

Fitz grunted, looked her right in the eye. How he despised little empire-builders. 'Calling them clients like you do. I'm just curious.'

She shot him a disparaging look. 'It's only the older members of my staff who have a problem with that word.'

'Really?' Fitz thumped his fist on McVerry's desk. 'Ian McVerry was stabbed in the face and neck twenty times with a broken bottle. He lost, what, six pints of blood in less than an hour. He lay in a gutter, half conscious, it must have taken him a good twenty minutes to die. When his wife identified the body she had to go by a birth mark on his upper arm. Now, we think one of your clients did that to him.' He held out a hand. 'So can we see that diary?'

He'd struck home. She reeled back, dropped the Filofax, looked around the bare room, clapped a hand over her mouth, gagged, and ran out.

Penhaligon picked up the Filofax, and said reprovingly, 'Fitz.'

'Either that or we'd have been fannying about here for another hour. These two have killed once, they might easily kill again. There's no time to waste.' He reached over her shoulder, flicked the wallet open, found the current week.

There were two entries for the previous day: *7:30 conference*; then, in capital letters, *B.N.!!!*

There was a Link cash dispenser outside a building society on the small parade of shops not far from Grady's digs. He advanced on it, card at the ready, tensed up, wary of the people passing about him. Every one of them, man, woman or child, felt like an enemy, a potential opponent. Now he had power, now he knew he could kill, and the sensation alternated between horror and exultation.

He punched in his number, requested a withdrawal of two hundred, his daily maximum. Anxious seconds passed as the dispenser assessed his claim, and he looked around nervously. An illogical fear struck him, that somehow everybody here knew what he'd done, and worse than that, they knew why, they could see into his head. They only had to look at him and at Bill.

The machine spat out the notes and he snatched them up, folded them into his wallet, and slunk back to the car.

He opened the door and was confronted by his own revolver. 'Bang! Give us your money,' Bill said playfully.

Grady felt a surge of anger. He lunged, smacked the gun from Bill's hand. An expression of infantile upset crossed the boy's face. Grady jumped in, kicked the gun under his seat, fired the engine and looked out. A young mother with a pushchair was emerging from the bank, staring directly at him, shocked and uncertain. Terrified, he drove off, twisting the wheel violently. 'It was a joke,' said Bill.

'Get your bloody head down,' Grady screamed. In the rear-view mirror he saw the young woman gesturing frantically at another shopper. He spun the car about, forcing another vehicle to brake sharply, drawing more attention. Furious, he put his foot down and tore off the main road at the next turning.

Everybody outside was looking at him, getting a good look at him.

Fitz pulled a cigarette from his pocket. 'Do you mind?'

Penhaligon shrugged. 'You never used to ask before.'

'Well, perhaps I'm being polite.' They sat in her parked car, outside number thirty Honeysuckle Road. Nobody was in. Being Saturday the Nash family were probably out shopping. They'd decided to wait, and Fitz could tell he was getting on her nerves. 'How's Temple's arm?'

She sighed. 'You're not really interested.'

He lit the cigarette. 'Well, it's something to talk about.'

'We don't have to talk.' It started to rain more heavily, and she switched on the wipers. They squeaked back and forth over the windscreen, the noise serving only to heighten the tension between them.

Fitz glanced out at the rows of redbrick houses and sighed. 'I'm glad I don't live in a backwater like this. Who designed these bloody places? No community, no shops, not even a bloody pub. Just bundle the kids in the car once a week and off to the supermarket, mow the lawn, feed the cat, go to the pictures and die.' She didn't respond. 'There, I was trying to change the subject.'

'What you really want to know,' she said, 'is what happened when I went to Alan's flat last night, because you're jealous.'

'I'm concerned, not jealous,' he protested.

'Very fatherly of you.' She turned to face him. 'I offered to make him better, and we fell into each other's arms and had wild sex until the small hours.'

155

He smirked. Defensive reaction. 'You're lying.'

'I was too tired so I just telephoned him.'

'Right.' Fitz nodded across at her, making sure to keep eye contact. 'You weren't planning to go there at all, you just needed an excuse to wind me up. An excuse to yourself, to justify your behaviour.'

She smiled. 'Do you really think you're that important to me, Fitz?'

Before he could answer they both saw another car, a Volvo, pulling up at their rear. There was a family inside, parents and two kids, small boys. 'This'll be them,' said Fitz. He surveyed them as they got out of the car. The mother was tall and blonde. She was smiling and laughing with her boys, but there was an anxious look about her, and he noticed the movement she made as she walked towards her house, an almost imperceptible sweep of the head. She was worried, looking for somebody. Interesting. The kids followed, healthy and squeaky clean, the younger boy clutching deflated arm bands and a lifebelt. The father locked the car, and he too gave that anxious look up the road.

Penhaligon approached the mother, flashing her warrant card. 'Diane Nash?'

The woman spun round. 'Yes?'

'Detective Sergeant Jane Penhaligon. Can I talk to you about Ian McVerry? Your husband rang him last night.'

Diane Nash's face fell. 'No, it was me, I called him.' She shot a nervous glance to her husband, and Fitz saw the glint of some secret understanding pass between them. Mr Nash started to shepherd his boys back to the car. 'Come on, we'll nip round and see your gran.'

'Are they police?' asked the older boy, staring at Penhaligon and Fitz, excited and puzzled.

'Just get back in the car, Steven.' The kids obeyed him.

Penhaligon indicated Fitz. 'This is Dr Fitzgerald, he's a psychologist who's working with us. You don't have to talk to him if you don't want to.'

Diane Nash looked doubtfully at Fitz and forced a smile. 'No, no, that's fine. I suppose you'd better come in.'

Temple arrived back at Anson Road to find himself the subject of rows of accusing glances in the incident room. For a moment he wondered if somehow his mistake had been uncovered, but then Skelton looked up and nodded to Wise's office. 'Guvnor wants to see you.'

Temple had his story prepared. 'It's my arm, it was playing up again.'

'Don't tell me, tell him,' said Skelton.

Temple swallowed, gathered his nerves, and walked to Wise's office. He knocked, took a deep breath and walked in.

For a second the surreal nature of the scene he found inside threatened to overwhelm him. Wise had his head down, and was shouting into the phone, and on the desk before him, still strapped upright into its carry-seat, was Fitz's baby, fast asleep, his tiny eyelids twitching in dreams. 'I don't care what he says,' Wise was shouting. 'Ten counts of handling, four of burglary, and probably another lot of breaking and entering when he decides to confess, OK?' He put the phone down and grimaced.

'Bloody Cooper. I've got enough on my plate.' The sociable moment passed and he bellowed, 'And where the bloody hell were you?'

He attempted a shrug. 'My arm, sir. Started playing up again. I went for a rest.'

'Look, you were offered leave. Are you on or off duty, would you mind telling me?'

'On duty, sir.'

Wise sat back. 'Slope off without permission again and I'll pull the other arm out, right?'

Temple bowed his head. 'Sir.'

He turned to leave. Wise called him. 'Make yourself useful. Phone Fitz's wife.' He nodded to the baby. 'I'm not having this.'

Fitz saw that Diane Nash was very proud of the fact she'd procreated. She'd made them cups of tea and led them into her almost suspiciously spotless lounge, one entire wall of which was taken up with a photographic montage of the two kids at various stages of their lives. They were fine-looking boys, obviously happy and well adjusted. Fitz felt an inward guilt at the thought of Mark aged ten, always stomping about tearfully, shouting at his parents to shut up arguing.

Penhaligon flipped her notebook open. 'Mrs Nash, can you tell us why you called Ian McVerry last night?'

She looked back fearfully. Treading on sensitive ground, Fitz could tell. And why would a family like this require a social worker, calling him out as an emergency? 'Well,' she began. 'Quite soon after we married, we put ourselves up for fostering. One of the kids we fostered came round and he was making a bit of

a nuisance of himself. It was all a bit silly, so I called
Ian. He came round –' her voice faltered '– he came
round and sorted the problem out, and left.'

'What was the child's name, Mrs Nash?' asked
Penhaligon.

'Oh, Preece. William Preece.' She shuddered as she
spoke, and the facts started at last to resolve themselves
in Fitz's mind. William, not Brian.

'Can you talk us through that?' he asked.

'Well, you know. He took him back to the children's
home. William's on a long-term care order, coming to
the end of it, I suppose.'

Fitz nodded, thinking of the younger, weaker killer.
'He's how old then, seventeen?'

'Yes. March the twenty-third.'

'And you fostered him when?'

She was getting agitated. '1985, to the end of '86.'

'Hmm.' Fitz looked down. 'Did he threaten you? I
mean, seventeen can be intimidating.'

'Not . . . threatened, no.' She was trying to shrug this
all off, play it down, negating how she truly felt.
Something very important, a crisis point in her life, a
bad decision she'd made, and she couldn't live with the
guilt, so made out it was nothing. 'William isn't . . .'
She broke off. 'Look, I don't really know him any
more.' She was reaching for something in the pocket of
her coat, a comforter; it was an automatic reaction to
stress that Fitz knew well. A pack of Silk Cut emerged.
She offered them round.

'No thanks,' said Fitz. 'I'll stick to my own.'

She lit up. 'Look, if you want a social history, you'll
have to ask McVerry.' What she really meant: nothing

159

to do with me, this child I brought up for over a year and washed my hands of, not my responsibility. 'Ask McVerry what happened last night.'

'Tricky,' said Fitz.

'He was murdered last night,' said Penhaligon, very bluntly. Fitz thought of his old Panhandle, pre-Beck. Then it would have been 'I'm afraid there's been an incident, Mrs Nash.'

As it was, Diane Nash stifled an exclamation. Her hand faltered. 'I'm sorry, I . . . it's . . .' Her eyes flicked involuntarily over the photographs on the wall, over to her boys. 'Oh God.'

'When he left with William,' said Penhaligon, 'were they alone?'

Diane shrugged, still shocked, but Fitz knew there was something she was holding back. She dragged on her cigarette and folded her lips together, trying to keep calm, trying not to expose herself.

Such behaviour was like a red rag to Fitz. 'B.N. and three exclamation marks. It was the last entry in McVerry's diary. The final entry, it transpired. We thought the initials referred to your husband. Now, B could mean William, but his name's Preece.' He leant forward, looking deep into her eyes. 'What do you think N could mean, Mrs Nash?'

It was a mistake. She flared up. 'I've no idea. Look, I'd like my husband here.'

Fitz raised a hand. 'Was William more important than the others? I mean, a year and a half, that's a long time to be fostering.'

'None of them are more important than the others,' she replied coolly.

'But if he's calling himself Bill *Nash*, he obviously thinks he's more special.'

The tactic worked, as he'd known it would. She shrank back from him, twisted slightly in her chair, then the tears came. She stubbed out her cigarette and brushed her eyes. 'Nobody asked for an eight-year-old. We asked for a baby. I wanted a baby.'

Fitz reached out clumsily, tapped her on the shoulder. 'Just let it out.'

'We were only supposed to be fostering him for a couple of months. But he just seemed . . .' She wiped her eyes. 'He just seemed so happy. He blended in. It felt like he'd been here forever.' She hid her face. 'We signed the forms and applied to adopt him.'

Fitz saw it now. 'And then you got pregnant, right?' She nodded. 'A shock, that was unplanned. You'd manufactured a new family, manipulated William to fill in the gaps, and then you got pregnant? Ironically, having him about probably helped you to conceive your first boy. So you're carrying a premier division player and looking at a sub in the spare room?' His own depth of feeling came as a surprise, because right now he loathed this woman and her calculation of what she'd done. 'So, the charm dissolves, up in a puff of smoke. You withdraw your love, flick it off like a light, there was no need to fake it any more?'

She kept her face pushed against the softness of the sofa, unable to confront his questions. She replied hotly, 'Look, it wouldn't have been fair. We'd never have treated him the same as Steven, could we? You'd have done the same.'

Fitz held back on that point. If a person's racked with

guilt, their first defence is to make their offence seem natural, commonplace. 'You cancelled the adoption?'

'Yes.'

He was unable to keep the venom from his voice. 'You cancelled William?'

'Yes!'

SIX

Temple inhaled deeply and knocked again at the door of Wise's office. Through the frosted glass he could see Wise slouched in his chair, shirt untucked and sleepless eyes red-rimmed, the phone cradled beneath his beard. He was writing something urgently down on a pad and shaking his head ruefully. As soon as the phone was down, he dropped the pen and beckoned Temple in. It was only at this point Temple realised that Wise wasn't wearing his glasses. Without their protection he looked both younger and more exhausted. Temple found himself wondering how he'd look without the beard. He said, 'Sir. Fitz's son's down at the front desk.'

Wise was up instantly, reaching for his overcoat and moving the baby-seat in his direction with a definite shove. He ripped the top sheet off his pad and slid on his glasses. 'That was Jane. She thinks she's on to something. A kid called William Preece or Nash, one of McVerry's cases. He's on a care order, at a halfway house, but they haven't clapped eyes on him since Thursday morning. He's supposed to be on work experience at the Cheltex factory, on that industrial estate down Bagley Road.' He gestured to Temple to get moving. 'The lad's got a history. A bit of nicking, nothing serious, and a caution for threatening behaviour.'

163

Awkwardly, Temple carried the baby into the incident room with his good hand, to be greeted by a chorus of jeers and titters from his colleagues, behaviour they couldn't risk on Wise. 'Have we checked the factory, sir?'

'Of course we bloody have,' replied Wise. 'He isn't there. But we need his records. You can come with me, make yourself useful.' He accompanied this statement with a long, penetrating look. Temple felt a moment's irritation at the unreliability implied. Then he recalled his error and stifled a protest.

Brand's Mill came into sight behind a row of derelict warehouses. It was four storeys tall, its windows long gone, muddy brown in colour. The nearest houses were a mile away, cramped terraces backing on to a massive gasometer. Human figures moved distantly. In spite of Grady's efforts to drive with care over the uneven ground, the suspension took a battering, and he and Bill were bumped up and down. The mill's entrance was a crumbling maw, above which was sculpted in foot-long letters the name of a long-forgotten trader, accompanied by a sunbeam design, vaguely twenties in character, now defaced by decades of pigeon shit.

'This is it,' said Bill. 'I hid out in there for the best part of a week once. A couple of years back.' He leant forward in his seat, craning his neck to look up at the imposing side of the ruin. 'I found it myself. The trick when you're on the run is to look like you know where you're going. Nobody ever comes out here. I was stupid, I gave myself away. I made a fire.'

I gave myself away. The words tumbled through

Grady's mind and he felt a surge of anger at the thought of the woman with the pushchair, and saw again her frantic gestures to her fellow shoppers. They'd lingered for a good fifteen seconds there, she was sure to have their number. So Bill could look after himself, he'd proved that by finding this place, trying to make up for things. But he was stupid, unthinking, couldn't plan.

As he brought the car to a halt Grady looked across at the beautiful button-nosed face of his partner. His eyes were shining with youth and enthusiasm, as if they were attempting nothing more than an afternoon picnic. He was grinning nostalgically. 'We'll be all right here, eh?' he prompted.

Grady couldn't trust himself to reply. He could feel the anger building again, felt his hands form fists as he removed them from the wheel and took the keys from the ignition.

'I'm sorry,' Bill said. 'All right? I didn't know she was there.' His face assumed a pained, pleading quality. 'Just talk to me.'

Grady leapt from the car, stormed around, yanked the passenger door open. 'Out.' Bill looked up at him, and there was real terror in his eyes. 'I said out!' The boy cowered, turning his head away. Grady lunged for him, grabbed his collar, pulled him out on to the waste ground. Bill was astonishingly light and unresisting, and Grady once more experienced a savage rush of blood to his loins as he tripped the boy, and decked him, laid him out with the brush of a fist over the Montego's bonnet.

Bill seemed aware for the first time of the real

danger he was in, and brought up his hands to shield his face. Grady bore down on him, bringing his upper body down, raising one fist, using the other hand to secure Bill's shoulder. 'It's not just you,' he shouted, 'it's me, you prick. I don't care where you want to go, but you're not taking me down with you, OK?' He pressed harder, brutally. 'OK?' His own exhalations roared in his ears. He raised the fist but kept the position, his face inches away from Bill's.

Nothing happened for a few seconds. And then Bill removed his hands from his face, and his wounded expression melted Grady's heart. He felt an over-whelming tenderness, an aching love mixed up with his rage and lust. Involuntarily he squeezed Bill's shoulder, gently. The move came quite naturally, auto-matically to him. A horrifying certainty occurred to him. He realised he knew what to do, he knew exactly how to proceed, how to attend to the quivering male body beneath him, how to satisfy himself and bring equal pleasure to his partner. It was a simple, easy, natural process to him, as effortless and undemanding as eating or sleeping. And it was a perversion.

Bill looked right at him and he saw there was no confusion, no denial in the boy's eyes. He wanted love, he needed desperately to be lifted away from the awful hurt that had been his life, to be caressed, wanted, *forgiven*. And Grady almost responded, almost let himself be taken. He held on, prolonging the accidental embrace for a good ten seconds, then pulled himself up and away.

'Would you rather I dropped you at the end of the

drive?' asked Penhaligon. 'I wouldn't want Judith to get the wrong idea.'

Fitz pulled a pained face. 'That's low.'

'I wonder where I get it from.' She nodded past him to his house. 'Hadn't you better get back to baby?'

Fitz opened the door. 'You'll keep me informed?'

'Of course.' More evidence of her forward thinking. Exploit his guilt, offload him now with the excuse of the baby, pick up the credit for getting on to Preece, pile up the plus points for promotion.

He swung himself out of the car. 'I'll most likely see you later, then.'

Without replying she set off, scattering gravel in her wake. Fitz turned and stared at the drawn blinds of his home with something rather less than enthusiasm.

The Cheltex supervisor wore a long brown coat and a long-suffering expression. His speech was painfully slow and toneless, and his movement through the deserted rows of machines was equally protracted. On the way in Temple had seen a skeleton crew of fork-lift drivers in the forecourt by the loading bay, stretching their Saturday morning overtime out to its limit. Flexi-time encouraged sloth, he supposed. There were a very few cutters at work also, all female.

'William Preece,' Wise told the foreman for the third time. 'Do you know the name?'

The foreman shook his head. 'Can't say I do.' He scratched himself behind the ear, where a pencil rested. Temple suppressed an urge to kick him. 'But, there again, I'm not in fact the registered supervisor on the weekday shifts.'

'Do you know if he works here or not?'

The foreman stopped and ruminated. 'Work experience, you said?'

Wise nodded, clearly exasperated. 'From Wiverton, the halfway house. He was supposed to start here Wednesday. Do you know if he did?'

'Hmm. We have definitely taken youngsters from Wiverton House beforehand, I know that.' He stared absently into a point in space directly between Temple and Wise. 'Strictly speaking, no. He doesn't work for us, not if he's on work experience. And he'll definitely not be in here today, because technically he's an ancillary, and ancillaries aren't allowed overtime, you see.'

Wise sighed. 'So where is he? 'Cause he's not at Wiverton.'

The foreman sighed and started moving again, leading them to a cabin-like office at the far side of the machine room. They ascended a small flight of steps. 'Well,' he continued, 'the bloke who'd know if anybody does is my counterpart, the weekday supervisor. This is his office, you see.' He tapped his thin lips, and surveyed a row of lever-arch files arranged on a shelf. 'It's awful when a young person goes missing, isn't it, officer? You have to wonder why. There are so many temptations nowadays, I suppose.' He trailed his finger across the files, scrutinising the numbers on each with unnecessary care. 'Not like in our day.'

Wise bristled at the notion that he and this individual could possibly share anything in common. 'We'll be here all bloody day,' he whispered to Temple.

'Ah, here we jolly well are.' The foreman reached

168

down one of the files and flicked it open. 'Porterfield, Pringle, Probert. No Preece, I'm afraid.' He contemplated. 'There again, sir, these records are updated only occasionally. It may be that the young man's name simply hasn't been added.'

'Well, can you give us the other foreman's number?' Wise demanded. 'You said he might know?'

'I can, sir, but I don't think you'll have any luck.' He pulled out a diary from his top pocket and flicked through it. 'He's taken a few days off, we think. In a bit of a state at the moment. His landlady was murdered, sir, a terrible business, I suppose you know about it, your colleagues are probably looking into it, or perhaps you read about it in the papers. Her husband did it, apparently, he'd beaten her about before. Terrible. You wonder why people don't get divorced, don't you?'

Temple felt himself blush. He watched for Wise's reaction. The big man seemed to flare up, and his jaw clamped open and shut before he spluttered, 'Mary Franklin?'

'Yes, that's right.' The foreman found his place in the diary. 'There we are, nine Banville Street.'

Wise shook his head, confused. 'You what?'

'Oh, is that an eight or a three?' The foreman squinted. 'Begging your pardon, sir. It's a three. Flat three, nine Banville Street. His name's Stuart Grady.'

Wise was already moving. Temple nodded to the foreman and hurried out, feeling as if he were about to throw up.

The old mill reeked of dust and decay. Grady sat on what remained of the wall of a demolished outbuilding,

169

eating one of the cheese and ham sandwiches he'd stocked up on yesterday afternoon. There was graffiti all along the wall, not of the modern type, but lovehearts and woz-eres, and proclamations of undying loyalty to forgotten pop groups and relegated football teams. Grady sat and ate in silence, feeling glad of the warmth of his lumberjack shirt in the chill air, surrounded by engravings of a youthful exuberance and lack of care he'd never felt.

He heard Bill coming, trailing a long stick through a puddle. He'd set off to circuit the building and look for signs of recent habitation. It was obvious there'd be nothing. 'You know,' he said, 'we need to work out some kind of call sign, between us.' His efforts to sound practical, to make up for his mistake, were endearing, and Grady smiled. Bill misunderstood. 'That's what you'd have done in the army, isn't it?' Grady said nothing, just grinned and threw over a can of Coke from his knapsack. 'Don't laugh,' Bill said, his tone uncertain. 'I mean, if they catch us, what's our story?' He looked out over the soulless, barren wasteland and the meshed enormity of the gasometer, vividly outlined against the white sky. 'I want them to know we're together,' he said proudly. He turned to face Grady. There was a silent moment.

Then Bill started to shake his can vigorously. He opened it in Grady's face, drenching it and laughing wildly. A boyish delight, totally unexpected, burst forth in Grady and he grabbed another can. Bill was already running.

He followed, boots pounding over the wreckage, over fallen masonry and inspection plates, swerving and dodging wildly from side to side to keep up with his quarry. Bill was strong and fast, and he yelped, waved his arms above his head, ran in a zigzag away from the mill. Grady was faster and cleverer, anticipated his moves, and cornered him finally against a concrete slab. Laughing manically he shook his can and sprayed Bill, soaked him. Bill leapt up and down, cursing, his face a picture of childish merriment.

To give Wise his due, thought Jane, the raid on flat three at nine Banville Street had been planned with meticulous accuracy. She'd returned to Anson Road to find him giving orders with a kind of resigned ebullience; angry they'd fouled up again, happy things were really moving at last. He detailed her to find out more about the tenant, Stuart Grady. According to the foreman at Cheltex he'd been in the army. The bare details of his service record was still warm from the fax when it was time to move out. She'd pulled it from the machine and read it in her car on the way over.

The house on the corner was as it had been, with only the addition of a few bunches of flowers at the door as a sign of the horrors perpetrated there. Taking no risks, Wise had officers waiting at the back and sides, and only when they reported in as ready did he advance, leading from the front, opening the front door with Franklin's confiscated key and tiptoeing in and along the hall. It occurred to Jane only now, as they neared the door of flat three, that it was Temple who'd interviewed Grady the day before. She felt a twinge of regret. After this he wouldn't last long. Wise was in need of a scapegoat.

Wise signalled for absolute quiet. He stepped back from the door, turned his tubby but muscular frame sideways, took off his glasses and handed them to Temple with a look that said *this is how you do it, boy*, and charged.

The door splintered under Wise's weight and he burst through. But the flat was empty. Jane looked around quickly. The single room was almost monastically bare. The only ornamentation was a couple of wood carvings resting on the windowsill.

Satisfied, Wise ordered, 'Rip the place apart. We're looking for a murder weapon.' He stood aside, and the lower ranks of Anson Road swarmed in, heading for the sofa bed, the kitchenette, the work table. Jane's own progress was slower. She was drawn instinctively to a small pile of paperback books which were leant against the side of the big wardrobe. All of the books were thrillers of the guns and girls variety.

Wise stood in the middle of the room, teeth gritted. He spoke levelly, with an air of suppressed menace. 'Somebody interviewed this guy yesterday morning, after Mrs Franklin's murder. I want to know who.'

Jane couldn't answer. She was reassured by the sound of Temple's voice. 'I'm . . .' he began. 'I'm not sure, sir, I think it was Skelton.'

Wise nodded outside. 'He's around the back. Fetch him, I want a word.'

Temple turned to leave. Jane flashed him a look that conveyed her feelings, told him that she remembered; he slid past her and backed out. He passed one of Anson Road's younger WPCs, who entered with her notebook open.

'Sir,' she said, 'I checked with the women at Cheltex. Both Grady and the boy – he was calling himself William Nash – arrived in work after midday, separately but only ten minutes apart. Nash told them he'd overslept, Grady wasn't due in until the afternoon anyway. They were both gone again by the end of the afternoon. Nobody thought to connect them, they assumed Grady was in shock about the murder of the landlady when they heard about it. Apparently he'd been in an aggressive state.'

'Righto.' Wise dismissed her with a perfunctory smile. He crossed to Jane and whispered, 'The Flying Scotsman wasn't far wrong, was he?'

'No, sir.' Jane's attention flicked distractedly outside; through the net curtains she could see Temple moving towards Skelton. She passed Wise the fax. 'That's Grady's service record. He was discharged eighteen months back.'

Wise digested the information. 'He was in there long enough. Thirteen years. What's this, "Incompatible Behaviour"? What's that supposed to mean?' He handed the sheet back to her. 'Find out, eh?'

'Sir?' One of the Forensics men was calling Wise. They'd found an ebony box in the drawer of the table, and inside were a set of carving tools. The implication was plain. There was the murder weapon. Jane turned and went out, her pace increasing as she passed through the activity in the hall. A powerful sense of injustice was building within her. Secretly she was glad she could still feel it, after all that had happened in the last couple of years.

She nipped between the vehicles once again strewn

across the Franklins' lawn, and advanced on Temple. He had coaxed Skelton around the back of the wagon, and was pacing up and down, running the fingers of his good arm through his hair. There were droplets of sweat on his brow and his face was flushed. 'Come on, Skelly,' he begged.

Skelton was shaking his head, resolutely. 'No way. This is the biggest chance I've had, so no way.'

'You're fresh in,' Temple pleaded. 'You're allowed a mistake. I've already had all mine. Wise is looking to save his own hide, he'll crucify me.'

'Hey, come on.' Skelton faced him, determined, jaw set. 'In case you hadn't noticed, Alan, I'm black. I'm not allowed any mistakes.'

Jane couldn't stand to see this, because she knew Skelton was easy prey, she knew that he was about to give way, and it was wrong, it was unjust. 'Skelton,' she said sternly.

He looked up guiltily. 'What?'

'You're going to Preston.' She handed him the fax. 'Bretherton Barracks. Grady got hoofed out of the army. Find out why.' Something else struck her, something Wise, typically, had forgotten. 'And we need a photograph.'

'OK.' He walked off, ignoring Temple's frustrated glare at his departing back.

Jane counted to three and vaulted forward, grabbed Temple by the shoulders and slammed him against the side of the van. He gave a pained cry that she found rather gratifying and raised a hand automatically to nurse his injury. 'What –' he began.

She held up a hand. 'We've only just got ourselves

rid of one selfish little shit, we don't need another. It was you who interviewed Grady.'

He said nothing, straightened up. Enraged, she slammed him again. 'Don't do that,' he said, straightened up again. She couldn't help it. The arrogance, the stupidity of the man was too much. He'd disappointed her, and she realised how much she'd invested in him. So she slammed him again.

He raised a warning finger. 'You do that again and I report you, and you can write your promotion off. Back off, Jane.'

She saw the sense in his words, stood back, still furious.

Temple looked down at his shoes. 'He said it was his son. He opened the door with a tin of paint and a Walkman on. The woman upstairs heard nothing, didn't she? So I wrote them off.' Her expression must have shown her contempt because he went on, 'I swear, Jane. I looked around the flat and there was nothing to see. Everything was calm, he said the boy was his son. He was a big guy, macho. You don't expect a feller like that to be screwing schoolboys.'

Jane shook her head in mock despair. 'So bloody thick. There's only one bed.'

'You'd never have thought it, Jane, you'd have believed him.' He fell back against the van. 'You would, honest.'

'So, you just try blaming a new DC and get on with rebuilding your career?'

He looked directly at her. 'Look, Skelly could've taken that one on the chin and carried on. I won't, will I? Wise already hates me.'

175

She sighed. 'Don't be such a kid, Alan. Look, you got a good look at both of them, you can describe the boy as well?'

'Yeah.' He licked his lips. 'So what happens now?'

'What are you asking me for?' She turned her back on him, trying to ignore her own sense of betrayal. She'd overestimated him, like she'd overestimated Peter and the rest. In the end they were men, all practically the same. Only Fitz had the nerve to be honest, face up to himself and his failings, acknowledge them and the fact he'd never beat them.

She hadn't got far when Temple said, 'October fifteenth. Penhaligon was being a cow.'

She whipped round. It was like a ghost had tapped her on the shoulder. The choice of words, the phrasing, the date. They could only have come from one person. She felt giddy, disorientated, her legs went weak. Temple was in front of her, and she could hear Wise arguing distantly with someone, but these things seemed suddenly to be far away, and she was in another place, struggling, kicking, in a dark corner, being dragged away, powerless, and at the same time she was on the rooftop, with the wind whistling around her, with Beck and Harvey just feet away. Beck.

'November fifth,' Temple went on. 'Woke up crying. More nightmares, Bilborough and Kinsella. I let the bastard go free and he killed my mate. And in the nightmare it's just the same and it's like I can't wake up.' She felt herself weakening, an uprush of emotion threatening to burst out of her. 'Catriona asked me to be Ryan's godfather.'

Jane realised she had walked back to within inches

of Temple. 'What do you . . .' Her voice sounded removed.

Temple swallowed and said calmly, without malice, 'I found Jimmy Beck's diary. When I was sent to clear out his locker.' His expression had softened, and it became clear why he'd been looking at her that way for the past week. 'I know what he did to you.'

Jane was uncertain of her reaction. Wasn't this the evidence she'd wanted so desperately? 'Where is it?'

'I've got it.'

She couldn't help herself. The mention of Beck, this revelation, empowered her. She pushed him back against the van, bellowed, 'Where is it?'

'It's safe, I swear. Nobody else has seen it.'

She put a hand to her head. 'Is this blackmail? You're telling me this, now, just to save yourself?' She raised a fist, lowered it immediately. 'You could have told me a week ago.'

'I didn't know how to bring it up,' he protested, apparently in earnest. 'You've not exactly been approachable.' He took out his wallet and produced a small key. 'It's in my locker. Stapled envelope. With your initials on it. I was going to leave it for you.'

She grabbed the key, shuddered, and walked away from him, breathing deeply, bringing herself back to reality. She would not let Beck beat her.

The house was apparently empty. Fitz had ascended the staircase manfully and thrown open the bedroom door to find his wife strewn out beneath the duvet, one arm sticking out at an odd angle towards a half-empty glass of water and a stack of ibuprofen. It was a situation that

177

had often been played in reverse, and he quelled his impulse to shake her awake, recalling how irritated he felt whenever she walked in on his hangovers and drew open the curtains. If he behaved blamelessly – and, he reminded himself, in the last couple of days his conduct had been comparatively exemplary – and took the role of injured party, any oddness on her part would be seen as malicious and unnecessary.

So he went back down to the living room, stuck on a CD, and proceeded to iron his way through a pile of clean baby things. The task brought out some nostalgic feeling, and he briefly pictured himself and Judith in their previous house, younger and in his case thinner, and their innocent joy in Mark's early upbringing. At the time, naturally, it hadn't felt like innocent joy. But the rows had been fresher and more spontaneous then, more enjoyable, mere disputes, and he'd been full of vigour at the typewriter, kidding himself that his theses weren't the warmed-up, hackneyed crap they were. He was lost in reflection, humming along gently to the music, when he heard, in short order, an enormous crashing and banging from upstairs. He assumed initially this was to tell him to turn the sound down, but then it ceased abruptly; and ten minutes later he heard Judith's tread on the stairs. He counted the steps, waited for her to enter the kitchen, assumed his most beguiling expression. It went unrewarded. He heard her going into the living room. He waited anxiously, caught by the dilemma. He had to hold out, wait for her to come to him, or his strategy was ruined.

Pointless. He turned off the iron and made for the living room. Astonishingly, she was immaculately made-up, wearing one of her smartest suits. He watched as she delved between the sofa seats and produced an earring, a casualty of last night's binge. The empty whisky bottle remained on the floor under the coffee table. Without a word she clipped the earring in and pushed past him and into the hall.

'Judith,' he called. She was already halfway back up the stairs. 'Look, will you please just stand still.' He was impressed; even to himself he sounded convincingly wounded. He heard the bedroom door slam. Deciding that such action constituted reasonable incitement, he bounded up after her.

He found her surrounded by chaos, drawers pulled from the chest, bedclothes thrown on the floor, his clothes lying crushed under the toppled wardrobe. In the midst of it she stood putting on her jacket and reapplying her lipstick with the aid of a fallen mirror. Displacement; she was angry with herself for neglecting the kid, she felt she'd failed. Fitz said, 'Look, I don't want you to do anything. We don't have to talk if you – if you don't want that.' He'd almost said *not ready*, but his experiences with Jane of late warned him against it. 'I just want to know where you keep his pyjamas and things.' A genuine, practical query. Still no response. 'Mark's with wee Jimmy right now, and I've called your mother, she can take him for the night, if you feel like a rest.'

She smiled acidly and moved to the *en suite* bathroom. He followed her cautiously. 'Come on, Judith, you don't have to feel like this.' Her reply was to hitch her skirt up and descend on to the toilet. 'You don't have to feel guilty about last night.'

That hit. 'Oh, I don't,' she said emphatically.

Fitz took up a concerned position, leaning against the jamb of the bathroom door. 'Look, you ought to talk to somebody, really talk. It doesn't have to be me. A woman would be better. I could recommend someone.'

She struck out with one leg and kicked the bathroom door shut in his face. 'Wrong!' she shouted, high-pitched, verging on hysterical. 'This is not post-natal depression.'

He rested his head on the door. 'You can't be certain of that, Judith.'

'I had post-natal depression!' she screamed back. 'I had it the first time, with Mark, and the resident shrink was too busy to notice the symptoms! The only reason you'd recommend a shrink for anyone is if it suited yourself, it's purely selfish. You want me better so that we can all get back to your twenty-six-year-old, terminal bloody existential crisis. You've had it so long it's made the house smell.' Fitz recoiled from the door, glad she couldn't see him. He hadn't planned for this. 'This one is mine, OK? It is mine, and I have never felt better, so keep your bloody nose out!'

She threw something at the door. He heard it break and then the toilet's flush.

Head swimming, he went slowly back downstairs. Something badly, definitely wrong this time. She was pushing herself to believe things. A couple of minutes of ironing later he heard the front door slam.

Bill watched admiringly as Grady parked the car in the very centre of the waste ground, got out and beckoned him across. They'd spent most of the afternoon exploring the mill, and Bill had been especially excited to find the spot where he'd dossed down before. The place reeked, and its structure was unsound, but right at the moment it felt more like a home than anything since Diane's house, back in Urmston. Grady didn't say much, and that was part of his appeal. He just got on with things, busied himself with the practicalities.

Grady reckoned it was for the best to get rid of the car. By now the police were sure to have their number. If they disposed of it here and now, covered their tracks, they bought some time. It might not be found for weeks and they'd be well away. He tried to give Grady some ideas about places to go, but he didn't seem interested. Just to keep going, survive together and plan only in the short-term was the best way.

Grady worked a plastic tube out from the Montego's engine system, cleaned it down with a bit of rag, and inserted it in the petrol cap. He turned to Bill. 'There's an empty paint tin in the boot.' Bill fetched it hurriedly and set it on the ground between them. He watched with growing wonder as Grady sucked at the tube, drawing the petrol up. There was a look of absolute determination on his face, the set expression of a trained military man. Bill felt the strength coming off Grady and inspiring him. He could never think of something clever like this. He needed a mentor.

Grady balked at the taste and redirected the tube down to the paint tin. Fluid streamed down and the tin was full in under a minute. Grady passed the tube, end-up, across to Bill, who instinctively capped it with his thumb. He realised that Grady trusted him, hadn't thought to give him precise instructions. He was viewed as an equal, as a man. Grady picked up the tin and splashed its contents over the back of the car. Then he knelt down, clicked his fingers. Bill handed the tube back and watched as the process was repeated. This time Grady opened the back door and sloshed the tin around, covering the upholstery.

'Right,' he told Bill, motioning him to pull out the tube. Bill did so and laid it down carefully by the nearer of the back set of wheels. Without looking at him, Grady shooed him back and away towards the mill, at the same time pulling his lighter from his shirt pocket and readying the piece of rag he'd used earlier to clean oil from the tubing. The operation was conducted with apparently effortless precision. He held the rag up by a corner and flicked the lighter's flame around the opposite end. To Bill, some feet away, this formed a strange, atmospheric picture: the fading light of the grey day, the lowering gasometer in the distance, the yellow light playing on Grady's determined profile.

The rag caught fire. Grady waited a couple of seconds, pulled back his arm and threw it, aiming for the petrol spills under the car. He sprinted back nimbly, still facing the car, one arm raised. Bill waited, watched. It was hard to tell what had happened from a distance of a hundred yards. It looked as if the rag had landed short of the spills and burnt itself out. 'It's burnt out,' said Bill. He saw how he could be of help, save Grady some bother and make himself useful. He sprinted forward, grabbed for the rag. His hand was just an inch from it when there was a sudden, horrible blast of heat, full in his face. It felt as if he was in the centre of an explosion, but for the first second there was no noise, no fire, only

182

the heatwave and a prickling sensation along his left leg. Stupidly he felt embarrassed.

The fuel ignited. He felt himself tumbling back, arms cartwheeling, head reeling, hardly conscious, then there was an enormous report and what felt like a wall of hot air knocked him flat on his face. He heard a high, panicked voice calling for Grady, and realised it was his own. For a moment there was no sensation in his left leg. The next instant he felt the fire, travelling up his body in a searing surge of agony, along with some part of his brain working out that a spray of petrol must have leaked over him from the tube. Then he was up on his feet, turning about wildly, shouting and screaming for aid.

He was knocked down again, by a second blast as the engine went up. He couldn't see or feel anything but the bright yellow flames crackling up him. Then something fell on to him, and he dimly glimpsed Grady, who tore off his shirt, scattering buttons, and flicked it at the leg, beating repeatedly at the fire. A gust of smoke came from the wreck, catching at Bill's throat, and abruptly the pain sharpened as the flames died out. He thrashed about on the concrete, consciousness receding. He felt himself go limp, and then was vaguely aware of being lifted up by a strong pair of hands. Grady's hands.

SEVEN

A meeting was set for half past six in the incident room.
Jane went about her duties unbowed, almost unthinkingly, compiling information on Grady and Preece
and printing out a digest of known facts that she
photocopied for general distribution. There were no
further leads that made much difference. She'd spoken
to Franklin on the phone and learnt that Grady was
reliable as a paying guest, and that he'd been up on
Wednesday, past midnight, going out and coming back,
waking them. Mary had said she'd heard movement and
conversation, and planned to confront Grady about
having women over. It was only at this point of their
conversation that Franklin realised why Grady had
become the focus of the investigation, and he'd been
stunned. Grady had been friendly, unassuming, quiet,
likeable. Jane compared that account to the service
records Skelton had prised out of Bretherton Barracks.
The photograph showed a tall, muscular, well-built
man, and there was nothing artificial about his build. It
hadn't been achieved in a gym but through hard,
constant physical drill. According to his ex-colleagues
Grady had been a fine soldier. Preece was something
else entirely, handed over to social services by a teenage
mother in the early eighties. As she skimmed through

his stack of social enquiry reports Jane felt some sympathy.

And all the while, the key was inside her jacket. An opportunity to resolve the past, point the way forward, bury Beck forever.

The meeting began, Wise calling things to order with an authoritative cough. He looked about the room, at the fifteen officers clutching their information packs like children with lunchboxes. 'Where's Fitz?'

'I have phoned him, sir,' said Jane. 'He should be here soon.'

'Right, well.' Wise nodded, looking somewhat comforted. 'Let's get into it, then.' He held up a colour photocopy of Grady's photograph. 'Stuart David Grady, 31. Born in Skibbereen, Eire, family moved to Belfast in 1965. Ex-army, blue eyes, six foot two. By all accounts built like a brick shithouse.' He nodded to Skelton.

Skelton consulted his notes. 'He served from June '81. Was kicked out in November '94, for incompatible behaviour. Two court martials for picking fights. Pub fights. Nothing major, just a pattern. He hospitalised one man, broke his jaw. They reckon he's a bright bloke, but impatient and volatile.'

'Right. Page two.' The team turned to the second page of Jane's precis. The face of William Preece stared back at them, compiled by Temple under her supervision. It was irritatingly vague; a good-looking child, high forehead and button nose. 'William Preece, or Nash, aged 17. Why haven't we got a photo of him yet?'

'The most recent anybody's got belongs to Mrs

Nash,' said Jane. 'And he's eight years old. Social services said he was very reluctant to have his picture taken.'

Wise faced her. 'You interviewed the pair of them yesterday.' He spoke evenly, making a statement, nothing more. Her confession to Temple's mistake had been made only an hour before; Wise had simply nodded and listened to the details. It was clear that he wasn't in the mood to bawl her out, clearer still how much he respected her judgement. None of the other DCs under his command would have got away that lightly.

The door opened and Fitz entered, hands deep in pockets, looking rather more cowed than she'd anticipated. Trouble at home, most likely. 'Sir,' she said. 'William Nash has brown hair and brown eyes. He's about five nine, slimmer than Grady –' she couldn't help catching the eyes of Temple and Skelton as she spoke '– and I think he had a Manchester accent. Could have been the Bolton area, I suppose.' She noticed Fitz's posture change, become more animated. 'Grady told me Nash was his son. I've checked, and Nash has no named father, so it's possible that might still be the truth.'

Fitz emitted a mocking snort. 'You don't believe that.' He moved towards Wise, taking the attention. 'Look, if they're father and son, there's no motive. Why kill Mrs Franklin?'

Jane took a deep breath and sneaked a glance at Temple. His hands were on his knees, plucking at the immaculate crease of his trousers, and his head was down, mentally willing Fitz to shut up.

Wise narrowed his eyes. 'So we don't let intelligence

get in the way of a good profile?' He dismissed Fitz with a cackle. 'Back of the queue, buggerlugs, these are facts, not half-arsed theories.'

Fitz swelled up. 'I said two people, you disagreed, I was right. I said one older, one younger, I was right. I said two men, one taller, one shorter, I was right. I'm telling you, these two met recently.'

'Still conceivable if Grady is the father,' Jane volunteered.

Fitz spun round, frowned at her, caught her eye. She gave him a momentary frown and a tiny shake of the head. He responded with a knowing look.

'Well,' said Temple. 'What does it matter if we know who we're looking for?'

Fitz's massive shoulders slumped in a childishly exaggerated gesture. 'Christ, is it small, deaf and stupid in here, or is it me? Yes, it affects how you take a confession. Fathers and sons do not operate in the way star-crossed lovers do.' He picked up a spare copy of Grady's army photo and shook his head. 'These two don't really know each other. This is ten minutes into *Thelma and Louise*.'

Wise was distracted by the phone in his office; as he moved to answer it, Jane caught Fitz's eye again and shot him a poisonous glare. This time he seemed to understand, and there was a brief, awkward silence.

Then Wise reappeared, looking lively. 'Catch on! Local station's just found Grady's car, burnt out by Carrington Wharf. It was torched deliberately. Two witnesses, kids, say they heard screaming, so one of them might be injured, so . . .' He pointed straight at Jane. 'Hospitals.'

187

She reached for the telephone. The meeting broke up immediately, Wise pulling on his overcoat and heading for the door.

At the very edge of the stretch of waste ground was a portakabin. Through the one lit window Grady saw a youngish man in a suit, talking to himself and attending to a filing cabinet. He seemed tired and dispirited. On the facing wall was pinned a diagram of the area around the mill, with industrial units pencilled in for the impending redevelopment. Already there was a wire mesh going up and pallets of bricks dotted about. Outside the cabin was a BMW, G reg, drawn up askew over a triangle of recently laid tarmac that debouched from the main road. Grady deposited the unconscious Bill behind a pile of bricks. He'd torn Bill's jeans up the seam, exposing a vivid purplish weal. It was a fairly minor wound but needed treating and dressing. For that they needed transport.

He watched the BMW's owner pottering about in the office, whistling through his teeth and washing out a coffee mug, mentally willing him to emerge. Again he was surprised by his own response to the dilemma. Something inside him was enjoying all of this, appreciating the opportunity to risk everything, to play a big game. This was war, what he'd trained for.

His thoughts was interrupted by a murmur from Bill. He looked back. Bill was stirring, and his previously set features were creasing with pain as awareness returned.

The cabin light switched off, plunging the waste ground into darkness. Grady whipped round, readied himself, felt the thrill of danger.

The suited man locked the cabin door and, still muttering, made his way to the car. He pointed a remote, the central locking clunked. Grady waited until the enemy's back was to him and sprang, his boots clattering crisply over the tarmac. His victim didn't get even a glimpse of him. Almost without thinking Grady tripped him, grabbed his head in the crook of his arm and choked him, pulling him backwards to the perimeter wire. It had been his intention merely to incapacitate him, but as he threw the half-conscious body down he felt inspired, felt the chance to let out some of his accumulated anger. He kicked once at the head, once, harder at the stomach. The enemy gave a strangulated cough and slumped. Grady leant down, frisked him, found his wallet and car keys.

He scurried back to the car and keyed the ignition, climbed in and reversed, off the tarmac and on to the waste ground, right up to the side of the pallet where Bill was laid. The tyres crunched dangerously over strewn chunks of jagged-edged rubble. He got out, leaving the engine running, and examined the boy. He was turning from side to side and whimpering. The trail of a tear glistened over one dirty cheek.

Grady raised an eyebrow. 'OK?' He knelt down, hooked his arms under Bill's body, and lifted care-fully, shunted him straight on to the back seat of the car, lengthwise. Satisfied he was comfortable, Grady sprinted to the front seat and pulled out on to the main road. From here it was only a quarter of an hour to St Martin's.

Resting on the dashboard was a bottle of Volvic. He grabbed it and threw it back over his shoulder. 'Pour that on, try and cool it down.' He watched as Bill straightened up and unscrewed the cap. He winced as the water made contact with the wound. 'It'll feel worse than it is. Lift your feet up.' Bill lifted his feet a fraction off the seat. Grady laughed in spite of himself. 'Lie down and lift your feet up, you prat.'

Bill attempted to join in the joke. He seemed aware of the plush surroundings for the first time. 'Hey, I've never been in one of these before.'

'Never lived then, have you?' said Grady. He reached forward, grabbed a cassette and slid it into the built-in radio. A muted chorus of guitars burst from all speakers. Grady found himself smiling. Ironic: the man he'd just thrashed shared his music taste. He found himself tapping along to the tightly controlled drum-beat.

'What's this crap?' came from the back. 'Is there anything else?'

'It's Dire Straits,' Grady replied, as if that settled the dispute in itself.

'It's wank.'

Grady grunted. 'Well, like I said, you've never lived.' He reached over and turned the music up. He remembered dancing with Jackie to this track, 'The Walk of Life', at regimental dinners. He couldn't picture himself dancing with Bill.

A solitary, unshielded lightbulb illuminated the locker room. Jane stood before her own locker, making a show of reordering her belongings, waiting for the last of the uniformed traffic to pass through and go home, her bag at the ready.

The door swung shut for what she hoped would be the last time. She counted to ten and brought out the key, found Temple's locker, and swiftly unlocked it. As he'd promised, there was the package, a medium-sized Jiffy bag with her initials written on the front in felt-tip. Her plan had been to grab it straight away and hide it. The sight of it paralysed her. She stared at the two capitals, transfixed, unable to move.

Then there came the fall of footsteps in the corridor outside. A familiar tread. Startled out of her trance, she grabbed the envelope, dropped it in her bag, and closed Temple's locker, with only a second to spare before Fitz was looking over her.

'The cheatin' Lolita!' he exclaimed, wagging a cynical finger. He jabbed a thumb in the direction of the incident room. 'What the hell was all that about? I don't respond to telepathic signals any more, you know, not since I fell out with Uri Geller over dinner.'

'What do you want, Fitz?' she asked directly.

He smirked. 'You were saving someone's testes from the grinder, Janet. I hope they weren't your own. Oh no, Doctor Finlay.'

'It was a misunderstanding,' she said levelly. 'It doesn't matter.'

'What, Skelton?' He shook his head and his mocking expression flickered for a moment. 'No. Temple.'

'I've got work to do.' She made to push past him, but he stayed her, rested a hand on her shoulder. His breath was surprisingly fresh. 'Well, if you're in a Julie Andrews sort of mood, I've got a favour to ask.' His tone changed, friend to friend. 'Look, could you give us a bed for the night? Judith's flat-packed our bedroom. I've a nagging suspicion I'm next.' He looked down at his shoes, putting on his best 'little boy lost' impression.

She considered. It would be very easy to succumb, to turn back the clock. Pre-Beck. She still found him attractive and still didn't know why.

'Look, I literally, honestly, just need a bed. You can put me on the floor if you're worried about the integrity of your sofa.' She said nothing, waiting for him to continue, waiting for a mistake. 'I just need somewhere to sleep, just for the one night.'

'Obviously.'

He was unsure what to make of that. He leant forward conspiratorially, lowered his voice. 'Well, I could be talked into more. I would like more.'

Jane was tempted, but her bag was under her arm, and the diary was inside. 'No,' she said flatly. 'I'm sorry. You don't like me pissed, so tonight might be a disappointment for you.'

Moments after Grady entered casualty, supporting Bill who held his bad leg a few inches off the ground, and for whom each tiny movement was agony, the heads of the others waiting in varying states of patience to be examined turned, looking them up and down, looking between them, registering the details. Grady felt hunted, threatened. He shored Bill up more firmly and smiled hollowly at a young female doctor who turned from the child she was tending to with a quick apology to its mother and hurried up to them. The bright, crowded hospital was dazzling and strange after the day at the mill. At any moment Grady expected to be pointed out, accused, attacked. It took him a few seconds to clock on that the curiosity of the faces surrounding him was symptomatic merely of ghoulish interest.

'Nasty,' said the doctor, kneeling down to examine Bill's leg.

Grady saw Bill's mouth opening to rebuke her, and leapt in swiftly with, 'We'd lit the barbecue and it didn't take.' She nodded, her interest taken up with the wound. 'I'm his dad,' he added nervously. 'I threw some fuel on it and it must have caught his jeans. It just went up. It's my fault.'

She looked up. 'How does it feel?'

Bill croaked, 'It's bleeding agony.'

'Right, let's get you seen to.' She summoned a nurse and they lifted Bill from Grady's shoulder carefully, suspending him between them, moving towards a curtained-off cubicle down a corridor. Grady tagged along anxiously, unable to prevent a nervous shudder.

Inside the cubicle, the doctor set to work, cutting the material of Bill's jeans above the knee. 'What's your name, please?' asked the nurse. She picked up a clipboard with attached pen, checked her watch and filled in the time of admission.

Grady butted in again. 'Peter Smith. I'm his dad.' It was weak, the first name that entered his head.

The nurse's face stared back blankly. Her expression was unreadable. 'Right, Mr Smith. Your address?'

Grady's invention failed him. He pretended to worry over the injury as Bill let out a cry. 'Is he going to be all right?'

The doctor laid the square of fabric to one side and

smiled in a businesslike fashion. 'I should think so. I'll need some fresh gloves.' The nurse put the clipboard to one side and searched a store cupboard. Grady sighed and sat down in a corner, his breathing coming in short, sharp gasps.

Fitz got back home to find the house still empty and the bedroom still trashed. Message from Katie on the answerphone, telling her mother she was staying over at Clare's. Mark was presumably out doing whatever he did until four o'clock in the morning. There was no evidence that Judith had been back at all, and as he settled himself in front of the telly with a fresh bottle of Scotch he started asking himself questions about where she'd gone. He'd been too absorbed in his own self-pity at the time of their earlier debate to really notice her immaculate dress. Why was she dolled up like that? What destination required such impeccable attire? Not her parents, not her friends in the daytime, alone. She was trying to reassure herself of her own beauty for a reason, for the purpose of some confrontation. He let the thought slip and sat, very bored, watching the lottery show. Its awfulness had by now ceased to amuse him, and sanctioned wagers at such ridiculous odds did not appeal.

He heard the car crunching gravel and immediately drank up, bottled the Scotch and hid it along with the glass behind the sofa. How best to appear? Trashed after a long day's fruitful work. He let his head slump back and closed his eyes, waited.

It was wasted. She came in, slammed the door, and went straight upstairs.

194

Another night on the sofa, then. He reached for the bottle and poured himself another big shot.

The nurse had slipped off somewhere, taking her clipboard along with her. The doctor was looking up from her inspection, rolling off her gloves with a snap. She smiled perfunctorily. 'It's not too bad, Peter, but I want one of the plastic surgeons to come and see it before we dress it, OK?' Bill nodded and sank back against the bed. His head was propped up against a large white pillow. 'I can let you have some painkillers in the meantime.' She faced Grady. 'Not allergic to anything, is he?'

Grady stammered. 'Er – no, no, I don't think so.' He sought Bill's confirmation, but his eyes had closed.

'OK. If you just wait here, I shouldn't be five minutes.' She pushed out through the curtain.

Bill's eyes opened. He turned a pleading face to Grady, as if he knew they were doomed, that now it was only a matter of time. Grady realised they hadn't discussed either murder since last night, as if yesterday hadn't happened.

'Are you glad you met me, Grady?' Bill asked weakly.

This time Grady held the look, tried to speak, tried to say how much, tried to break through. He shook, screwed up his eyes, and managed a nod, converting the action halfway through to make it seem more natural, more ordinary. His heart rate raced and he felt his legs shaking. Before he knew what he was doing, before he could stop himself, he reached out and took Bill's hand, made contact, felt tears brimming to his eyes. Neither of them had wanted any of this. Why were things so difficult?

He nodded again and pulled his hand back.

The diary was standard Police Federation issue, the size of a small paperback. Beck's writing was frightening, large and uncontrolled, his thoughts on each day squared off into separate sections. There were many blanks, and illustrations and doodles, of blank grimacing faces and disembodied eyes. Fitz might have been able to make much of it. But neither Fitz nor anybody else was ever going to see it.

She ripped the pages out one by one and fed them into the mouth of the shredder, keeping her eyes off what had been written. She was alone in the stationery room, and stood facing the door, ready for any intruder. Six months ago she'd have quite literally been prepared to kill for evidence like this. Now, what did it matter? She thought of Beck's sister and felt a brief twinge of compassion. She wasn't going to let Beck destroy anybody else. She would erase all trace of his existence. It would be as if he had never been. She would fight on, as herself, and succeed.

Another page disappeared. The shredder shook, disgorging thin strips like vermicelli into its waste pan. Jane watched dispassionately, her hands moving automatically stripping and feeding, stripping and feeding.

Beck's destruction took under fifteen minutes. And when it was over, she tore the diary's cover into eight sections and threw them in the dustbin. She felt hollow, numb, and in desperate need of a drink.

She stepped from the stationery room to find herself

face to face with Skelton. There was activity going on behind him, she heard Wise bawling somebody out again. She hoped it wasn't Temple.

'Grady and Nash,' Skelton said breathlessly, bringing her rudely back to the present. 'They've just checked in to St Martin's casualty.' He was away down the corridor before she had time to respond. The interruption, she realised, was welcome. She needed distraction, some stimulus, she needed to prove herself.

She got to Skelton just before the doors of the lift shut.

A strange calm settled over Grady. He knew that in minutes he'd be fighting for his life, for a principle he wasn't sure of, for Bill. The corridors of the casualty ward were filling up as the night went on. Trolleys whizzed by outside the cubicle, there was shouting and tears, muffled exclamations and soothing words. He knew this was the end, the last hour of freedom he might ever know. Bill was silent, his eyes closed, his hair standing up in little tufts against the pillow's whiteness. The young doctor had been gone ten minutes. There might well be a reasonable explanation for that, but he doubted it. It was time to fight again.

He lifted the curtain's edge and peered into the corridor. There was no sign of any enemy activity. He needed to be sure. With a last longing glance back at Bill he went out, walking nervously, every sense alert, back towards the large waiting room. The scene looked much the same as before, and he relaxed. It was just possible that the police were still holding Franklin, that they hadn't connected the murder of his wife with the

197

murder of McVerry. Even if that were so they'd be looking for Bill. And where had Bill last been seen? With him, parading openly through the city centre yesterday afternoon. He felt giddy, sickened. The entire operation, if it could be called that, had been a disaster. There was a drinks machine in a corner of the waiting room and to justify his appearance he inserted fifty pence and collected a can. If the wound was dressed in the next half-hour they could get out, get away, far away this time. They'd have to change cars again, but that was no problem. He started walking back down the corridor to Bill. That was when he saw the doctor. She was talking to another nurse frowning, and as he appeared she glanced over, warily, their eyes connected. And he saw, for definite, that she knew. The anger returned, misting his vision with a familiar redness.

He leapt into the cubicle. The first nurse was back in there, inserting a drip into Bill's arm and murmuring to him about painkillers and allergies. Grady pushed her aside with a swatting motion, shouted 'Move!' and took a firm grip on the metal edges of the trolley. He swung it around and pushed, only distantly aware of Bill's howl as the cannula was yanked out and the screams and cries of the fallen nurse. He shoved the trolley through the curtain and back down the corridor to the waiting room, towards the car park. He heard the doctor shouting, calling for security, registered the startled expressions on the faces of the waiting hordes, and then was out past the admissions desk and into the night, the trolley clattering as it descended the ramp at speed. Bill was sitting up, blinking, looking dazed. The BMW was only a couple of hundred yards away. Grady pounded between rows of cars, breathing hoarsely. He heard police sirens, caught a flash of blue light through hedgerow, and swore, loudly and repeatedly. He pulled back, slowing the trolley.

'Grady, just go!' Bill shouted. 'Go on!' Even as he spoke he was trying to get off the trolley and failing, each movement of his leg causing him to wince.

'No,' Grady told him. He knew he was powerless alone. He pulled out the car keys and raced for the BMW, wrenching open the door. The sirens came closer, louder, a square of blue light dazzled him, he heard shouting, orders being given, a growing hubbub from spectators gathering at the hospital entrance, their own ailments temporarily overwhelmed by relish at the prospect of violence.

With the door still open he fired the engine. The Dire Straits cassette sprang to life as he jerked the car back out of its plot a fraction. He swung himself out, looked back for Bill, preparing himself for swift action.

The trolley was empty. He turned a full circle, saw the police cars approaching, what seemed to be a whole fleet of them. Cursing, he climbed back in the car and wrenched the wheel around. There was a horrific screech and he smelt burning rubber. He turned the wheel back. The car's response was to splutter dangerously.

Two police cars darted nimbly in, one from ahead, one from behind, boxing him. He slammed the flat of his hand against the dashboard and jumped out. Two plain-clothes officers leapt from the first car, a young woman and a black guy. He heard the doors of the other police vehicle slam and then footsteps on the tarmac, blocking any hope of escape. There was no way he'd go down without a fight. The black guy loomed up, flashing his ID. Grady readied himself, but as he moved to strike he was grabbed from behind, a strong pair of arms encircling his waist. He attempted to kick back, but against two opponents he was helpless. The black guy decked him and he crashed to the ground. 'Stuart David Grady,' a voice said, in an unbroken litany, 'I'm arresting you on suspicion of murder. You do not have to say anything but it may harm your defence if you do not mention, when questioned, something which you may later rely on in court. Anything you do say may be given in evidence.' He struggled as they took his arms, pulled them behind his back, clamped on handcuffs and then heaved him to his feet. He found himself looking into a familiar face. The Scottish copper, arm still in its sling, standing back from the others, his hair out of place, looking flushed.

The woman was at his side, barking harshly into her radio, 'Grady's down. Repeat, Grady's down. Main gate, we need a van.'

A reply crackled back. 'Where's the kid?'

The black guy shouted in his ear, 'Where's William Nash?'

A remnant of his instruction on resisting interrogation came to Grady. 'Who's William Nash?'

'Just Grady,' the woman said. 'Nash must be in the grounds somewhere.' As she spoke she looked keenly about, scanning the brightly lit car park as he had done. The van loomed up through the car park's gates and he was dragged towards it, limp, unprotesting. Despite everything he smiled to himself.

Bill could do magic. He could make things vanish. Even, so it appeared, himself. They hadn't a hope.

Fitz really was asleep when the telephone rang. He opened his eyes, focused blearily on an almost empty bottle of Glenfiddich, and shook his throbbing head. The television was still on, offering a football match in black and white. He shook his head again and the shirts of the teams turned bright orange and the pitch turned silver. A third shake and the picture resolved. That was happening more and more nowadays, he ought to get it seen to.

He stumbled into the hall and grabbed the receiver. 'Fitzgerald.' His voice was throaty and an octave lower than usual.

'Is that you?' said Wise.

'If it isn't these y-fronts are a good fit,' he grunted.

'We've got Grady, but he's clammed up. There's twice the going rate if you can come over now and make him talk.'

Fitz eagerly grasped the chance to assert his superiority, emboldened by the alcohol. 'No chance, you windy bastard. You didn't listen to me, and I was right. I'm not running out in the middle of the night to save your skin.'

'Have you had a few?' asked Wise.

'I'll get in early, and I'll want all you've got on both of them.'

Wise coughed awkwardly. 'We've only got Grady. Nash has vanished.'

Fitz sneered, admiring his expression in the hall mirror. 'You're really piling on the effort to lower your league position. They operate together, they only function together, they stuck together like the babes in the wood, what do you mean you haven't got Nash?'

'In tomorrow,' Wise said curtly. 'You're no use to anyone pie-eyed.' He rang off.

'Daft bugger.' Fitz staggered back slowly to the living room, with a last glance up the stairs.

No sound came from the bedroom.

Bill kept to the back roads, turning back on himself several times to avoid passing patrol cars, hobbling on his good leg. He knew the area well from his previous flight. Around here it was easy not to be seen, if you observed a strict routine, took no risks. He could have walked back to the mill in fifteen minutes going along the main road but they'd have picked him up for sure, and he had a duty to Grady to survive. The important thing was to look like you knew where you were going. He passed several strangers and made a special effort to walk naturally, nonchalantly, trying to keep his injured leg in the shadows. Every time his throbbing right leg touched the ground a sharp, digging pain surged through his whole body. He hated being alone again.

He made it back to the mill just before ten, and skirted the waste ground, keeping right at the edges, his senses alert, looking out for any sign of Grady or the BMW. Should be here by now. They needed another car and then they could clear out. Perhaps if he drove and Grady got down in the back it'd be better. They could go to London, hide themselves properly, get some work. If Grady grew a beard and he dyed his hair they'd look totally different, and they could steal a couple of passports, alter the details and leave the country, head for the Netherlands or somewhere.

There was no sign of Grady or the car.

Bill hobbled sadly into the mill. Light came weakly from the city, spilling through the rows of empty windowframes. The place reeked of neglect and disuse, the odour overwhelming his other senses, because there was nothing to see or hear.

'Grady,' he called hesitantly. 'Grady!'

He went on calling for another half an hour, rooted to the same spot, crying uncontrollably for himself.

EIGHT

Very faintly a church bell was tolling. The peals filtered their way into Bill's dozing awareness, reviving him, making him cognisant of the cold, the aching loneliness, the searing pain of scorched tissue. He snivelled and shifted his head against his pillow, a folded blanket Grady had salvaged from his car. The significance of the bells occurred to him. It was ten, and he was still alone. His mate was gone. He felt hungry and lost in this huge, shattered building. At this distance, the continuous rumble of passing traffic was reduced to a gentle murmur.

Suddenly, so quickly it caught him unaware, a profound hatred, a blind rage, rose inside him and he shook himself fully awake. None of it was fair. He'd never done anything wrong. His fists clenched and he beat them against his own head, savagely, inflicting pain on himself, hitting hard, again and again, aiming to wound, to mark himself. It wasn't a new way of behaving. Without Grady he was back to being useless and worthless, and nothing mattered, because love was always rejected, friendship was crushed, loyalty rewarded with betrayal. And if you grasped that you could set yourself among the gods. Because you could do anything you liked to anybody. It was the only way to be happy. Diane had seen that, nine years ago. And he was going to do it today, until he had what he wanted. Grady.

He brought his hands down from his aching, bruised head at the sound of footsteps. Urgent, scurrying, kicking over debris. Only one intruder, it sounded like. Not Grady, he'd keep quiet. Bill dug under his bedding, pulled out the gun, clicked off the safety, waited, preparing himself for his first solo kill.

A black shape shot from the darkness up ahead. A dog. It scampered into view, half-starved, mangy-looking. It saw him and paused, its mad eyes weighing his threat, its tail wagging crazily.

Bill, confused and terrified, fired. The loudness of the shot, the force of the jolt as the bullet was ejected, sent the gun flying from his hand. It fell a few feet away, clattered metallically. His aim was hopeless. The dog fled, legging its way back to the outside world.

Bill blinked and fumbled for the gun. Next time he'd be ready for the noise and the recoil. Next time.

This obsession for mini-rolls had to stop, Fitz thought as he despatched another in two bites. He was leaning against the snack machine, a bundle of stuff on Grady and Nash in his hands. It had made good reading, and he revelled in the rare delight of being proved correct on all counts. At the moment he simply wasn't paying any thought to Judith's bad mood. It would blow over, and there was a good interview coming. He could make Grady talk. It'd be easy. Press the usual buttons, winkle out the repression.

Wise poked his head around the door of the rest

room. He looked slightly perkier, although plainly still worried. 'Are you ready?'

Fitz thwacked the files against his side. 'Is he?'

'Still not a dicky bird,' said Wise as he led Fitz along to the interview room. 'He says he doesn't even know William Nash.'

'There's your services training. Protect your oppo, or in this case your teenage sweetheart. He's devoted to the guy.'

Wise bit his lower lip and frowned. 'Are you sure about all this queer business?'

Fitz chuckled. 'What, he doesn't look the type? How long have you been in the force? Long enough to bust a cottage or three, I'd say. And what did you find? Odds on, six out of ten of those queers were married men.'

Penhaligon was waiting at the door of the interview room. Something was up. She looked ruined, as per, but there was an unhurried, casual quality to her movement that had been lacking ever since Beck. He supposed he ought to feel pleased. Ignoring Fitz, she said to Wise, 'Sir, Grady's lawyer's backed out.'

'I'm not surprised,' said Wise, head drooping. 'Get him another.' He addressed Fitz. 'Do you want to wait?'

Fitz blew out his cheeks. 'Do you want to wait for Nash to kill again?'

'All right.' Wise signalled the officer on the door to admit them to the interview room. As he walked in Fitz felt a thrill of anticipation. It felt great to do something you enjoyed, and for it to be consequential.

In spite of his objections to Wise, the sight of Stuart Grady pulled him up. The man was big, and with real presence, a dominant figure even when silent and under guard. He sat with his arms laid out on the table, looking straight ahead into nothing. He had clear blue eyes like ice chips. Fitz felt a brief twinge of envy for his handsomeness. It was evidently easy to fall under the spell of such a person. 'Hello, Stuart. I'm Doctor Fitzgerald, they've probably warned you about me.' He sat, hugging the files to his chest. 'If you like you can call me Fitz. Everyone else does, among other things.' He made himself sound bright and chatty, turned up his potential to irritate to maximum. What would offend a man like Grady more than cosiness, small talk?

'Do I have to speak to him?' Grady asked Wise, avoiding Fitz's eye.

Fitz answered. 'You don't have to do anything, Stuart. Just listen.' He made a show of looking around the bare room, under the table. 'Where's that lawyer of yours?' There was no response. 'An hour ago, when I turned up, he was down with you in cells, briefing you. I go to the lavvy, cast my eyes over these' – he tapped the files – 'get my breakfast' – he waggled the empty box of mini-rolls – 'come back and he's off out the door like a whippet. Not the man for a challenge then?'

Grady said simply, 'I sacked him.'

'Ah.' Fitz cogitated on repression, saw the way forward. 'You know, my most vivid fantasy is to sit like this, face to face with a lawyer. He's desperate for my wisdom but there's been a virus flying about and my voice has gone, so I have to keep writing everything down.' He chatted on, studying Grady's reaction. He maintained his unmoving reserve but his eyes were twitching, he was disorientated. 'So I'm scribbling away and I'm smiling like a fool because I know every note I push across the table I'm charging the bastard twenty-five quid plus VAT. Wouldn't that make you cream, Stuart?' Reaction still negative, so probe deeper, go direct. 'No? So, what's your most vivid fantasy?' He slowed his delivery, stretched the words. 'What would you most like to be thinking about now? Just close your eyes, forget you're in this shit and get a taste of it. Go on.'

The corners of Grady's mouth turned down. 'No.'

'They can't touch you for it.'

'I don't want to.' There was a slight tremulous note in his voice.

'It'll relax you, do you some good.'

'I don't want to be relaxed.' He turned to Wise again. 'Do I have to talk to him?'

Wise grinned. 'Ask your lawyer, son.'

'Arsehole,' Grady hissed.

'No thanks,' said Wise, still grinning. Fitz repressed his own fantasy of telling Wise to sod off. He registered an urgent tapping on the glass transom of the door. Penhaligon pointed to him and beckoned. Her expression was puzzling, half urgent, half amused. What could cause that, apart from his humiliation? Yeah, the baby.

He gathered his things up. 'OK. I'm off. I won't stay where I'm not wanted.' He noted Wise's nonplussed reaction to this announcement, and told him, 'When Perry Mason found out the other guy was a seventeen-year-old male his Rotary Club card started twitching. Bad for business. When he shot through the doors he looked a very happy family man. There's a lot of them about.' He stood, turned back to Grady. 'Good luck,

Stuart.' Use of the first name always butters them up nicely. Grady's brow twitched, as if he sensed he was throwing away an important lifeline. Fitz acted on that, leant over him. 'Stuart, this is the one day of your life when you have to try and account for the terrible things you've done before they send you down. I wanted to help you through that. Nobody else will.' He nodded to the officer on guard duty and the door was thrown open. 'Your lawyer wouldn't,' he told Grady finally, 'because he knows you're gay.'

Number thirty Honeysuckle Road looked empty. Bill lobbed a stone up at the kids' bedroom window. No response. In his time he'd learnt how to judge a property. He'd lifted stuff from a dozen places, small things, ghetto blasters, jewellery. Number thirty had window locks, but there were high wooden fences out the back protecting him from the gaze of neighbours. In such a set-up, doors were the weak spot. He bunched his fist, wrapped the material of his sleeve around it and knocked through the small panel above the door handle. The glass shattered and tinkled. He knocked out the jagged edges and, keeping his hand wrapped, reached through, felt for the key. There. Diane hadn't changed. He knew her ways. The year he'd spent with her, the only good time in his life, he'd committed in detail to his memory. Nothing else had been worth remembering.

He turned the key, pushed the door open, moved in, the gun raised.

As Fitz followed Penhaligon into the incident room he was conscious of a murmur of amusement and a stifled laugh. She opened the door of Wise's office and he saw why. Danny was sitting there, the pram at his side, eyes accusing, the baby in his arms. Fitz was reminded of illustrations of the Virgin Mary in the missal they'd shared as children. 'What's happened?'

'Nothing,' said Danny in his extra-smug, extra-godly mode. 'Everything's fine.'

'Where's Judith?' he asked, sounding contrite because he wanted to get this finished. He wanted to get back to Grady.

'She's in bed, apparently.' He looked out through the window at the police officers, shaking his head at the photographs of Mary Franklin and McVerry that had been pinned up. Briefly, Fitz felt he was being blamed for the murders. 'For God's sakes, Eddie, why can't you at least try to make her feel better?'

Fitz sat opposite him. 'Perhaps she doesn't actually want to feel better, have you considered that?'

'I have,' said Danny vehemently, raising his voice a notch. 'And perhaps she doesn't because she knows you're waiting for it, so you can get back to hogging the attention and scrub out your own bloody guilt.' He shook his head. 'Our mother's money. After all she did for you, the sacrifices she made.'

Fitz thought of asking him to leave. Instead he reflected for a moment. ' "I have no guilt about the people I sacrifice." Who said that?'

Danny raised an ironic eyebrow. 'Judas Iscariot?'

'Or was it Jeremy Beadle?' Fitz pointed over his shoulder. 'I'm working, if you hadn't actually noticed, working for money.'

Danny's face flushed. 'Your own guilt about making

her feel worse. You promised her no gambling, you arrogant tit.'

Fitz held up one hand in mock surrender. 'Heard it, heard it. Don't lecture me, Daniel.' He smiled. 'When a man thinks tits are arrogant it's time to reach for the raincoat.' He stood. 'I shouldn't be long.'

Danny sat back. 'You know she's divorcing you?'

Fitz felt only minor irritation, as if a wasp was buzzing around him. 'What?'

'According to her mother, she went for a drink with her solicitor yesterday.'

Fitz was hurt, so he shrugged. 'I should have guessed when she started dolling herself up. She's pulled that stunt before. She flirts with her solicitor, then lets me know where she's been. Just bloody childish. Sad and childish.' He turned to go.

Danny shouted, 'Your wife's having a breakdown, Eddie!' loud enough to turn heads in the incident room, among them Penhaligon's.

Fitz rounded on him. 'Don't try to tell me about my marriage, you overgrown, underqualified, impotent shite!' He raised a fist, and might well have struck if the baby had not started bawling. Both went for the pram. Fitz was first. Gently he lifted his son, shushing him, rocking him. 'There you go, Jimmy. Ignore your wicked uncle.'

The door opened and Wise appeared. He nodded to Danny, said to Fitz, 'Hey, who is it you're supposed to be interviewing?' He looked between the three of them, tutted. 'Grady's asking for you.'

'What, somebody wants me?' Fitz asked in mock surprise, making sure Danny heard. The baby quietened gradually.

211

Danny looked away, stared out of the window. 'Go on. You're needed.' His holy voice again. Fitz opened his mouth to say something about a halo and closed it again quickly. He'd triumphed and there was no need to crow. What would be best? An apology?

He handed the baby over. 'I'm sorry,' he said. Like most sincerely voiced sentiments, it was easy to say that without meaning it. 'Right.' He rolled up his sleeves and followed Wise out, making a mental note to attempt an apology to Judith when he got home.

Bill surveyed Steven's room, the neatly turned duvet, the Discman, the games console, the wall of football posters. He pulled open the wardrobe, examined the stacks of carefully laundered and folded clothes, tee shirts, socks and underpants. By rights these were his clothes.

Exhausted, still in pain, he threw himself down on the bed. It felt instantly familiar. He turned over gently, mindful of the burns, and rested his head just over the edge of the bed, tucking his arms one over the other under his head, as he always had. This was his bed. He was Steven. The boy who had this room now was the impostor. He let the gun dangle, rolled it around his finger like a cowboy. For a full minute he rested, looking up at the pattern of Glo-Stars on the ceiling and the lampshade, at the stack of games and Power Rangers stuff in the corner. Then he felt something under the pillow. Pyjamas. He pulled them out, threw them across the room. The action reawakened his anger and he jumped off the bed, reached for the wardrobe, toppled it. Grunting gutturally, he pulled off the

212

bedclothes, kicked the toys over, and lurched out, heading back downstairs. This was his house. He could do anything, he belonged here.

Fitz settled back in his chair and smiled. 'I hear you wanted me back, Stuart.' No response. 'Ah, the strong, silent type. On the surface at least.' He tapped the file. 'That's what it says in here. Convincing.' He leaned forward, indicated Wise. 'Strictly *entre nous*, you convinced the boss. But then he's not on the lookout, is he?'

'I don't know what you're talking about,' said Grady.

Fitz opened up the file. 'Those fights you picked in the army. They were special. Real men, like you. You thrashed 'em to put 'em right. One or two of your mates singled you out, spotted an oddity.' He assumed a lisp, waved a limp wrist. 'Said something sensitive, did they?'

'I just lost my temper,' Grady said levelly, but Fitz saw the rage flash across his face, just for a second, at the suggestion of effeminacy.

'You decked them, Stuart. Wallowed in the brutality, the thuggery, the testosterone. To re-establish your credentials. "Volatile temper" on your record. Hardly Larry Grayson, a man to be feared, a real man. Puts you back on track with the lads, eh?'

Grady bunched his fists, frowned, and for the first time drew his hands off the table, folded them. That was telling. 'I'm not . . .' he began, angrily.

Fitz held a hand up, cut him off. 'Hold on. Did it never once occur to you how these guys knew? The ones who spotted your secret? Think about it, Grady. As

213

I said, takes one to know one.' He flicked through the file's pages casually. 'Any one of those boys you chinned could have been your future. Instead of this.' He unclipped a photograph. Grady, a young twenty-seven, in full regimental kit, with his arm around the waist of a young woman, a blonde, curvy and disproportionate in all the right places, a man's woman, archetypal army wife. In her arms was a baby in swaddling. She was smiling as broadly as her husband was grimacing: protectively, like a bulldog, at the camera. 'Did you tell Bill you've a wife and child?' Fitz asked softly, knowing what the answer would be.

Grady looked away from the photo. He raised a hand, said flatly, 'I don't know this Bill.'

'You didn't tell him, did you, Stuart?' Fitz moved closer. 'No? Why not?' He was breaking through, using the tactic opposite to custom. Apply tenderness, forgiveness, be gentle, coax out the soft centre. And he was getting there, Grady was shaking slightly, forcing down tears. 'You know why, Stuart. Because Bill Nash was different. He was honest. He dared to look at you for long enough to say what he meant. He offered himself to you, a strong young man. Did he make the first move?' Grady broke, hugging himself, let the tears flow. He shot an anxious glance over at Wise.

Fitz turned while Grady was looking down, made a shooing gesture to Wise. Wise replied with an outraged shake of the head.

Grady buried his head in his hands and sobbed. On cue, Penhaligon moved in, set a box of Kleenex down with a thump. Fitz examined her briefly. She also appeared confused.

214

Fitz took up a tissue and offered it over. 'Come on, Stuart. You looked at Bill and you saw a braver version of yourself. Look, like I said, this is your one chance to let the light in.'

Grady struck out at the box of tissues, swatting it savagely across the room. Fitz observed this, and nodded sagely.

Judith made herself a mid-morning salad and took it out to the garden. The weather was improving, the wind warming up for summer, and most joyful of all, divorce proceedings were under way. If she got what she wanted, and this time she intended not to settle for anything less, the house, three-quarters of the fittings and the baby would be hers. Fitz could eke out the remainder of his days in a bedsit somewhere. Without the safety net of her money, her hard bloody work. She smiled briefly, rather wickedly, at the thought of him attempting to hang that massive picture of his on the wall of a boxroom. She crunched on a cube of celery, enjoying the sensation of healthiness after two days of consistently poisoning her body.

The garden gate opened and she looked up, expecting to see Katie. But this was Danny, pushing the pram along, looking inside and burbling with his lower lip at young James. For a second, Judith felt a strange twinge, a mixture of memory and mournfulness, because Fitz had once looked like that, twenty-six years ago. Stocky but still slender, pushing through the quadrangle of the main Uni building with a stack of books under his arm, with, it seemed, so much to look forward to.

Danny waved and gave her a big smile. She returned a small one and patted the seat next to her.

Bill staggered downstairs wearing one of Steven's tracksuits. He helped himself to Steven's breakfast, a bowl of Coco Pops and two slices of toast with crunchy peanut butter. Cup of milky, sugary tea the way he'd always liked it, only half a cup because he couldn't manage any more. It was easier to move now, though he wasn't sure if that was the pain of the burns dying away or only him getting used to it. He sat at Steven's place at the kitchen table, fed up with waiting, tapping the edge of the bowl with the spoon. Where were they? Gone to see Diane's parents, Nanny and Grampy? He'd gone there about every third Sunday in his time with Diane, a big house with an old metal climbing frame in its back garden and friendly kids next door. They'd be grown up now. He wondered if they recalled him, if they'd asked Diane or Brian what had become of him, and the thought made him angry again. He started nudging his mug, the one with Steven's name on the side, to the edge of the table. It ought to be his name on there, by right. Steven had no right to appear and destroy him. Steven had no right to exist. He'd prove that to the world.

The phone rang, startling him so that he jumped up, the spoon raised in defence. There was nobody about but he still felt stupid, thankful Grady couldn't see him behaving like a scared girl. The answerphone message cut in. Tellingly it mentioned no names, just 'We can't come to the phone right now. Please leave a message.' Nine years and they were still covering their tracks. He felt touched, in a strange way. They were thinking of him. He'd left some impression then, even if it was a negative one.

Then Brian's voice. 'It's only me, love.' That sickly husbandly voice. Perfect bloody family man, a fine example to the community. That was what really made Bill sick, the way Brian and Diane pretended to be good parents, good people, and nobody but him could see their real evil. 'I'm still at the yard but I'll only be half an hour. I can't remember whether I'm meant to be coming home first or what.' There was a pause, during which Bill had to suppress his urge to pick up the phone, tell Brian exactly what he thought. No point giving himself away. 'Well, I'm obviously talking to myself, so I'll see you down Castlefield.' The call ended.

Castlefield. The word resounded through Bill's mind. He'd seen it recently, since coming into the house . . . since coming into the kitchen. He looked round. On the pinboard by the sink were a sheaf of bills, a couple of recipes, and a small, brightly coloured flyer. Castlefield Carnival. Today's date.

He had them. He stood, picked up Steven's mug and threw it at the board.

Grady lay across the table, destroyed, his whole body shaking, tics twitching over his eye. Oddly, and she wasn't sure why, Jane found herself watching Fitz. She'd lost count of the times they'd been together in this room, the atmosphere charged like this, the revelations, the human wastage. Seeing Fitz at work was, she had decided long ago, one of the privileges she'd been granted in life. He promised salvation, redemption; for a few minutes at the least you could see your whole life in perspective. For bystanders like herself and Wise the effect was close to a religious experience. This occasion was different. She was accustomed to Fitz displaying pity and sympathy along with bile and anger, but never before had he exhibited such plain compassion. He was getting older. Or was it all a part of the strategy? Still they were no nearer to a confession.

Fitz waited a few minutes, allowing Grady a good sob, before asking, 'Who's the worst person you could imagine telling? Your mother? How old's your mother, Stuart?'

'She's fifty-four,' he croaked.

Fitz nodded sadly. 'How old was Mary Franklin? Late forties. Not much difference.' He reached out for the box of tissues and handed Grady another. 'You haven't cried in a long time, have you?' he asked gently. 'And that seems stupid now, you wished you'd been brave enough.' Grady took the tissue. Jane noticed how often his eyes flicked over her and Wise, expecting some kind of judgement. With a shock she realised he was more afraid of being exposed as a gay man than as a killer. Fitz took a breath, and ploughed on. 'Your father would be difficult for all the obvious reasons. Same reason your lawyer walked out. One man smelling of two men's aftershave. It brings out the antibodies. Your mother, that's different. She's invested a quarter of her time on this earth into personally supervising your development. "Mum, I've got something to tell you." No way, not ever. She'd be devastated.' He shook his head. 'When Mrs Franklin found you with Bill you were looking at her and you were letting your mother down.'

Grady looked up. 'Nothing happened.' The words came slowly, he really had to force them out. 'Nothing happened between . . .'

'Between you and Bill?' Fitz raised an eyebrow. 'A whole generation of women screaming "what a waste", and other blokes, real men like yourself, who'd never look at you the same again. And you just couldn't face that, not even the suggestion of it. You attacked Mrs Franklin because she saw you for what you were, you attacked her because you couldn't face letting people down.'

'I didn't attack her,' he gasped.

Fitz raised a finger, said more calmly, 'I know you didn't. Bill attacked her. She tore into you, so Bill attacked her. He sprang to your defence to keep you happy, because he loves you.'

Grady scoffed, managed a weak ironic smile. 'For Christ's sakes, I only offered him digs for the night.'

'But that was an investment, Grady. You might not have known that up here' – he tapped his temples – 'but your mid-brain was plotting away. Getting what it wanted, fighting back after all those wasted years. It saw the opportunity, it responded. Nature struggling back.'

Grady seemed bemused. Dazedly he said, 'She was going to ring the police. He's on a care order, he'd have got into trouble.'

'Which you couldn't bear, because he was just beginning to open your eyes. The mid-brain sensed the only chance it might ever have slipping away, and you forced it back down, and that made things worse, and you cracked.'

Grady turned from him, appealed directly to Jane, then to Wise. 'What is he talking about? What the hell's the mid-brain?'

Fitz responded to that, puffing up like some threatened tropical bird. 'Yes, Stuart, say it, yes, you know it's true, you know exactly what I mean.'

Grady blinked back another wave of tears. 'Look, I keep telling you, nothing happened, I never touched him.'

'Look at me, Stuart,' said Fitz. 'Nothing happened because you've always prevented it from happening. Avoiding love in all the right places. The wife, the child, the army, the factory, always surrounding yourself with real men, so you wouldn't dare weaken. You've got to face it, Stuart, you're hardly unique. You're in the middle of Manchester, for God's sakes. Big city, huge gay scene, no thanks to James Anderton, God rest his larynx. You killed because you couldn't face up to the fact you're not unique, because it would have overturned your world view and you were terrified of that, that was an abyss.' He shook his head with genuine sadness. 'Yeah, chances are you'd have to listen to a lot of really crap disco music, but it's a small price to pay for a better self-image.'

Grady leapt up, angry again. Jane found it incredible; it was the word disco, the implication that he might dance with another man, that riled him. He shouted over Fitz's head, right at Wise, 'I want another lawyer.'

'Sit down,' barked Wise.

Grady bunched a fist. 'I want another lawyer.'

'You'll get one. Sit down!'

Fitz sighed. 'Like clockwork. Look, you don't have to take it from me. I'm a dyed-in-the-wool heterosexual, no man would have me. You could walk ten yards from here and find some honest answers. Two hundred coppers in this place, ninety per cent of them male. Rough estimate, ten of them feel exactly as unique as you do.' Jane stifled a smile at Wise's uncomfortable reaction to that.

Grady sat, folded his arms. 'I swear, I never touched him.'

Fitz slammed the flat of his hand down on the table. 'Exactly. That's the waste, Stuart. You never did it. You never said it.' Just perceptibly Grady was shaking his head, but he was defenceless against Fitz on full power. 'Bill Nash put himself out on the line and dared to break the rules. Not in some club you avoided, but in the factory, in broad daylight. He looked at you and offered you your best chance yet to make your life mean something. Your legs went, your stomach went, you could barely breathe.' He was warming to the theme, hammering the point, staring directly into Grady's eyes. 'I understand that so completely it's breaking my heart, Stuart. I'm looking at a man who fell so spectacularly in love that he wiped every obstacle out of his way.' He waved a hand at Penhaligon and Wise, at the officer on the door. 'Look at their faces. Whatever else they're thinking about you, they're jealous. In three days you've had the biggest adventure of your life. It's tragic you've achieved all of that, you feel like that, and you still can't say it. You love him, Stuart.' Grady buried his face in his hands, sobbing relentlessly, nodded. 'And if you love him, you'll tell us where he is.'

'I can't,' said Grady through his fingers.

Fitz spoke calmly, pointedly ignoring Wise's frantic hand motions urging him to step up the pace. 'We need to speak to Bill.' He contemplated Grady's shaking head. 'You didn't go home Friday night, after you killed McVerry. Where did you sleep?' Jane recognised a tried Fitz technique; offer sympathy, then slip in some detail pertaining to a victim, encourage the subject's violence and loss of control under a cloak of understanding.

Grady spoke more animatedly. 'They'll take him back to Sowerby Park and that'll do his head in. He's had years of all of that.' His voice rose and his eyes clouded. Jane recoiled from the callousness in there, and the image of McVerry's smashed unrecognisable face came into her mind's eye. 'That's why the social worker went down. That –' he faltered, lips juddering '– that bastard deserved to die. All Bill wanted was time with his family, a chance to talk, after all the shit they'd put him through. And that bastard started dragging him away like a convict. He's seventeen, he's been through all that shit, and all anybody wants to do is mess him about.' He ran his fingers back through his hair. 'I mean, at that age I was signing up for this country. Bill's owned by everybody but his bleeding self. I'm the only one who's ever showed him any respect.'

Fitz said gently, 'Mr and Mrs Nash aren't Bill's parents.'

Grady nodded. 'Oh, he told me that, yeah. He told me what they did to him.'

222

'Oh, yeah,' Fitz said, not without irony. 'But he got them back all right, and did he tell you that, I wonder?' He opened the file on Nash. 'Phone calls. Eighty times a night.' Grady nodded, smiled back, proudly. That's my boy. 'Broke into their house. Never took a thing, but he was always there when they got home. They changed their number a dozen times and eventually they changed their address.'

'Good,' said Grady bluntly. He leant forward defiantly. 'Straight in there. Make 'em suffer. They're the bastards who should be sitting here.'

Fitz waved a hand airily. 'Sure. But now he's met a man who's shown him the light. Shown him how to get what he wants. You killed for him.'

'We did it together,' said Grady, and Jane saw that she'd been right. He despised his sexuality, he glorified in his savagery. 'We helped each other.'

Wise stood up, popping up like a jack-in-the-box, with a daft half-smile plastered across his hairy face. Results. 'You murdered Mary Franklin?'

'Yes!' shouted Grady. Just perceptibly Fitz was frowning. He didn't dispute the confession; Jane got the idea that he was dismayed at this macho display.

'And Ian McVerry?' Wise pressed, getting the idea, sounding more aggressive.

'Yes!'

Fitz spoke, addressing Grady. 'Three days of intensive training, and you're like that –' he crossed his fingers '– your own little two-man cell?'

'Right, yeah,' said Grady.

Now it was time for Fitz to look smug. Surprise coming. 'He stands up for himself, does Bill. You admire that in a fighter? Better than most of your mates in the army?'

'Yeah.'

'A young hero. Up for it, unafraid, he didn't care what people thought. He could fight, he could pick a man and let him know, offer himself like a man, not like a queer.'

Grady said loudly, 'I'd have given anything to have been like him. Anything.' He looked insolently at Wise and the guard, measuring their reactions. His shoulders were tensed, his fists clenched. Jane saw the power there. One well-aimed punch of those massive fists could kill.

'Well done,' said Fitz. 'At least we're getting somewhere. Now, Bill fell in love and killed in the same week, just like you. And now he's been separated, just like you, and we happen to know he doesn't cope very well with separation.' He smiled smugly once again. 'We need to find him for his own sake.'

'No chance,' sneered Grady. 'He's going to fly now. You wouldn't think so to look at him but he really does know how to survive.'

'Really,' Fitz said. 'How close were you looking?' Grady frowned, bemused. Fitz pointed to his left wrist, then his right, then to his neck. 'Here? Here? Here? Did you not see the scars, Stuart?' He flung Nash's file down on the table, opened at a series of medical reports, a photocopy of his history. 'Attempted suicide five times. Two overdoses, three razor blades, two near-fatal. That's what Brian and Diane Nash arrived home to, a twelve-year-old lad smothered in his own blood. If he's led you to believe he's a survivor then he's lied. If

224

he's led you to believe he's a man he's lied. Bill Nash is still very much a child.' He spoke casually but the effect on Grady was profound. 'You must help us to find him. If you really love him.'

Grady slumped back in his chair. 'Brand's Mill. Back of the canal.' Wise leapt for the door. 'Wait!' shouted Grady, and Jane jumped up, almost standing to attention. 'He's got the gun.'

Wise's shoulders slumped. 'What gun?'

'Mine. Standard issue domestic service revolver. Webley 455 Mark 6.'

Fitz leapt up, put a hand to his head. He stared across the room at Jane, already five steps ahead, appealing to her as an equal. She felt quite proud, in an odd way. 'Bloody hell. The Nashes.' He made a strange pointing gesture with his finger, as if unravelling the consequences of the revelation. 'The kids.'

Wise looked askance at Grady and summoned them out of the interview room with a nod of the head. Jane noted how Fitz seemed suddenly to have lost all interest in his subject, who was left slumped, exhausted.

In the corridor outside she collared Fitz. 'You think the Nashes are in danger? If he's suicidal?'

Fitz shrugged. 'Depends how good a shot he is.'

Wise was already through the far doors on his way back to the incident room, calling, 'ARV to Brand's Mill. Find somebody who knows the layout.' He turned back to her and bellowed, 'Tool yourself up and follow a van to the Nashes.' He hesitated a moment and gestured to Fitz. 'Take him with you.'

To Jane's surprise Fitz reacted very badly to that. He shot after Wise, banging the swing doors aside with both fists. 'You've got to be bloody joking. That was my bit, just now. Razor blades I can cope with, the occasional rope job at a push. But I don't do guns.'

Wise was already bounding up the stairs, taking two at a time and not listening. Jane came up behind Fitz, beckoned him towards the armoury. 'I'll cover you,' she said simply.

'Is that a promise?' he yelled as he followed her.

There were side stalls and attractions down either side of the Liverpool Road, and the carnival noise, an outpouring of simple, massed human joy, drew Bill on like a magnet. Dimly he recalled coming here before, on an outing from the Park, being sneered at and picked on by other kids. Where's your mum and dad? they'd ask, and when he couldn't answer they'd call him a reject, a strange one. He'd shout back that he had parents, believing every word.

The carnival seemed to have got smaller. Perhaps that was just him growing up. He pushed through the crowds, hobbling and resting his weight on his right side, the revolver hidden beneath his shirt. Nobody looked twice at him, and for once he was glad of that. It wasn't yet midday, and the crowd was fairly thin. It should be easy to find them, and have a word or two. Up ahead were the fairground rides, a wall of death, a fun house, a mighty, fast-turning centrifuge, the scene dominated by a whirling wheel with cars shaped like small space rockets. He recalled a trip to Whitley Bay with Diane and Brian, sitting between them in a car like that, all holding hands. He'd felt no fear. He'd trusted them absolutely.

He snarled as he limped on, head turning, seeking them, seeking his family.

The ARV team made no secret of their approach. Fitz shook his head pityingly as the van in front of them, its siren wailing, swung in to Honeysuckle Road, and its occupants sprang out, rifles at the ready, each man in padded black bulletproof coverings. Penhaligon brought the car to a halt and took out her own gun. 'A fantasy come true, real Angie Dickinson stuff,' he said wryly. 'This is what you've been wanting to do since that first day at Bramshill.'

She checked the magazine, rolled the barrel, and didn't reply. Worse than that, she smirked. But there lingered some doubt, some bemusement about the situation. One of the ARV men signalled to her with a thumbs-up and unhooked a megaphone on a long coil. He started barking something along the lines of come out with your hands up, we have you completely surrounded. Fitz switched off listening, turned to her. 'Very macho. The adrenalin's really flowing. You're loving this, a chance to test yourself.'

'The interview finished fifteen minutes ago,' she said curtly, her eyes on the front windows of number thirty, the drawn curtains and dimly discernible family photographs on the living room wall.

Fitz thought a moment. 'You're wondering why Grady just didn't go ahead and do the deed? Dip his wick and have done with it, stand up loud and proud like any good member of the gay community?'

She didn't move her eyes off the scene outside as she said, 'He seemed very afraid of himself. It was sad. I mean, I've . . .' She faltered.

'You've known plenty of gay blokes in your time,' he completed. 'Oh yes. Some of my best friends, et cetera. Bet you didn't know any like Grady.'

'Grady is a killer.'

'He's also a working man, Jane.' The use of her first name came automatically, and was a mistake. In these circumstances he sounded deliberately patronising. 'The sexual revolution passed a lot of people by. Grady considers it more shameful to kiss another guy than kill him. With his background it's not surprising.'

'Wait.' She hushed him, raised her hand. The megaphone man had elicited no response, and had sent another couple of officers running up to the door with a thick black battering ram. As it struck home, knocking the door clean off its hinges so that it fell inwards with a crash of breaking glass, Penhaligon sprang from the car. In spite of himself Fitz followed. He couldn't decide why; did he feel protective of her, or was he just letting thirst for material lead him on?

Two other marksmen dived into the house, shouting challenges, moving like lightning, and Fitz felt an unaccustomed envy of the youth and strength of their bodies. There was a brief, shouted conversation, then one of them popped his head back through the now empty door frame, and beckoned to her. Interesting. They really looked up to her, all heads were turned in her direction, attentive. She was going to make a good boss. His boss, one day, and the day couldn't come soon enough.

She stepped into the house, gun still raised, carefully manoeuvring over the fallen door and the jagged shards of glass. Fitz followed, unchallenged by any of the marksmen.

First thing he saw in the hallway, at the foot of the stairs, was the remains of some computer games console. It had been thrown down, very violently, and its spewed electronic innards trailed across the meticulously Hoovered carpet. The other marksman stood at the top of the stairs, weapon lowered. 'One of the kids' bedrooms is wrecked,' he shouted.

Fitz grunted and went through into the kitchen. Penhaligon was there, holding the two halves of a smashed mug, fitting them together to make the name Steven. The radio at her belt crackled into life, and Wise's voice came through, unnecessarily loud. 'Jane, have you found him?'

She looked to Fitz for confirmation as she said, 'We're certain he's been here, sir.' Fitz nodded. 'Came in through the back door, but there's no sign of him or the Nash family.'

'Same here,' Wise said desperately. 'No sign of him at the mill, but the gun's gone. Just a –' There was a bizarre sound, a bark and a loud gun shot. 'Shit. I was going to say just a mad dog.'

Fitz surveyed the kitchen, the empty bowl at the kitchen table, sat where Bill must have sat, squeezing himself into place at the breakfast table. He looked out of the window into the garden, at the swings and the slide. A high wire fence at the bottom of the garden. And in here nothing but serried ranks of plates in a wooden unit fixed to the wall, a mug tree, a cloth drying, neatly folded on a tap, a pinboard arrayed with recipes, bank statements and bills. Young families, where might they go, on a Sunday?

'I've got Fitz here with me now, sir,' he heard Penaligon saying.

'Tell him we need to know where Nash'd go next.' He sighed. 'Tell him it'll be worth a few quid.' He sounded desperate.

Fitz raised his voice. 'You've come to life all of a sudden. Check relatives' addresses, check the children's home. And if you're looking for the Nashes, these are close people, the woman really lo–' he checked himself '– she really gets a kick out of being with the kids. Check if there are any exhibitions or events for children going on today.'

'Fitz!' Penhaligon reached forward, grabbed a small handbill from the pinboard. 'The Castlefield carnival.'

'Yes,' he shouted.

Wise's voice crackled, bemused, from the radio. 'What's that?'

'Castlefield, sir,' Penhaligon said urgently. 'They've gone there, almost definitely.'

Fitz swallowed. 'And what's more, Bill knows they've gone there.'

It took a good twenty minutes to find them. Several times Bill thought he'd seen one of the boys, only to get closer and find they belonged to another happy family. The throng swelled to a few thousand strong, mostly congregating at the central area, the bigger attractions. Bill was whimpering with pain and for some reason it was getting more difficult for him to see things properly; the bright primary colours were blurring, and a shoal of silvery lights kept passing through the lower

230

half of his field of vision, with a corresponding surge of pain through his leg. But he wasted no time on thoughts of giving up. A day from now he might be anywhere, doing anything. He controlled his destiny, his life was in his own hands, and he wasn't going to pass up the chance.

He saw Brian first, dangerously close, almost right next to him, moving through the swell in a definite direction. He had the youngest kid with him, holding his hand. Bill considered, and his hand flickered momentarily under his shirt, but the moment passed. These were not the primary targets. As long as he kept them in his sights they would lead him to the goal. He waited a second and loped on after them, the sudden stimulus overcoming his weakness. Brian was a six-footer, making it easy to track the top of his head. He was murmuring some rubbish to the boy, a daft smile playing across his lips, so happy with the results of his treachery. Bill was going to enjoy changing that, enjoy making him remember. He slowed down to match Brian's pace, and watched closely from a position of safety, concealing himself around the corner of a dodgem ride, mingling with the punters waiting their turn.

Diane. She was right there, waiting with Steven at a coconut shy. The kid was playing up a bit, and she was telling him off mildly, ineffectually, slapping him very lightly across the back of the hand. Bill sneered. He'd never misbehaved, not once, never earned even that much reproof. His replacement was an ungrateful little sod. Brian and the other boy arrived. There was a brief conference, Diane pointing to her right at another stall.

231

Bill couldn't make out the words. The next moment they were splitting up again, Brian and the younger boy one way, Diane and Steven the other. Bill, breathing deeply, started walking after the second group. He wasted no time on thoughts of good behaviour. Smile, McVerry always used to say, smile and you'll be rewarded, and it doesn't take much effort.

Bill's Caterpillars squelched in the mud churned up by the carnival crowds. Time seemed to speed up around him, and reality took on a more vital aspect. The sky was bluer, the fume-filled air more pungent. This was going to be the greatest moment of his life.

Diane and Steven were at a rifle range. Diane handed over a pound coin, the stallholder indicated a vacant place to the wide-eyed Steven. They were both turned away from him, concentrating on the line of wooden ducks as it jerked to life. He had a clear point of entry. He closed on them.

Steven's aim was all over the place. First time he'd ever seen a real weapon, something that could do some damage, however small. Wouldn't be the last. Bill had learnt of such things from other bad lads at Sowerby Park. If Diane had kept him on he'd never have become what he had. It was all her fault.

'Don't pull the trigger,' he heard her say. 'You're meant to keep your arm very still and then squeeze.'

The words galvanised him. He sprinted the last few steps towards them, pulling the revolver from its hiding place, flicking off the safety catch.

'Good boy,' said Diane. 'Now squeeze.'

Bill took aim and fired into the ducks, blew the stall down with a retort that was appallingly loud, even over the din of the crowd. Diane and the kid whirled round; there was a general commotion, much screaming and fleeing; the stallholder backed away, cursing.

Diane stared right at him, and the look of terror on her face was a joy to behold. 'It's time you apologised, *Mum*,' Bill spat. He gestured with the smoking tip of the revolver, indicating to the left, towards the exit on to the Liverpool Road. 'Move.' Not moving his eyes an inch away from Diane, because this moment was sweet to savour, Bill pointed the revolver straight at Steven. 'Move.' The boy and his mother seemed frozen.

Bill lunged, took hold of the kid by the scruff of his neck and swung him under his free arm. He insinuated his gun hand under Diane's armpit, nudged her along. Quickly he surveyed the crowd, who were milling back, a chain reaction passing through them, faces turning to him with a mixture of terror and morbid fascination.

Diane spoke. 'Please. William, please. Just let us go.'

'Shut up,' he growled, tightening his grip on the boy's neck.

'Let Steven go, William, please.' Her voice was breaking. God, she cared about the kid, the bitch.

'It's Bill,' he shouted in her ear, making her sob. 'Bill!' he added to the world, screaming the word loud. 'Nobody calls me William any more. You should know that. You would know that if it wasn't for him.' He shook Steven, relishing the power he had. Power to do things, get what he wanted. And there was one thing he wanted more than any other.

There was a guy in a bright yellow stewards' vest moving in, summoned by the shot and the screams. Bill singled him out, still pushing his captives on as he screamed, straining his voice to hoarseness, 'Tell 'em I want Grady back. I want Grady back right now, or he dies.' He emphasised the threat by jerking the gun up against Diane's shoulderblades. Her reaction was to emit a kind of shuddering groan. 'She dies, he dies, him first.'

The steward looked on in horror, a collection tin still held in one hand. 'I don't understand,' he said falteringly.

Bill was now choking back his own tears. 'I want . . .' He regathered his strength, toughened his stance. 'I want Grady!'

NINE

'I might have known this would bloody happen.' Fitz listened with increasing alarm to Wise's urgent radio reports.

'He's threatening to kill both Diane and Steven Nash,' Wise went on. 'Are you listening there, big lad?'

Fitz took the radio from Penhaligon's hand; already she was spinning the wheel of her car, making for the Liverpool Road. 'Don't tell me, he wants Grady.'

'Yeah, well,' said Wise, in tones thick with prejudice. 'I want you there.'

Fitz stifled an exclamation. 'Me? If you'll allow me a moment of self-deprecation, I'm hardly his type.'

'I want you to talk to him.'

'No point,' said Fitz flatly. 'He wants Grady, you'll have to give him Grady.'

'I can't bloody do that, the feller's a self-confessed bloody murderer!'

Fitz took a deep breath. 'Diane and Steven Nash have a gun to their heads. Bill will have not even a second's hesitation in pulling the trigger. Get Grady.'

Penhaligon turned the car about again; distantly Fitz saw the activity of the fair, the top of a big, immobile ferris wheel. A moment later came the sirens, the screeching blue lights. The ARV truck from the Nashes' place overtook them.

Bill had Diane where he wanted her. He'd found a good place of shelter, at the base of one of the smaller wheels that backed on to a line of hedgerow and a generator. Nobody could get behind him without being seen, and as he had the revolver wedged in the hollow of Diane's cheek they were unlikely to try. The police arrived in just five minutes, armed men in a black van, pouring through the entrance gates and pushing back the gawping crowd. Bill boggled at the sight. He'd caused this, he'd brought all of this activity about. He felt strong, and suddenly very frightened. It wasn't just something you could walk away from.

Grady would find a way to save him.

Diane twisted in his grip, sighed in a strange, unnatural way, and said quietly, 'Bill, Steven's only eight years old.' She started crying, and that was awful because it made him want to cry, too. No sympathy, he reminded himself.

He retorted, 'I was only eight. Then.' To emphasise his point he gripped the boy by the hair, pulled his head back viciously. 'That's how old I was, Diane.'

Wise summoned Fitz and Penhaligon, led them over to a white van that was just pulling in, its siren wailing. 'You've got what you wanted,' he said gruffly.

'Grady?' asked Penhaligon.

Wise jerked a hairy thumb at the van's door as it opened up. 'In there.'

Grady emerged, handcuffed to Skelton; Temple

scrabbled out of the van after them. Fitz noted a momentary flash of eye contact between him and Penhaligon, filed it for later assessment, turned his attention on Grady. Grady's head was twisting anxiously over the heads of those around him, seeking Bill, a look of almost paternal concern written on his pinched features.

Fitz licked his lips. He didn't like the way they were all, from Wise down to Skelton, looking at him, as if expecting him to perform some huge bloody miracle. Any other time it'd be appreciated, but he was too aware of the potentially tragic consequences of his actions to take any pleasure. He thought a moment, then, uncertainly, he addressed Grady. 'He's desperate for everyone to like him. It's a fostering instinct. That's how those kids find freedom, they just smile until some bugger latches on.' He shrugged grimly. 'No pun intended. He'll be desperate to do the correct thing for you, so you have to make him believe that the gun's no answer. Smile a lot, use his name a lot' – a betrayal of his own methods, he registered Grady's slight grimace – 'and make him give up the gun.'

Grady shook his head. 'I can't do that. He's just going to think I'm letting him down.' He paused, and said almost embarrassedly, 'He'll know I won't mean it.'

Fitz sighed, reminded himself of the remains of McVerry's face, the puncture in Mary Franklin's lower back. 'Shit,' he mumbled. 'Granted.'

There was an uncomfortable silence between the small group. Wise broke it. 'For Christ's sake, do something.'

Grady kept his eye on Fitz, who found how much he resented the persuasiveness and strength in there. 'If he's that qualified he should be saying it all.' From the look on the faces of Temple and Penhaligon Fitz realised he was only voicing the general opinion.

He faced the centre of the commotion, over at the wheel. 'Look,' he said, 'the last person he'll want to see over there is a shrink. The last person I want to see there is me. He chose you, Grady.'

As if on cue, Bill's voice called Grady's name. Wise shuffled uncomfortably, clicking his fingers together.

Fitz called on a new tactic. 'He trusts you,' he said, 'because he thinks you care.'

Grady bristled. 'I do.'

'So go and save his life.' Fitz pointed to the marksmen, who were scurrying to take up their positions, some of them climbing the scaffolding that propped up the Wall of Death adjacent to the wheel. 'They're trained marksmen. You know what that means.'

Grady swallowed. 'I'm not moving, unless you come with me.' He reached out, prodded Fitz in the chest.

Fitz felt himself blanch, acutely aware suddenly of the limits of his desire for emotional intensity. He had no passion for real, physical danger. And, from the look in Grady's steely blue gaze, no alternative this time.

Wise saw that too. He gestured to Skelton, indicating he should unlock the cuffs. 'Fine by me, mate.'

And then it was too late to protest. Fitz offered up his wrist with attempted nonchalance, but his insides were churning.

Bill saw the marksmen climbing nimbly up the scaffolding tower opposite, their rifles on black slings over their backs. When each man settled the rifle seemed to spring into his hand. Bill fought back a wave of fear, tightened his grip on his captives, pushed the revolver even harder against Diane's head. One squeeze and they were both dead. No satisfaction in that.

Then the police gathered across the way started parting, stepping back to let somebody through. Bill's heart skipped a beat and the silvery lights swam in his head; he shook it, cleared it. Grady was before him, strong, tall, beautiful. In cuffs, chained up to a weird-looking fat guy dressed all in black. Didn't look like a copper. Was this an attempt to throw him?

'On his own, I said,' yelled Bill. 'On his own!'

'It's OK, Bill,' Grady cried. 'It's OK, he's with me. He's not a copper.' There was a moment's silence. 'He's my lawyer.'

Penhaligon watched the scene tensely, her eyes flicking between the base of the ferris wheel and Wise, who was grappling with the switches on a megaphone. A crackle of radio communication surrounded them. At this distance they could now see quite clearly Fitz and Grady walking towards Nash and his hostages.

She heard raised voices, turned to see Temple and Skelton pushing a man and a small, crying boy behind the hastily improvised security line. Brian Nash and his son.

She came forward, addressed them coldly. 'We're doing all we can. Please try and stay calm.'

Brian Nash shook his crumpled, tearstained head. 'That's my wife and child . . . my wife and child . . .'

'Please, Mr Nash,' said Temple. Again he looked across at Penhaligon, imploring her to step forward and deal with the situation. She nodded and crossed over, because there was more information shared in that glance than it might have appeared. An understanding, and an empathy, a selflessness and regard on his part, that Fitz could never display.

Fitz studied Bill Nash's snot-streaked face. He'd been right; outwardly a young man, still very much a child. Grady led him a few steps forward, causing Bill's eyes to dart everywhere, up at the marksmen, across at the police vans, over to the remains of the watching, strangely silent crowd of bystanders.

'I don't want anybody but Grady near me,' Bill shouted, and with a jolt Fitz realised he was being addressed directly. He tugged on the chain, brought Grady to a halt. They were about ten yards from the ferris wheel, nothing between them and Bill but churned-up grass. 'We want a car,' Bill went on. 'We'll put the kid in the car, but if we get away, and nobody follows us, we won't touch him.'

Fitz saw the slight increase in tension in Grady's posture. At last he was seeing the mistake he'd made. 'They won't do that, Bill,' he called.

To Fitz's annoyance Wise's voice, amplified, rang out suddenly. 'We'll find you a car, but not until you put the gun down, Bill.' He turned; Wise was standing at the very edge of the police presence, megaphone in hand, face lined with worry, most of it for his career.

'Do you think I'm brain dead, you wanker?' Bill cried, his fingers curling about the trigger. Diane Nash had gone limp, eyes closed, but the little boy was rigidly upright, bright eyes open shockingly wide. Fitz felt a moment's revulsion for Bill, then calmed himself. There was a way round this, everyone could go home happy. Bill nodded to the child. 'Grady, that's him. That was me. Do you know?'

Fitz saw Grady preparing to speak and leapt in quickly, whispering, 'Not his fault, let him go.'

For a moment he wondered if Grady was going to take his cue. Then: 'I know, Bill. But that's not his fault. Let him go.'

'I can't, can I?' Bill said, trying to sound casual, matter-of-fact, a child's idea of grown up. 'If he goes, there's only her left, and I can't trust her, the lying cow.'

As he spoke, Fitz saw that Grady was moving very slowly forwards. He allowed himself to be led on, praying to whatever he believed in in such desperate times that Wise would keep his mouth shut. They were now sufficiently close to hear Diane Nash's cry. 'I'm sorry.'

'Y'what?' cried Bill, tightening his grip on the revolver. 'Y'what?'

Grady took another cautious step; as Fitz followed, he shot a nervous glance up at the marksmen perched on the scaffolding. There were two of them, stock still, squinting through their sights. Fitz swallowed. There was, after all, more of him for a bullet to misfire at.

Grady spoke again. 'You don't need the gun, Bill.' Better. He sounded calm, poised. That's nice, Fitz willed him, gently does it. 'You don't need the gun. Put your arm around her neck and squeeze with your elbow.' Clever, might even work, Grady was a smart guy. 'You don't need the gun, Bill.'

Bill's face creased up and tears came. 'But . . .' he stammered. 'B-but then . . . she'll get away. They'll have me, they'll get both of us, and . . .' Fitz got a chance to see why Grady had been attracted in the first place; Bill's helpless pleas moved him. 'And that's the end of everything.'

Those words struck Grady, forcefully, and Fitz felt a flicker of danger. Grady was still walking forward, but his lower lip was quivering. The moment was coming, the moment Fitz had tutored him for, back in the interview room. He cast his mind back a couple of hours. *'You never said it, Grady. You couldn't tell him you loved him.'* There was still time.

'It's the end of everything,' Bill repeated. He was manipulating, coaxing Grady.

'It's not,' Fitz whispered.

'It's not!' called Grady, sounding like he hoped he meant it.

'He's changed your life,' Fitz prompted.

Grady fell silent. Then: 'Put your elbow over her throat and just squeeze.'

Oh Christ. Fitz looked more closely at Grady, saw the way his eyes kept flicking back to Wise, to the policemen, the men among the bystanders. 'Make him feel important,' he whispered urgently. 'Forget the macho, Stuart, you *have* to make him feel important.'

Grady rounded on him, barked 'Shut up!' so loud Fitz jumped. 'I don't need telling.'

'Telling what?' Bill asked, suspicious.

Grady took a deep, shuddering breath. 'You are important,' he said. Close to hyperventilation. Fitz made a mental note that if he got out of this he was going to personally wring the neck of the next homophobe he encountered. 'I understand, Bill. I know why you're here, now, doing this.' Still he kept glancing back at the onlookers. To Fitz's horror, people in the crowd were *giggling*.

'Say it now,' he said quickly. 'Say it now and you'll get another chance in fifteen years.'

'You're half my age,' Grady continued, now starting to lose control, 'and I really admire you for what you've got through, being honest and just doing it, going for what you wanted, not . . .' He dried up, his face spasming, wracked by the wounds of the past.

'You love the bloke,' Fitz urged, 'just tell him, *tell him!*'

Grady shuddered, and then pulled up his shoulders and bellowed, 'I love you!' The tears were running down his stubbled cheeks, and still he kept looking round, terrified. Not for himself, not that he was going down for double murder, but that he was exposing himself as less than a man. 'I swear to God, I swear . . . I loved you more than I ever . . .'

'The gun, the gun,' Fitz whispered urgently, looking back at Diane Nash. Her eyes were open, and along with the fear she was looking at Grady with a mixture of horror, confusion and disgust.

'Bill,' said Grady, 'if you don't put the gun down, I'll never get the chance to say it again. Just put the gun down, mate. All right?'

Bill started shaking, badly, head to toe, the revolver, still pressed up to Diane Nash's head, wobbling crazily.

'If you're scared,' said Grady tenderly, 'give it to me, Bill.'

'No,' Fitz said firmly, feeling the advances slipping away.

'Put the gun on the ground, Bill,' Wise blurted over their heads.

Grady stepped closer. Fitz had no choice but to follow, and he had a sudden vision of himself being used as a shield. With a start he realised that was exactly what Grady was proposing. 'Give it to me, Bill.' He held out his hand, moving closer all the time. They were now mere feet away.

Fitz couldn't stop himself. 'Don't!' he called to Bill.

'I'm going to take it,' said Grady, 'and I'm going to put it down on the ground so we can talk properly, all right?' He stretched out his hand.

Bill nodded, and, still shaking, he shifted the gun, very slowly, gently, its tip brushing through the blonde tresses of Diane's hair and towards Grady's hand. For Fitz, sympathy for Grady was fading fast. The man was a killer. He swallowed as he saw the gun passing through the closing gap between the teenager and the man. Vaguely he saw Diane Nash sag with relief; her hand reached behind Bill, and she placed it reassuringly on her son's shoulder.

The revolver was almost there, inches from Grady's grip. There was a strange and horrible silence, and Fitz wondered how this might look in his obituary. He had no intention of going out as a hero. He wanted all his misdeeds remembered untainted. People might think of him fondly, and the prospect gave him even more of the shivers.

'I swear I'll never let you down, Bill,' said Grady, softly. 'I'll never let you down. I love you.'

Bill's hand twitched and he broke down, finally. 'I love . . . you, Grady.' The revolver brushed Grady's fingers.

Diane Nash shifted minutely, and she muttered, disapprovingly, letting out the tension, 'Oh my God.'

Bill swung round, suddenly livid. The gun came up. Grady lurched forward, reached for the weapon. The kid, Steven, ran.

Then the noise. The crack of rifles. Seven shots.

The blood from Bill's twisting body splattered the screaming face of Diane Nash.

The crowd surged forward, Wise barking orders through the megaphone. Nobody listened, least of all Fitz.

He was pulled down by Grady, only dimly aware of Diane and her son running off and the crowd's screams as all twenty-three stone of him was knocked off its feet by the sheer strength of Grady's fall.

Grady had thrown himself down next to the dead, red face of William Nash. He stared into the boy's unseeing eyes and let out a howl of tortured, animal grief.

Fitz turned away and let his face sink against the grass. He breathed deeply, slowly, recalling all he knew about traumatic stress. It didn't work. Grady's anguish echoed in his ears like the cries of a new-born child.

Judith had waved Danny goodbye and was back in the kitchen, making up the baby's midday meal. It was with a renewed sense of purpose that she filled the bottle, and she flicked on the radio unthinkingly. She was ready to confront the wider world once more, because things were finally going to get done. She felt almost exultant. A new age was beginning.

The local news report came in on the hour, just as she was lifting up the baby and angling the teat to his mouth. 'A youth has been killed after an hour-long siege at the Castlefield carnival,' said the newsreader. 'Psychologist Dr Edward Fitzgerald, of our own phone-in show *Fitz in Your Face*, was involved in attempting to free a mother and her young son, who were being threatened by the youth, who it appears was armed. Details are still coming in . . .'

Judith put the bottle down and, feeling numbed and strangely weak, allowed the baby to settle back softly on its bedding. She held up her hands; they were trembling.

The telephone rang. She ran to the hall, snatched it up.

'Hello, is that my wife?'

'Fitz!' She shuddered and let out a long breath. 'What the hell have you been doing?' And she couldn't help it; she really was concerned.

'It's all right,' he assured her. 'Apart from a couple of bruises, I'm fine. More than can be said for the other guy.' There was a pause, replete with significance. 'Look, Judith, I'd better go . . .'

'OK. I'll see you later. You're sure you're all right?'

'Yes, I'm fine.' There was none of the wordplay, no conceit behind the words. Just the level acceptance of the truth. They were staying together.

She put down the phone and put her hand to her mouth, holding back tears. For Fitz? For herself? For the baby and the future he would live in with feuding, ageing parents?

Then she went through to the living room, drilled two large holes in the wall, and hung the painting, his gift, up above the fireplace. It would probably stay there for the next twenty years.